C000163045

The Sleepover Club

Three fantastic Sleepover Club
stories in one!

Have you been invited to all these sleepovers?

Mega Sleepover Club ⑥

Sleepover Girls Go Snowboarding
Happy New Year, Sleepover Club!
Merry Christmas, Sleepover Club

Sue Mongredien
Fiona Cummings

HarperCollins *Children's Books*

The Sleepover Club ® is a registered trademark of HarperCollins*Publishers* Ltd

Sleepover Girls Go Snowboarding first published in Great Britain by Collins 1999
Happy New Year, Sleepover Club! first published in Great Britain by Collins 1999
Merry Christmas, Sleepover Club! first published in Great Britain by Collins 2000

First published in this three-in-one edition by Collins 2002

HarperCollins*Children'sBooks* is a division of HarperCollins*Publishers* Ltd
77-85 Fulham Palace Road, Hammersmith
London W6 8JB

The HarperCollins*Children'sBooks* website address is
www.harpercollinschildrensbooks.co.uk

3

Sleepover Girls Go Snowboarding
Merry Christmas, Sleepover Club!
Text copyright © Sue Mongredien 1999, 2000

Happy New Year, Sleepover Club!
Fiona Cummings 1999

Original series characters, plotlines and settings © Rose Impey 1997

ISBN 0-00-733102-9

Sleepover Kit List

1. Sleeping bag
2. Pillow
3. Pyjamas or a nightdress
4. Slippers
5. Toothbrush, toothpaste, soap etc
6. Towel
7. Teddy
8. A creepy story
9. Food for a midnight feast:
   chocolate, crisps, sweets, biscuits.
   In fact anything you like to eat.
10. Torch
11. Hairbrush
12. Hair things like a bobble or hairband,
    if you need them
13. Clean knickers and socks
14. Change of clothes for the next day
15. Sleepover diary and membership card

Sleepover Girls
Go Snowboarding

HarperCollins *Children's Books*

CHAPTER ONE

Yo! How's it going?

It's Kenny here if you hadn't guessed – yep, I'm back, fans! Well, let's face it, there was no way I was letting any of the others tell you this story. I mean, puh-leeeze, it was all down to me that we went snowboarding in the first place...

Oops – getting ahead of myself as usual. My mum reckons I'm always doing that – charging off without warning. Maybe I'm just a bit too impatient to do everything properly all the time. So what, though! That's just me – the original Action Girl – I like everything to happen fast! Hanging around is for wallpaper, that's what I say...

So where was I? Oh yes. Snowboarding. Have you ever tried it? It is AWESOME!!!! It's the most exciting, dangerous, scary, fun thing I can think of – well, except our sleepovers, of course... Mind you, not that I'll be able to go on the slopes again for a while, 'cos— oops, I'll have to tell you that later. Better not ruin the story on the first page, eh!

I like all sports really – especially football. And gymnastics. And I'm mad about swimming. And running. You get the idea. But snowboarding is something else altogether! As soon as I'm a rich and famous surgeon, I'm going to splash out on a no-expense-spared snowboarding holiday for the Sleepover Club, off in Colorado or somewhere – Nick says there are some WICKED slopes there.

Now I know you'll be confused. Who's Nick, then? you're thinking. And you might even be thinking, who are the Sleepover Club when they're at home?! Don't worry – I'm about to explain everything!

There's five of us in the Sleepover Club – me and Frankie, who are best mates, plus Fliss, Lyndz and Rosie. As a quick intro to the others, I'll do this thing Mrs Weaver got us to do the other day at school.

OK, say the five of us were all different types of... I don't know... bag. So I'd be a sports bag, right? That one's easy. Frankie would be a sparkly, space-age kind of bag with cool gadgets and inventions all over it – she loves that sort of thing. Some people at school think Frankie is pretty weird because she comes out with these off-the-wall ideas all the time, but she's just an original, which is a good thing if you ask me. You'll recognise Frankie when you see her – she's really tall and she'll probably be wearing something freaky as usual.

Who next? Well, Fliss is another easy one. If Fliss was a bag, she would be a pink and fluffy girly kind of handbag with a lace trim and frills all over it. Yuck!!! Just the sort of thing I hate. Oh, and it would be a designer model too, of course – and very expensive. Fliss is big on things like that. She loves clothes, make-up, jewellery, doing people's hair and the colour pink. Say no more! I suppose she's quite pretty if you like that sort of thing – but there's being pretty, and then there's being pretty and really boring about it. Unfortunately, our Fliss is more like the second of the two...

That's enough of me being horrible. Lyndz next – let's see. Lyndz's bag would probably have pictures of animals all over it – especially pictures of horses and dogs. Oh, and when you bought it, some of the proceeds would go to a kittens' orphanage or a sanctuary for retired donkeys. Yes, Lyndz is truly nuts about animals – she'd do anything for them. Lyndz is kind of soppy sometimes too, but only in a nice way. She also gets the loudest hiccups you've ever heard in your life. Scary!!

Last but not least, Rosie. I've left her till last because she only joined our school fairly recently. Surprise surprise, Lyndz felt sorry for her 'cos she didn't know anyone, and invited her to join our club. The rest of us were a bit mad at first because we don't let just anyone join – but it turned out to be a good thing as

Rosie is brilliant fun. The best thing about Rosie is her sense of humour though, so I reckon her bag would be quite trendy and nice, and would have something that made you laugh on it.

Anyway, the five of us are all in the same class at school, and we do just about everything together out of school too. Best of all, every weekend we have a sleepover at someone's house. And guess what? That's why we're called the Sleepover Club! DERRRR!

Ever been to a sleepover? They are just the coolest thing. We all take our night stuff and torches and Sleepover diaries, and everyone brings loads of sweets that we can munch through the night. We play loads of ace games and then stay up all night telling horror stories or jokes. Sleepovers are the best!!

I tell a pretty mean horror story if I say so myself – Fliss gets scared sometimes and says she feels sick (what a wuss!!) while the rest of us get all giggly and screechy. You know when just the slightest thing gets you all scared and hysterical, and your heart starts beating dead fast, and then someone makes you JUMP?! Like that. EEEEEEK!!

Like the other week, when we were sleeping over at Lyndz's, I told the others this story I'd got from my dad (he's a doctor, so he tells me all the goriest, grossest things!!). He told me that in the olden days, about five hundred years ago, the doctors used to cure people by sticking leeches on them – 'cos they thought that while the leeches were sucking out your blood, they'd suck out all the bad stuff in you that was making you ill as well! Is that just gross or what?! YUCK!!

You know what's it like if you're lying there in the dark and getting all scared about something, though. Anything sets you off! Everyone was groaning and making "ugh" noises at my leech story – and of course Fliss was saying she felt sick as usual – so I decided to play a trick on Frankie, who I was lying next to.

"Imagine all those leeches on your body slurping away at your blood," I said in a deep spooky voice, "and imagine them slithering over you to get to another juicy bit!" And then I made this huge slurpy noise and scrabbled my fingers through Frankie's hair.

"Aaaaaargh!!!"

She let out this ginormous scream and I collapsed in giggles. Frankie can be mega LOUD sometimes! All the others jumped – but then when they heard me laughing, they all cracked up too.

Frankie whacked me round the head with a pillow. "Cow!" she yelled at me.

"Leech-brain!" I yelled back, whacking her so hard I toppled over and landed on her.

Somehow we had totally forgotten it was the middle of the night and we were meant to be quiet. Soon all five of us were having this free-for-all pillow fight in the dark. Ever done that? It is so funny! You don't know where anyone is, and you're just whacking away, hoping to get someone – and now and then you hear a scream and know you've hit a target!

Suddenly – *crash!* The door was flung open and there was Lyndz's dad standing in the doorway.

"It's a giant leech!" Lyndz yelled and we all screamed hysterically.

Lyndz's dad switched the light on and blinked at the mess everywhere. Pillows thrown all over the place, sleeping bags tangled up where we'd scrambled out of them – and the five of us all out of breath and looking a bit spooked! Lyndz's dad is a teacher at the comprehensive, so he's a pro at telling kids off if he's narked. He was a bit cross 'cos we'd woken baby Sam up. Uh-oh...

So sometimes my horror stories get us into trouble – but most of the time we can get away with it!

Anyway, back to this story. Ready? Tell you what – why don't we go and sit in my garden while I tell you the whole lot? We can swing on the swings while I'm telling you – and then we can do some of those flying swing jumps off when we get really high. Come on – this way. Then I'll tell you EVERYTHING!

CHAPTER TWO

Right. Story. Well, I suppose it started on a Saturday. It was the beginning of November, and of course Fliss the Virgo wanted us all to go Christmas shopping. No offence if you're a Virgo or anything, but they're just a bit too organised for me. You should see Fliss's bedroom – everything's arranged in neat little piles or hidden away in storage units, and everything matches. Pink. Very pink. Personally, my "storage unit" is the space under my bed, where I stuff everything. At least that way if I lose something, I'm pretty sure where it will be.

But anyway, Felicity "Miss Organised 1999" Sidebotham wanted us to go Christmas shopping, even though Christmas was absolutely weeks and weeks away. Christmas shopping's for Christmas Eve, that's what I say, but sometimes you just can't argue with Fliss. She gets that stubborn look on her face, and you know that's it! You've got to go along with her.

Rosie talked me into it in the end. "I'm not going to be buying anything either, 'cos I'm skint," she said, frank as ever. "But we could go Christmas *wish*-shopping – where we look for things we want as presents from other people!"

Ooh! I liked the sound of that much more. "Brilliant one, Rosie," I said. "The new sports shop it is, then!"

The others all groaned. "Ooh, surprise us," said Frankie, rolling her eyes. "Let me guess... Could it possibly be something to do with..."

"Football!" everyone yelled out together.

I grinned. Did I mention that I love football?!

Ahh. I already told you.

"C'mooooon you Foxes!" I shouted, jumping up and down. "I want to have a look at the new strip – I mean, we're three months into the season and I haven't even got the new top yet!"

Us five always have a good laugh in town – even if Fliss does drag us round every single clothes shop most of the time. YAWWWWWN! First of all, we went into Boots because Lyndz wanted to get some bubble bath for her mum. Fliss spent ages examining every type of nail varnish while we were in there, leaving me, Frankie and Rosie in front of this shelf of all sorts of yucky things like wart cream and sprays for smelly feet.

"OK, who can find the grossest thing?" Rosie said. "We should club together and buy it for someone we don't like."

"How about these drops for hard ear wax?" Frankie suggested. "That's pretty gross."

"Here's some athlete's foot powder," I said, and started reading from the label. "*For flaky, itchy feet.* Yuck!! No thanks!"

"What about this spray for bad breath?" Rosie giggled. "Ugh! Just imagine how embarrassing it would be, buying that!"

Lyndz came up just then. "What are you lot all sniggering about?" she asked. "Fliss wants us to help her choose some perfume – she's going to ask her mum for some for Christmas."

I couldn't help groaning. "Poo, you won't catch me wearing any stinky perfume," I said, as we started walking to the perfume counter. "It all smells horrible!"

"What – even this one?" Frankie said – then grabbed a tester bottle and sprayed this yucky sickly perfume all over me.

"Aaaargh!" I shouted, coughing and choking. It really was *foul*! "Right, Frankie Thomas," I said, "you've asked for it now!" And I grabbed another tester bottle and squirted her with it. "Now you stink too!"

Fliss was so embarrassed, she dragged us out of the shop. As we all walked along the street, people kept giving us funny looks. We really did pong!!

Then I stopped dead on the pavement. "My

turn!" I said. "We're going in here next."

The others groaned as I led them into the new Mega Sports shop that had just opened in Cuddington. I'd been badgering my mum and dad all week to take me into town to check it out – and at last I was going to get to see it.

Woweee! It was a wicked shop. Heaven! I wanted to move in! Loads and loads of footy stuff, which of course I checked out straightaway. Loads of nice trackie tops and trainers – definitely a few to put on the Christmas wish-list there...

And then I found this whole surf and ski section at the back of the shop, which was just *awesome*. Lots of boards and all the gear – and there were these three tellies on the wall showing snowboarding videos. The sight of the snowboarders skimming down impossible slopes, doing jumps and turns, just made my legs go wobbly with excitement. It looked f-f-fantastic!!

"Hey, Frankie, check this out!" I shouted, waving some snow goggles in the air. "Snowboarding!"

I think I must have shouted quite loudly – me? Loud? Impossible! – because suddenly this guy appeared next to me.

"Ahh, a snowboarding fan!" he said. He sounded like someone off *Neighbours* so I guessed he had to be an Aussie.

"I wish," I said to him. "I've never tried it, but it looks wicked."

"Oh, it's the best," he said, enthusiastically. "It is so cool! You go so fast, the world's like a blur – and then once you get in the half-pipe, you can really start having some serious fun."

"Wow," I breathed. I wasn't quite sure what he was on about, but it sounded good.

"Yeah, it is pretty wow!" he laughed. "You should try it – get out on those slopes. It's the most exciting thing you can get into. Believe me, I'm an addict!"

"Mega!" I said, just as Frankie wandered over.

"Well, it's quite easy to pick up," he said. "You should give it a go. All you need is good balance, good co-ordination – and nerves of steel!"

"And snow," I pointed out.

"Snow helps," he agreed. "Fingers crossed we get some soon, eh?"

"Fingers crossed," I said fervently, crossing as many as I could.

"Well, if you ever want any advice or tips about snowboarding, just come and have a chat with me any time," he said, smiling. "The name's Nick."

"Kenny," I said, suddenly feeling shy as we shook hands. "Thanks."

Nick suddenly coughed and wrinkled his nose. "Can you smell something?" he said. "I think the cleaner's gone a bit mad with the air freshener this week!"

I could hardly keep a straight face as he went off to serve someone. As soon as he was out of earshot, Frankie elbowed me and we collapsed in giggles.

"Air freshener!" I snorted. "I knew that perfume smelled horrible!"

"Maybe Fliss should just ask for a can of that for Christmas instead!" Frankie giggled. "Save her mum a bit of dosh, anyway!"

Once we'd pulled ourselves together, I noticed the others had left the shop and were waiting outside for us. "We'd better go, I suppose..." I said reluctantly.

"Found the footy top you want, then?" Frankie asked.

"I think I've found something better," I told her, pointing up at one of the videos where someone was going a 90-degree turn in mid-air, like it was the easiest thing in the world. "Snowboarding," I said. "That's what I want!"

You know what I'm like. Once I get one of my brilliant ideas in my head, it's impossible for me to think about other stuff. Suddenly I really really *really* wanted to go snowboarding, more than anything else in the world!

I could just imagine myself whizzing down those slopes, a spray of snow flying up behind me, hat and sun-goggles on, arms out to keep my balance... WOW!! What a thought!

Lyndz had something else on her mind, though.

"Lunch time!" she said loudly as soon as we

got out of the shop. "I'm STARVING!"

"Lyndz, you're always starving," Fliss said disapprovingly. Fliss's mum thinks we should all live off carrot sticks and sunflower seeds – and sometimes I think Fliss agrees with her. Fliss even went on a diet once – I mean, D-U-M-B or what?!

"Maybe you've got worms, Lyndz," I said to wind her up. "Dad says they make you feel hungry all the time."

"*Eeeeugh!*" Rosie said, pretending to be sick. "Gross, Kenny!"

"I have not got worms!" Lyndz said hotly. "I just feel like a cheeseburger, that's all."

"Yeah, you look a bit like one, too," I said, dodging out of her way as she tried to whack me with her bag.

"You're in a good mood for someone who hates shopping," Fliss said suspiciously. "What's got into you?"

"I wish a cheeseburger would get into me," Lyndz was moaning. "Like, now."

"I'm on a mission, that's what," I said mysteriously.

"What, with that bloke in the shop?" Frankie said, winking at me. "They looked very cosy when I walked over there!"

"Get knotted!" I said crossly, but they'd all creased up giggling and Lyndz started making smoochy kissing noises in my ear.

"He was quite a babe actually, wasn't he?" Fliss said thoughtfully. "Not as nice as Ryan Scott, though."

"Well, now we know what Kenny's type is like," Lyndz said between giggles. "Action Man! What a perfect couple you two would make! *Mwaaah!!*"

"Shut up!" I said.

"Ooh, getting a bit hot and bothered, are we?" Rosie teased, elbowing me. "You must like him!"

"I don't like him – well, he was OK, I suppose," I said. For some reason I was blushing like anything. "It's snowboarding I'm into now! That's my mission!"

"Oh, here we go," Fliss sighed. "I thought it was trampolining you wanted us all to get into?"

"That was last week," I said. "But this sounds much more fun! Even better – it sounds much more *dangerous!* You have to have nerves of steel to try it, Nick said!"

Fliss did this big dramatic groan like she'd rather eat worms. As I told you, she's a bit of a wuss sometimes, especially when it comes to my brilliant ideas. Nerves of steel? Nerves of cotton wool, more like!

In fact, me and Fliss are pretty different in a lot of ways. When we have a sleepover at hers, she always tries to get us to play hairdressers and girly stuff like that – and sometimes she won't join in my ideas for games because she thinks they're "too rough" or she doesn't want to mess her hair up. Honestly! The only time I ever even think about my hair is when Mum is brushing out the tangles and I'm yelling with pain. Some people are weird, aren't they?

"This way," Lyndz said, shepherding us into the burger joint. "Unless you want me passing out from hunger, that is?"

I started telling them all about the things I'd seen on the snowboarding videos in the shop while we were queuing up to get some lunch.

"And then I saw this one bloke doing a jump like this, right," I said, whizzing round quickly in the queue just like the guy on the video.

Uh-oh. Bad idea...

"Whoops!"

"Oh, look where you're going, young lady!"

I'd just sent someone's vanilla milkshake flying! It shot through the air and splattered all over the floor, spraying our feet with sticky white goo.

I bit my lip. Things like that are always happening to me – I don't know why.

"Sorry," I said to this lady who was looking furiously at me, and I scrabbled in my purse. "I'll get you another one."

"I should think so too!" she snorted. Stuck-up prune. Didn't she know a snowboarder in the making when she saw one?

We finally got to sit down with our lunches and the others all started teasing me again about Nick. Rosie started doing her terrible Aussie accent, every time she said anything.

"I bet he likes hanging out in Summer Bay,"

she drawled. "Awww, surf's up – chuck another shrimp on the barbie, willya?"

"You sound like Rolf Harris – go back to *Animal Hospital*, will you?" I growled. "And get yourself a brain operation while you're there!"

"Ahh, fair dinkum, Sheila!" Frankie giggled.

"Tie me kangaroo down, sport!" Lyndz added, laughing so hard that milkshake shot straight out of her nose – both sides!!

"*Eeeeurggghhh!*" squealed Fliss, turning away hurriedly.

"Gross!" Frankie said, sticking her tongue out and laughing at the same time.

"Yeee-uck!" Rosie wailed.

"Can you tell what it is yet?" I yelled, doing my own Rolf impression.

By now we were all laughing hysterically, and were creased up over the tables. For a minute I even forgot all about the idea of going snowboarding. Not for very long, though...

CHAPTER THREE

Well, the next thing that happened was that I went home and found out that my parents had been abducted by aliens – and even better, the aliens had taken my gross sisters too!

Nah, not really. Just checking to see if you're paying attention, or if you're skimming through to get to the best bits. Sneaky, eh? Mind you, I'm the biggest skimmer in our class. Sometimes you just want to skip ahead to see what's going to happen at the end, don't you? I can't stand waiting!

Anyway, no aliens in this story unfortunately. No, the next thing that really happened was that after being dragged around a few boring clothes shops by Fliss, we all went back to our own homes.

Saturday tea-time means chips and everything in our house. YUM! My favourite tea – I'm a champion chip-eater. Even better, Emma (oldest sister – OK but a bit bossy) is going through this teenage "Don't want to get fat, don't want to get spots" phase at the moment so she isn't touching anything remotely greasy. You know what that means, don't you? All the more for ME! I've got her so sussed that if she even looks at a chip, all I have to do is say, "Terrible for your skin, Em," and she'll back away as if it's going to infect her with the plague, just by sitting there on a plate. Fantastic!

Of course, Molly (other sister – and horrible pig I have to share a bedroom with) still shovels them down her neck like the Cuddington Potato Famine has broken out, worse luck. And she wonders why I call her

Molly the Monster... Plus, she's skinny as anything and hasn't got a spot near her, so I can't use my Emma tactics on her. YET!

Anyway, I decided I might as well start on the Kenny-Goes-Snowboarding campaign straight away.

"Mum, you know for Christmas this year..." I started saying through a mouthful of sausage and tomato ketchup.

Mum raised her eyebrows. "Yes..." she said.

"I sense our daughter is about to put in a request for something," Dad said, clapping a hand to his forehead. "I just get that feeling..."

I ignored him. "Well, you know we always go to Grandma's, or Granny Mack's for Christmas?"

"Yes..." Mum said in a suspicious what-does-Kenny-want-this-time? kind of voice.

"Spit it out, love," Dad said.

"Well, what do you think about going abroad this year? Going on holiday? Maybe somewhere snowy," I said, crossing my fingers under the table so tightly I nearly cut my blood supply off.

"Laura, what are you getting at?" Mum said. "What's all this about?"

"I just thought it would be nice to do something different," I said casually, shrugging as if I hadn't really thought about it. (Yeah, *right!*)

"She wants to go snowboarding, Mum," Molly the Monster said smugly. "I heard her talking to Frankie about it on the phone."

"Shut up!" I said crossly, kicking her. "Mind your own business!"

"What's snowboarding?" Mum asked, looking puzzled.

"It's like skateboarding but without snow," Dad said. "Kind of." He didn't look very impressed. "Andrew McCarthy broke his leg doing it – he's still on crutches because of it."

"Oh, it's not dangerous," I said breezily. "You could always go skiing if you didn't want to snowboard."

"I don't know why we're even having this conversation," Mum said, putting her knife and fork down. "What makes you think we can afford a holiday at the moment anyway? Because I'll tell you now – we can't."

"PLEEEEEASE," I said, going down on my hands and knees in front of them and making my eyes go as puppy-dog as they could. "Please, please, please – you don't have to buy me a Christmas present or anything if you say we can go!"

"Who said you were getting anything anyway?" my dad said – joking, I hope.

"Oh, go on, Mum," I said, trying to ignore my dad. "You'd say yes if you luuurrrved me..."

"I'm saying no *because* we love you – because we don't want our little girl to break her leg!" Mum said. "Now eat your tea before it gets cold."

I scowled. Little girl – ugh!! Sometimes I can't wait to be old. It's so unfair that parents get to decide everything all the time.

"Don't cry, little girl," Molly said sarcastically, pulling a horrible face at me. "Ahhh, diddums!"

I whacked her one. "You'll be crying in a minute," I warned her.

"Girls, if you keep fighting, we won't be going anywhere – not even to Grandma's," Dad warned.

I sulked and stabbed a chip, wishing it was Molly I was plunging a fork into. GRRR! Sometimes she is just...

"How about one of those indoor places?" Emma said suddenly. "Maybe you could go there for a day instead – there's meant to be one around here somewhere."

"Not the same," I growled, through a mouthful of chip, too cross with my mean parents to be interested.

"Suit yourself," she said, shrugging. "*Little sister.*"

I had a moan about it to the others at school on Monday.

"I can't believe they won't even think about taking us on holiday," I said mournfully. "Why do parents have to be so boring?"

"I'd rather go and lie on a beach for my holiday," Fliss said, wrinkling her nose up. "I agree with them – I wouldn't want to go, either.

All that cold snow, ugh! You wouldn't get much of a tan."

"Christmas would be weird in another country anyway," said Lyndz. "I like being at home with everyone around. Waking up in my own bed on Christmas morning, you know."

"And it would cost a bomb, all of you going away," Rosie pointed out.

"I can't exactly imagine your dad snowboarding either," Frankie said, with a laugh. "His glasses would come flying off and he'd crash straight into something!"

"But *I'd* love it," I said, wistfully. "I'd really, really love it. There must be a way round it somehow..."

"Oh, no," Rosie teased. "Kenny's got her thinking head on – and you know what that means!"

"She'll be building her own snow mountain in the village!" Lyndz said, giggling.

"And pushing Molly down head-first," Frankie said. "I'll help you, Kenz!"

I sniffed. No-one was taking this very seriously! "You may scoff," I said grandly. "But you wait – I'll get my snow one way or another!"

On my way home that night, I got thinking. If *they* weren't bothered, *I* was! What could I do?

As I was kicking my shoes off in the hall, I spotted Emma's skateboard. Aha! Snowboard, skateboard – well, it would be a start, anyway. Now all I needed was some snow – and a slope!

Well, snow was out of the question; it had been as clear as anything all day with no sign of any snow-clouds. Hmmm.

And then I had another brilliant idea. The stairs!

I stood at the top with the skateboard and took a deep breath. Well, here goes! I said to myself. I got on the board and pushed myself off and...

WOOOOAAAHHHHH!! I hurtled down the stairs, bump, bump, bump – crack. OUCH!

Results – one cracked head.

One furious sister.

One cross mum saying it was my own fault.

One mad dad saying stairboarding was banned for life in his house.

I'm telling you – don't bother. Far too much aggro for about five seconds of excitement!

The only thing to do was to go back to Mega Sports to get some advice from Nick. He was the one person who could help me in my hour of need – and this time, I'd make sure I didn't stink the shop out, either!

Next day at school, as soon as Mrs Weaver said it was home time, I charged out of the classroom like Roadrunner with ants in his pants. ACTION!

The others cornered me as I was taking off my bike lock in the staff car park. The five of us usually hang around together after school a bit, waiting for our mums to pick us up – or we walk or cycle part of the way back home together.

"What's the big hurry, Kenz?" Frankie asked curiously.

"Mum says I can go to Mega Sports before I go home today," I said, strapping my helmet on. "I want to talk to that Nick bloke again."

"Oh, yeah," Rosie said, all sarcastic. "I see. We see, don't we, girls?"

"Kenny, you're going all red," Fliss said smugly. "Over a boy!"

"He's not a boy, he's a man," I said. Bad thing to say, Kenny! As soon as the words were out of my mouth, they all started giggling.

"Ooh, he's a real man!" Lyndz said, laughing so hard that she was holding her tummy and bending over.

"Shut UP!" I yelled, getting on my bike quickly. I couldn't stand much more of this!

"Well, now you've got a boyfriend, don't forget about your friends – us," Frankie said, sounding a bit put out.

"He is not my boyfriend!" I shouted. "For the last time..."

"Ooh, has Laura got a boyfriend?" someone cooed in a sickly kind of voice. "Who would go out with her? He must be blind!"

"Or mad!" another voice simpered.

Oh, great. That was all I needed. We'd made so much noise, the M&Ms had heard us!

(If you don't know – the M&Ms are Emma Hughes and Emily Berryman. They're our sworn enemies and just totally vile girls that should be put down for the good of the human race. But you'll see that for yourself, before too long anyway.)

"Don't call me Laura," I said through gritted teeth, as they walked over, giggling stupidly. "And get out of my way before I run you over!"

"Oh, I am scared," said Emily, or Goblin-features as we sometimes call her. "Look, Em, I'm just shaking in fear of Laura."

"Right, you asked for it, Berryman!" I said, and charged my bike straight for her. She squealed and dodged out of the way just before I got to her. Rats!

"I'll get my brother on to you if you lay a finger on me!" she yelled after me, sounding a bit shocked.

"Ooh, puh-leeeze don't scare me!" I shouted back, grinning to myself. "Bye, you lot!" I called out to the others. And with that, I shot off, pedalling as fast as I could.

CHAPTER FOUR

I love sports shops. I must have been in a million of them and it's like being in Kenny paradise, surrounded by all the football stuff and tennis racquets and swimming costumes. Every time I go in I have this stupid fantasy where I'm a millionaire, come to spend, spend, spend – and I end up buying the whole shop!

I walked around slowly, and then I saw Nick again, sorting out a box of sunglasses at the far end of the shop, just near the surf and ski section. Aha!

He looked up and smiled as I walked over.

"Hello again," he said. "Kelly, wasn't it?"

I blushed horribly. Oh, no! Blushing! I was turning into a right girl!

"Kenny," I said. "It's a nickname."

"Oh – sorry, Kenny," he said. "What are you up to, then? Come back for another look at this snow gear?"

"Yeah," I said. "I haven't been able to stop thinking about it."

He shook his head, eyes twinkling. "Oh, mate," he said. "You've got it bad, haven't you? You're as bad as me! Only problem is, there's no snow, right?"

"I've been practising on my sister's skateboard, but it's not really the same," I confessed.

"It's not a bad idea, though," he said. "It'll help you practise keeping your balance, I suppose." He looked thoughtful. "Want to have a go on a real board? Just standing, I mean?"

I nodded, feeling all shy again. For some reason, I couldn't think of anything to say. Yeah – I know what you're thinking. Me, motormouth, lost for words! I'd never had that feeling before.

He got a turquoise-coloured board down from the rack and put it on the shop floor. It looked massive!

"Are they all that big?" I asked, my eyes popping.

He grinned at me. "There are junior sizes too, but we've only got the adult ones in the shop at the moment," he said. "Take your shoes off, anyway. What size foot are you?"

"Three," I said, hoping it didn't sound too babyish. I unlaced my school shoes and stood there in my socks.

"Try a pair of these on," he said, passing me a pair of black boots.

I could hardly tie up the laces, my fingers had suddenly gone so trembly. "There," I said finally. "Blimey, they're heavy, aren't they?"

"Need to be, mate," he said. "You need good, solid support round your ankles when you're 'boarding. Don't want you toppling over to the side, do we?"

"Suppose not," I said. I'm telling you, my feet

43

really did look cool in those boots. I suddenly wished the others were there to see me, Kenny, about to have a go on a real, humungously big snowboard!

"Now, step on to the board," he told me. "Let me fix the bindings for you." He fastened up some straps and clasps – and then suddenly my feet were firmly joined to the board. It felt dead weird!

I tried lifting a foot up experimentally – and nothing happened, except I gave this sort of wobble...

"Whoooaaaa!" I said, arms flailing about.

Nick grabbed hold of me. "Easy, tiger," he said, laughing at my face. "Not as easy as it looks, is it, just standing still?"

"It's so weird!" I said. "And you can really slide down snowy mountains on one of these?"

"Oh, yeah!" he said, chuckling. "And it's a lot more exciting than just standing in a sports shop in Cuddington, I can tell you! To take a corner, you just have to lean to the left or right – and round you go!"

I closed my eyes and put my arms out to the sides to keep my balance. "OK, I'm in the Swiss Alps," I said, imagining as hard as I could. "It's a gorgeous sunny day and there's tons of snow everywhere."

"And you're right at the top of this awesome mountain and... you're off!" Nick said, going along with my pretend. "And you're whizzing down as fast as you can go, snow spraying up on either side of you – to the left, to the right – watch out for that tree!"

I opened my eyes with a jump, and we both started to laugh.

"You're pretty good for a beginner," he teased. "Shame about the tree, though!"

"Oh, well, it shouldn't have been in my way," I joked. I looked down at my feet and sighed. "I wish Leicester wasn't quite so... flat," I said.

"Not many mountains around, are there?" Nick agreed.

"I'm trying to talk my mum and dad into a snowy holiday over Christmas," I said hopefully – even though I knew it was about as likely as them taking us to Mars after my stairboarding tricks. "Where would be a good place to go?"

His eyes brightened at the thought. "Well, at this time of year, France would be good enough, if you don't want to go far. The Alps would be great – there are some wicked resorts there. Or Italy. Or Switzerland. Or Austria. And we Aussies get snow too, in Victoria..."

He groaned out loud, then laughed as he started unfastening my boots. "Now we're just torturing ourselves," he said. "There's always those indoor places if you can't talk your parents into a holiday."

I frowned. "It's not really the same though, is it?"

He shook his head. "It's not the same, but it's better than nothing." He yanked the boots off my feet and put them back in a box. "At least you can learn how to do it before you get on the real slopes, eh?"

"True," I said, thoughtfully. I'd just remembered Emma saying something about it the other night, only I'd been too cross to pay any attention. Hmmm!

"Well, pop in any time you want more info – always happy to help out a fellow fan," he said. "I can bore you with more of my stories about surfing and snowboarding my way around the world for as long as you like!"

"Thanks!" I blurted out, feeling myself going pink. "Brilliant!" (I know it sounds like I'm being Flissy but he really did have a nice smile. Honest!)

"No probs, Kenny," he said. "See you around!"

I cycled home as if I was cycling on air. As you know, I'm not the soppy type AT ALL, but Nick was really... *amazing*. The kind of person I just wanted to talk to for hours and hours and hours. He was so COOL – to think he'd been to all those places and could do all those excellent, exciting, dangerous things! I was just totally *totally* impressed, and suddenly understood what Mrs Weaver was on about when she talked about role models. I'd never really paid much attention to it before, but now I had my very own role model – I wanted to be just like Nick!

*   *   *

After school the next day, I went round to Frankie's house for tea before Brownies. I love going round to Frankie's house. For starters, her parents are really cool and friendly and speak to you like you're grown-up and not just some school kid. Plus she's got no horrid brothers or sisters (well, not yet, anyway – her mum's having a baby in a month or two actually) so she has a bedroom all to herself. *Plus* 'cos she's an only child, she has everything a kid could possibly want – a computer, loads of games, a telly in her bedroom... She is seriously kitted out, that girl.

When I went round there that night, it was all a bit different, though. Like I said, Frankie's mum is nearly eight months pregnant and apparently her blood pressure has gone dead high (that's how fast your heart pumps blood round the body, by the way – and if it gets too fast or too slow, you're in trouble, Dad says). So she's not working at the moment and Frankie's been a bit worried about her.

Maybe it was partly my fault that everything

had gone a bit strange there. You see, I'd asked Dad if he could help Frankie's mum at all, with him being a doctor and that.

"No," he'd said. "There's nothing I can prescribe for her – she'll just have to relax and take it easy." Then he pushed his glasses up his nose thoughtfully. "Maybe your friend Frankie could do a bit more around the house to help out – I'm sure that will be good for both of them!"

Typical parent remark, so I was kind of expecting Frankie to ignore it when I told her. "Help out around the house?" she'd said at the time. "Right." And I'd thought that would be the end of it. I wasn't expecting Frankie to turn into a housemaid!

Usually when I go round to her house, me and Frankie go straight up to her room and get stuck into some Playstation games. Or, if it's summer, we go out and mess about in the garden, or take our bikes out, or… Have fun, basically.

This night, though, we went straight into the kitchen. Now, I don't know about you, but

I tend to leave the kitchen area to parents. The only time I go in there is to make myself one of my hunger-buster sandwiches or to sneak some biscuits out of the tin while Mum's not looking. If I'm really unlucky, I'll be in there to wash up if I'm trying to get in Mum and Dad's good books. But that's about my limit!

This time though, Frankie was straight in there, apron on, filling the kettle with water and emptying the dishwasher. I hovered in the doorway, wondering what she was up to.

"Camomile tea, Mum?" Frankie called through to the living room where her mum was lying on the sofa.

She caught me looking at her with my gob hanging right open, and wiped her hands briskly on the apron. "It's relaxing," she told me. "Good for her."

"Frankie, you're acting like someone's aunt," I told her. "Shall we go and play Tomb Raider or something?"

"I'll just sort Mum out first," she said, like an old mother hen. She got out a tray and put this cup of yucky-smelling camomile tea and a banana on it, then frowned at the heating switch on the wall. "It's a bit cold in here," she sniffed.

"Frankie, it's boiling!" I said in disbelief. "What are you on about?"

"I don't want Mum getting cold," she said. "Kenny, don't look at me like that! I'm just trying to help her, that's all."

"Help her boil alive, you mean!" I snorted, pulling off my school jumper.

Just then, Mrs Thomas came waddling into the kitchen. I'm not being rude about her – Frankie's mum is ace – but you know how ginormous pregnant women get? They just start looking like ducks waddling around, if you ask me!

"Mum! What are you doing up?" Frankie said, and grabbed the tray off the table. I think she was about to give it to her, but you know how clumsy Frankie can be if she gets in a flap. Suddenly – *whooosh!* She'd stumbled on something, and hot stinky tea went splashing everywhere!

Mrs Thomas flopped weakly into a chair.

"Oh, Mum, I'm sorry!" Frankie wailed, rushing to the sink to get a cloth. "My foot skidded, and I..."

"What's going on in here?" came a voice. It was Frankie's dad, standing in the doorway.

"Frankie's 'helping' again," Mrs Thomas said to him. The two of them exchanged this weary, eye-rolling sort of look. I got the feeling they were both getting a bit sick of poor Frankie's help.

"Come on, Frankie, let's go and play upstairs," I said quickly.

"But I was going to cook dinner," Frankie began.

"No, you two go upstairs," said Frankie's mum. "I'm not totally useless yet, you know!"

"But..." Frankie started objecting, but her dad ushered us out of the kitchen.

"I was only trying to help!" she shouted as we went upstairs.

Honestly – parents. You can't win, can you?

CHAPTER FIVE

I've got to admit, I was a bit freaked out by Frankie's odd behaviour. It was like there was some other girl dressed up as Frankie, she was acting so out of character. Frankie is usually fun, fun, fun – not fuss, fuss, fuss. We leave all the fussing to Fliss! So as soon as we got to Brownies that night, I gathered the rest of the Sleepover lot together when Frankie was talking to Brown Owl about something.

"Emergency cheer-up sleepover required for Francesca Thomas," I said urgently. "She needs some laughs, badly! Look at her – she's gone all stressed out about her mum!"

"Dr McKenzie prescribes again," Fliss teased.

"Yeah, too right," I said. "I'm prescribing her a sleepover tomorrow night with lots of sweets and stupid games – what do you reckon?"

"Let's do it," Lyndz agreed. "We could have it at my house, if you want. We haven't had one there for ages. I'll check with Mum tonight if it's OK."

"Cool!" I said, turning a cartwheel. "And we all have to bring lots of exciting ideas for things we can do to cheer Frankie up."

"No prizes for guessing what yours will be," Rosie groaned. "Or are you into something else today?"

"No, still got a one-track mind," I said cheerily – and then I suddenly remembered the indoor snowboarding centre again. Maybe what Frankie really needed was a day away from home, having fun on the slopes. YES! What a fantastic idea. Oh, who was I trying to kid? *I* needed it too! BADLY!

* * *

Sleepovers are always good at Lyndz's house. I mean, they're ace everywhere but somehow they seem to be especially ace at Lyndz's house. This is why:

Lyndz's mum has the wickedest dressing-up clothes in the world so we get to play lots of cool games in them.

We take Lyndz's bed down and all sleep on the floor in a line in our sleeping bags.

There's always lots of yummy food – and big portions too, 'cos Lyndz has got four brothers.

Lyndz's dog Buster usually sleeps in with us and joins in all our games.

Her mum and dad let us stay up really really late (as long as we don't wake up the baby...).

Sleepovers are just the best bit of the week. For a start, they're often on Fridays so it's the beginning of the weekend. No school – YEEEAHH! And even better – this week I had some megadocious news to tell everyone. After tons of begging and please-ing and promises to do lots of chores (yeah, right!), I'd talked my parents into.... Oh, well I won't say it now. You'll have to wait and see, like the others did!

It's so hard keeping your mouth shut when you've got a secret though, isn't it? I'm the worst person in the world – I always manage to blab it out, I just can't wait! But this time, I really tried to save it for the sleepover. I wanted to spring it on everyone as a surprise.

Lyndz's mum picked us up from school at three-thirty. "Hello, girls!" she said warmly as we ran out of the school gates. "Looking forward to the weekend?"

"Yeah!" we all shouted, squeezing into the car.

Sleepovers are always different, but usually the first thing we do is change out of our yucky school uniforms and play a few rounds of International Gladiators to work up an appetite for the sweets. This week, as soon as we were all in our jeans and T-shirts, Lyndz picked up a sleeping bag.

"Squishy-poo fighting first," she announced. "We haven't played that for ages!"

What did you say? You don't know what

squishy-poo fights are all about? It's one of our favourite things – even Fliss loves it! What you do is, you stuff your sleeping bags full of clothes and pillows so they are like giant, long, squishy cushions, and then you whack each other with them. Anyone falling over is out – and the winner is the last one on their feet! The problem is, you get so giggly doing it, it makes you get all weak – and before you know it, you've fallen in a heap!

We all raced to fill our squishy-poos. The rule is, as soon as you've stuffed your sleeping bag, you're allowed to start whacking.

"Aaargh!"

"Ooof!"

"Squishy-poo to you, too!"

In the end, it was just me and Rosie left, whacking away between fits of giggles. And then – doink! Rosie got me so hard on my left side that it winded me completely and I crashed on to the floor. "Mercy!" I gasped.

"I am the champion!" yelled Rosie, jumping up and down and waving her squishy-poo around.

I had a quick look at Frankie, who was acting a bit quiet. Still worrying about her mum, I guessed. "Let's play Zombie next," I suggested – one of Frankie's favourite games. "It's a dark and spooky night, and there's a Zombie on the prowl..."

"Good idea," said Lyndz, jumping up and drawing the curtains.

"Oh, no," said Fliss with a shudder. "Do we have to?"

"Oh yes," I said. "Ibble, obble, black bobble, ibble, obble, out!" I counted round everyone's fists. "Frankie, you're the Zombie!"

She gave a blood-curdling growl. "I'll give you five minutes!" she warned and left the room.

Lyndz switched the light off and Fliss gave a whimper. You're meant to play Zombie in a whole house 'cos you need lots of hiding places, but Lyndz's room is just about big enough. We all scurried about in the dark, trying to find somewhere to hide from the Zombie. I squashed myself under Lyndz's desk – I had no idea where the others had got to.

It had suddenly gone very quiet...

"Time's up! The Zombie is on the prowl!" Frankie called in a spooky voice. And then – *crrreeeeak!* She pushed the door open slowly and did a Zombie shuffle into the room. "Zombie... zombie... zombie..." she moaned hoarsely, feeling her way around the room.

I felt my skin prickling. Even though I knew it was only Frankie, I was still going all tingly and scared.

"I'm coming to get you," she whispered, and I shivered as I tried to work out where she was.

"Zombie... zombie... zombie..." she groaned in this creepy voice. Then there was a squawk from Lyndz. Caught! Now there were two Zombies!

"Zombie... zombie... zombie..." the pair of them moaned. I could feel my arms go all goosepimply as they shuffled closer. It's such a scary game!!

I scrunched myself up tight under the desk as I heard Frankie go past. Then, as Lyndz followed, I couldn't resist it – I shot an arm out and grabbed her ankle!

"*AAAAAAAAAARGH!*" she screamed, completely freaked out. "Who was that?"

"It's the Zombie-eater!" I boomed – and then *everyone* started screaming!

Fliss ran over and put the light on. "I hate that game!" she said.

"We hadn't even finished it!" Rosie complained. "I had a wicked hiding place, as well."

There was a knock at the door, and Fliss nearly jumped out of her skin.

"It's only me," said Lyndz's mum, opening the door. "It sounds like there are some scary things happening in Lyndsey's bedroom – you might need a treat to calm yourselves down!"

She handed Fliss a box of Magnums and winked.

Fliss smiled weakly at her. "Thank you, Mrs Collins," she said, sounding relieved.

It wasn't until I'd taken a huge bite of Magnum that I remembered. I'd been so distracted by all the squishy-pooing and zombie-ing, I'd forgotten all about my amazing secret surprise.

I choked on my mouthful, trying to swallow it as fast as I could. "Hey, I've got something to tell you," I said excitedly, through a chunk of ice cream. "Guess WHAT?"

"You're entering the World Talking While Eating Championships?" Rosie suggested.

"You've decided never ever to scare me again?" Lyndz tried. "I hope?"

"No, I know," Fliss moaned. "You want us to run away to Switzerland together or something. I can tell by your face."

"Wrong, wrong and wrong," I said, smugly. "Although Fliss is kind of on the right track."

"I knew it!" she groaned.

"We don't have to run away to Switzerland to go snowboarding though," I said triumphantly. "There's an indoor skiing and snowboarding centre in Tolbury – only about half an hour away in the car. Emma told me. How about us all going there for a day's snowboarding?"

I was practically bursting with excitement.

"Well? What do you think? Mum and Dad have agreed to take us and everything!"

"Wow!" said Lyndz. "Really?"

"It sounds a bit dangerous to me," Fliss said, nibbling daintily at her Magnum. "I don't know if my mum would let me."

"It's not dangerous – you have a lesson and they teach you how to do it!" I said. "Honestly, Fliss, you're with an instructor all the time!"

She pursed her lips up and I could see she wasn't convinced. "You'd be good, anyway," I said to her. "What are you worried about? You're really good at sport!"

OK, so I was buttering her up a bit. But Fliss isn't bad at sport – she's quite OK at running and things like that, so it wasn't totally false of me. All right, so snowboarding was a bit different – so what?

"Do you think so?" she said, sounding pleased. "Really?"

"Yeah!" I said. "And you can ride a bike, can't you? So you must have good balance!"

"I suppose so," she said. Then she went a bit pink. "And I do like those fleecy tops they wear – I saw a thing about it in one of Andy's magazines..."

Good old Fliss! You can always count on her to say yes to something if it means an excuse to go shopping for a new outfit!

"What about the rest of you?" I said. One down, three to go...

"It sounds wicked!" said Lyndz. "Is it real snow?"

"Yeah, it is!" I said, grinning. "Real, white, wet, slippery snow! They make it with these mega snow-machines."

"Cool!" she said. "When you kept going on about it, I thought it was going to be something you could only do abroad – but if you can do it here... sounds brilliant!"

Two down...

"Rosie, what about you?" I asked.

Uh-oh. Rosie wasn't looking so easy to convince.

"How much is it going to cost?" she said cautiously. "Only it's coming up to Christmas and I don't know if Mum's got much cash to spare right now."

"It's not that much," I said quickly. "I'm sure you could ask for it as part of your Christmas present anyway – that would save her going shopping for it, wouldn't it?"

"I'll see what she says," she said, but I could tell she was feeling as excited as Lyndz underneath. "But hopefully yeah, count me in too! Sleepover Club on the slopes!"

"What do you reckon, Frankie?" I said anxiously. Frankie was the only one who hadn't said anything yet. "Won't be a proper Sleepover thing without you..."

She pulled a bit of a face. "It sounds ace and normally I'd go like a shot, but I don't know whether I can leave Mum at the moment."

I thought back to the way Frankie's mum had rolled her eyes about Frankie's 'helping'. Somehow I didn't think Frankie's mum would have a problem with Frankie going at all!

"She might like having the house to herself for the day," I said, trying to be tactful about it. "Give her a chance to really relax in peace."

"Maybe," said Frankie. "I'll ask."

I jumped in the air. "Whoopeeee!" I said.

"We're off! We can have a sleepover at ours on a Friday night and then go on the Saturday! It's just gonna be *sooo* excellent!"

"Even better – we can really rub it in with the M&Ms next week," Lyndz said with a wicked giggle. "They'll be sick as anything!"

"They'll hate us for it!" Fliss said, beaming broadly. "I can't wait to see their faces! We're going snowboarding, we're going snowboarding!"

Frankie leapt to her feet and pretended to snowboard along Lyndz's bedroom floor. "Look out, everyone – here I come!" she yelled. *"Neeeyyyoooooowww!"*

I grinned to myself. My best mate bouncing around like a nutter again was the best thing I'd seen in ages!

CHAPTER SIX

The whole of the next week was just unbearable. Like I said, I hate having to wait for anything – and this time it practically *killed* me! First of all, before we could all get really excited about going, the others had to check with their parents that it was OK for them all to come. Lyndz's parents said yes right away. Then Rosie's. Fliss's mum was a bit worried about the whole thing, so I had to get my mum to phone her and reassure her that everything was going to be OK and her precious daughter wasn't about to break her neck on the slopes.

Then Frankie rang. "Hi!" I said. "What did your parents say about the snowboarding trip?"

There was this awful silence. "Well," she started – and then stopped.

"*What?*" I practically screamed down the phone. "Won't they let you go?"

"Well, they said I could go..." she started hesitantly.

I gave a huge sigh of relief. "YEEEEAHHH!" I shouted. "Oh, thank goodness for that! I thought you were going to say you couldn't come!"

There was another silence.

"Frankie?" I prompted.

She sighed heavily down the phone. Uh-oh. This wasn't sounding good.

"What's up?" I asked. "What's the matter?"

"It's my mum," Frankie said slowly. "She's got a hospital check-up that day."

"And?" I asked. It was starting to sound worse by the second.

"And... I want to go with her," Frankie said. "So I'm not going to go snowboarding."

"What?!" I screeched. "Why do you have to go with her? What's wrong with her?"

"Well, it's just a regular check-up but her blood pressure's still too high and... you know, I just want to be there," she said.

My heart sank. "And she wants you to go with her, does she?" I asked.

Frankie hesitated. "Actually, she said she'd rather I went with you lot and had some fun, but..."

I pounced on her words. "You should then, if that's what she wants! You can't really do anything to help her at the hospital anyway, can you?"

Another pause. "Noooo, but..."

"Tell you what," I said, thinking quickly. "Come with us and you can have a great day out and take your mind off it all. And you can ring her on her mobile if you're worried, can't you?"

"Ye-e-e-es," Frankie said doubtfully, "but..."

"She'll feel happier knowing that you're enjoying yourself and not getting all worried," I said, pulling out all the stops to try and convince her. Then I played my trump card. "Besides, you hate hospitals – I know you do!"

She sighed. "Yeah, you're right," she said, kind of reluctantly.

"Yipppppppeeeeee!" I yelled. "So you're gonna come with us, then?"

"Yeah," she said. "But only if I can ring her while we're there."

"I'll even give you 50p for the phone call if it makes you come with us!" I said, a big grin stretching across my face. "It wouldn't be the same without you!"

After that near-miss, there came another blow to the plan – and this one was far more seriously BAD. We were all sitting and having tea on Monday night, and Mum only went and asked Molly and Emma if they wanted to come too, didn't she?

I choked on a bit of potato and Dad had to bang me on the back. "Oh, Mum!" I protested in horror. Those two would just wreck everything, I knew it! "Can't it be just the Sleepover Club?"

Mum pushed her glasses up her nose. She has this real thing about families doing everything together, worse luck. Just because she gets on with the rest of her family, it doesn't mean *I* do!

"Fair's fair," she said (one of her favourite phrases). "I'm going to phone up the snow centre tomorrow so I need to know how many people to book the lesson for. And it's only fair that Emma and Molly can come too if you're going."

"But there won't be enough room in the car," I argued, desperately trying to think of reasons to stop them coming along.

"We can take both cars," Mum said calmly. "Emma? Molly? What do you think?"

"I've got a netball match on Saturday so I can't," Emma said. "And even if I could, I wouldn't want to spend my Saturday with a bunch of ten-year-olds, thanks all the same!"

I gave her a cold stare but secretly was pleased that she didn't want to come. Good! Now there was only Molly the Monster I had to worry about...

"I'd love to come!" she said, smirking at me in that horrible way of hers. "Can Carli come too?"

Worse and worse and WORSE! Molly is a monster and a half but Carli... Carli's practically in the M&M league of yuckiness! And when Molly and Carli are together, it's *really* bad news. Suddenly my heart seemed to have sunk right down into my trainers.

"Of course she can – as long as it's OK with her parents," Mum smiled. "Right, that's that settled then."

"Oh, Muuum!" I groaned, but she gave me one of her looks.

"You're very lucky to be going at all, Laura – and don't you forget it!" she said sharply. "Now eat your dinner!"

I knew when I was beaten. GUTTED!!!

Once I'd just about gotten over the shock that it was going to be the Sleepover Club on the slopes plus yucky Molly plus even yuckier Carli, the rest of the week dragged by agonisingly slowly. Why is that when you're on holiday or it's the weekend, time whizzes by dead fast, but when you're waiting for Christmas or your birthday – or a snowboarding trip – it goes reeeeeaalllly slow, as if all the clocks in the world have broken down?!

The only good thing about the week was winding up the M&Ms. Ahh, a speciality of mine, don'tcha know! I can never resist the urge to make those two SQUIRM!

At school on Thursday morning, I broke the news to the others that my mum had booked us all in for a snowboarding lesson on the Saturday coming.

"Yahoo!" Lyndz said excitedly. "We're really going!"

"Hooray!" shouted Rosie.

We all jumped around cheering and yelling, even Frankie. Even Fliss!!

"What? Going where?" I heard two familiar nosey voices ask. AHA! The M&Ms had been eavesdropping!

"Maybe they're going back to Mars, where they belong," sniggered Emily.

"Hope so," Emily agreed. "Good riddance, wherever you're going! Don't hurry back, will you?"

"I'd never hurry anywhere to see you," I sneered back at her. "Don't flatter yourself, *darlin'*!"

"It's none of your business where we're going, anyway," Frankie said, her nose in the air. "Although it's going to be great getting away from you two for a while!"

"Can't wait," Rosie said. "No smelly Ems around, polluting the air..."

"Just clean, fresh snow," Lyndz said teasingly.

That got their curiosity going! "Snow?" Emily said. "Who said it's going to snow? It's not cold enough yet!"

"Where we're going there's always snow," Fliss said smugly. "So poo to you!"

I snorted with laughter. Fliss thinks "poo" is the rudest word in the world! "Well said," I agreed. "Double poo to you with a cherry on top!"

"And a cocktail umbrella!" Frankie chuckled.

"And a snowboard sticking out of the top!" Lyndz spluttered, between giggles.

"Snowboarding! Is that what you're doing?" Emma said, disbelievingly.

"Yeah," I gloated. "Jealous by any chance, are we?"

"I can't wait to go snowboarding, can you?" Rosie said to the rest of us. "It sounds so wicked!"

"So exciting," said Frankie solemnly.

"What, you mean you've never been?" Fliss said to the M&Ms sorrowfully. "Never mind – we'll tell you all about it next week!"

Do you know – for once, we had the M&Ms well and truly speechless. It was *ace*. They just couldn't think of any comeback! They both stood there, looking red-faced and totally jealous, and then in the end, Emily growled, "Hope you break your necks!" and they both stomped off in a huff.

We all collapsed into laughter. Definitely one–nil to the Sleepover Club!

At long last, Friday finally rolled around and

we all charged back from school for the sleepover at my house. Sleepovers are a bit tricky at my house because of me and Molly sharing a room. Molly usually sulks if she has to move into Emma's for the night, and makes a big fuss about letting my friends sleep on her precious half of the room. Like we're really going to trash the place! Us!

This week we had a bit of a result though, as she went to stay with Carli for the night. YES!!! Mum was going to pick them up on the way to the snow centre. So I suppose something good had come out of Molly going snowboarding with us – just about...

The first thing we did at Friday's sleepover was make an assault course in my bedroom. The only good-ish thing about sharing with Molly is it means we have a fairly big room between us – plus there are two beds which are good for playing trampolines on!

The assault course went like this. Three big bounces on my bed and a leap off, then a forward roll over to Molly's bed. Then we had to get on the floor and swarm under Molly's bed (past the smelly trainers, poo! That was an assault course in itself!) then cartwheel over to the bedroom door. Finally, a wriggle under our big saggy beanbag, a jump up to the windowsill, crawl along it and jump from there back on to my bed. Phew! What a brilliant course!

The only problem was the cartwheels. We were all going round in turn, but somehow Lyndz managed to kick Rosie in the face and then we all got a bit bunched up and kept bumping into each other. Excellent fun, though!

When we'd gone round a few times, I jumped up. "I know!" I said. "I'll teach you a few snowboarding tricks that Nick showed me."

"Ooh, Nick!" said Rosie at once.

"Nick says..." giggled Frankie.

"Nick knows *everything*!" said Fliss, clasping her hands to her chest and looking all dreamy and pathetic.

"Very funny," I said sarkily. "Now, then, I'll tell you how to strap your feet to the— *aaaargh!!*"

"Know-all!" said Lyndz.

"Show off!" said Frankie.

I couldn't get any further because suddenly the others were all pelting me with pillows, school bags and Molly's teddy bear. Somehow we ended up having this huge throwing match, all screaming and giggling hysterically.

"Knickers to Nick!" Lyndz screeched. "Big baggy white knickers to Nick!"

"Big Dad's Y-fronts to Nick!" Rosie gurgled. "He's not going snowboarding tomorrow – and we are!"

CHAPTER SEVEN

I could hardly get to sleep that night, I was so excited. And then when I finally did get to sleep, I dreamed about skimming around corners, deep white snow, speeding down mountains. I guess you could say something was on my mind!

I was the first to wake up, as usual. Why is it that on a school day, Mum has to practically drag me out of bed, but on a Saturday, my eyes ping open about six in the morning and I'm ready to go-go-GO!?

I lay in my sleeping bag, listening to the

others breathing, and I hugged myself tight with excitement. My tummy felt like it was fizzing up as I lay there, grinning away to myself like an idiot! HOOOORAY!! It was Saturday! We were going!!!

Mum was being super-nice that morning, and when we all came down for breakfast, she put plates of bacon, egg, mushrooms and fried bread in front of us. "It's a snowboarder's breakfast," she told us with a wink. "Need to build your strength up, don't you?"

"Definitely," I said, through a mouthful of eggy toast. "Thanks, Mum!"

Once we'd eaten our snowboarders' breakfasts, we piled into the cars. As Fliss, Lyndz and Rosie all got into my mum's car, I glumly agreed to go in the other car with Molly and Carli and my dad.

"I'd better keep you company, then," Frankie said, climbing in next to me. "Can't leave you to face the monsters on your own, can I?"

"Thanks," I said, sighing. "You're a true friend, Frankie Thomas!"

On the way to Carli's house, Dad made the

mistake of asking Frankie how her mum was. Instantly Frankie got her worried face on all over again.

"I didn't really like leaving her today," she confessed. "She's got her hospital check-up – and then, even worse, her and my dad were talking about going shopping! I mean, the stress of going into Leicester will send her blood pressure right up again, don't you think? She'll be on her feet all day – and there'll be all those people bumping into her..."

Frankie looked out the window as we sped along the road. "Maybe I should have stayed with her," she said softly.

"Don't be daft!" I said in alarm. Frankie looked like she was about to change her mind about coming with us – which would be AWFUL!

"She'll be fine, pet," Dad said gruffly. I think he's got a soft spot for Frankie, even if he does call her "Mad Frankie Thomas" sometimes. "The doctor will tell her if she's not fit to do anything strenuous, I'm sure. And just think, if she does go out, and has a really awful day shopping, at least it'll put her off going again for a good while, eh?"

"That's true," I said quickly. "And we're gonna give her a ring from the snow centre to check she's OK, yeah?"

"Yeah," Frankie agreed. "I'm probably worrying about nothing."

Phew – that was a close one! I found myself breathing out so heavily, I steamed the window right up.

It took us about half an hour to get there – and boy, was I glad to get out! Molly sat in the front with Dad, which meant that Creepy Carli sat in the back with me and Frankie. Triple YUCK. I'm not joking – nearly all the way there, she was digging her elbow into me. You know me – just can't ignore anyone if I think they're trying to have a pop at me, so after a bit, I was digging my own elbow into her, just as hard. Next thing you know, we're having an elbow fight on the back seat, and Dad has to pull over and shout at us to stop scrapping.

Why does Molly have to have such a HORRIBLE best friend?!

I was just thinking up plans to bury Molly and Carli in deep, deep snow, when Frankie nudged me. "Look – that must be it!" she said excitedly, pointing to a big white building in the distance.

The snow centre – COOL!!!

"Wow!" I breathed, unable to take my eyes off it. I felt like I was about to burst!

It was about eleven o'clock when we got there, so we had an hour to kill before our lesson at twelve. We met up with Mum and the others in the car park. I started jumping up and down, partly with excitement and partly 'cos it was so cold.

"Right, girls," Mum said. "Me and your dad are going to go to the gym for an hour while you have your lesson, OK? Then we'll meet up with you and we can all go for a swim. Then we can have a late lunch before coming home. What do you think of that?"

"Perfect!" I said. "Can we go in now? It's freezing!"

Dad laughed. "I really don't think the

snowboarding area is going to be any warmer, do you?" he said.

Mum and Dad took us round the complex so we knew exactly where everything was. We finished up in the spectators' gallery.

"Look," Frankie said with interest, "there's a snowboarding lesson going on!"

We all looked down eagerly. A row of people were wobbling about and falling all over the place.

"It looks a bit difficult," Fliss said uncertainly. "Do you think we'll be able to do it?"

"Oops! Over she goes!" Lyndz giggled, pointing to a large lady in a bright yellow puffa jacket who'd just toppled over into the snow.

"Look at him – right on his bum!" I said, laughing my head off at some poor bloke who was scrambling to his feet again.

"Ouch!" Mum said sympathetically. "Are you sure you still want to do this?"

"Definitely!" Molly said, eyes glued to the action below.

Fliss opened her mouth to say something.

"Yeah, of course we do!" I said quickly. "And anyone who doesn't dare is a CHICKEN!"

Fliss's mouth shut again, and I grinned to myself. I had her sussed!

"Hang on a minute – isn't that Nick?" sharp-eyed Rosie said, pointing to a guy in a blue woolly hat who was slithering about all over the snow.

I snorted. "I don't think so!" I said scornfully.

Lyndz scrunched up her eyes and peered in the direction of Rosie's finger. "Well, it looks like him," she said, slowly.

"Well, it isn't!" I said. "He can snowboard already – he's been snowboarding all round the world, he told me! Anyway, you've only seen him once, so what do you know?"

"I went into Mega Sports with Andy last week," Fliss chimed in. "And it does look like him, if you ask me!"

"Well, no-one *is* asking you, are they?" I said defensively. "And you lot think *I've* got him on the brain! Come on. We'd better go and get ready for our lesson."

*   *   *

Once we got into the boots-and-boards room, I found myself getting a bit bossy. Well, not bossy. Just... telling the others what to do, I suppose.

We went over to the junior boards section, and I pounced upon a turquoise board just like the one I'd stood on in the shop, although this one was about half the size! "Ah, Nick says this is a good make," I said, feeling grand. "It's the one I went on last time, actually."

"What – do you mean, when you just stood on it, in the shop?" Frankie said scathingly.

"Yeah, well, it's more than *you've* done," I pointed out. "And Nick said—"

"He didn't!" Rosie said sarcastically before I'd even had the chance to finish.

"What, Nick did?" Lyndz teased, joining in. "Your hero!"

"Nick really said that?" said Fliss. "You should have told us before!"

Honestly – you'd think they were jealous of my cool friend Nick or something! I couldn't help it if he was an experienced sporting hero, could I?

"Nick, Nick, Nick!" Frankie said suddenly. "It sounds to me like you'd rather be with him than with us!"

"Of course I wouldn't!" I said in astonishment. "I'd much rather be with you lot!"

"Good," she sniffed, not looking me in the eye. "Well, that's all right, then."

I was shocked. "Just 'cos I've been to see him a few times!" I said hotly. "It doesn't mean anything!"

Was Frankie jealous? I couldn't believe it!

"Oh, stop showing off in front of your friends," Molly said with a smirk, elbowing me out of the way. "Come on, Carls, let's get the best boots."

When Molly says things like that to me I really want to punch her one, but this time, I managed to hold my tongue all the time we were putting on our boots and collecting our boards. Then I held it a bit longer as we all trooped out in the snowy area where we'd be having our lesson.

Then I just couldn't hold it any more, and

picked up a *huge* handful of snow and stuffed it down Molly's neck. I'd give her showing off in front of my friends!

"*Aaaargh!*" she screeched as the freezing snow hit her bare skin. "You little..."

"Snow fight!" yelled Rosie in delight, and grabbed an armful of snow to hurl at Carli.

Suddenly we were all screaming with excitement and chucking snow about like anything. As it was five against two, Molly and Carli were getting soaked, fast!! I was starting to feel quite glad they'd come with us after all!

But then – *screeeeee!* A whistle blew, and we all jumped. I jumped so hard that I chucked my last snowball over my head and behind me.

"Girls, this is a snowboarding lesson, not a zoo!" came a sharp voice. "Stop that imme—"

Then there came this awful spluttering sound like someone trying to cough through snow...

We turned round in horror to see a tall woman in a fleecy red tracksuit wiping snow off her face. She glared at me as if I was a cockroach or something, and I suddenly had a very nasty feeling about where my last snowball had gone. WHOOPS!!!

"My name's Suzi and I'll be teaching you today," she said. "And I think you'd better all calm down before we do anything." She looked straight at me. "Now, is that clear?"

"Yes," I said in a small voice.

Her icy look seemed to thaw a bit, and then she gave us a smile. "Good," she said. "Let's get snowboarding!"

CHAPTER EIGHT

I hate to say it, but you know what? At first, I was just the *weeniest* bit disappointed by our snowboarding lesson. I know, I know – after all that fuss I made and everything. But in my head, I'd imagined us all on the main slope pretty much straightaway, cruising down dead fast, just like Nick had told me he'd done, and learning all these ace tricks.

Instead, we were on this baby slope – and even worse, Suzi told us there was no way we could go on the main slope until we'd had a few lessons and knew what we were doing.

Doh! So much for my big ideas, eh?

Suzi caught sight of my disappointed face and laughed. "Can you imagine if we just let anyone on the main slopes?" she said, shaking her head at the thought. "There would be all sorts of crashes and injuries – it would be very dangerous. Before you can go on, you have to prove you can control your speed, know how to stop and make turns properly. It's only fair on everyone else, don't you think?"

"Yeah," everyone said.

"I suppose so," I said grudgingly.

But I soon cheered up once the lesson got underway. It was such fun! And then I started to feel really glad we *weren't* on the main slopes, as one by one, we wobbled, fell down and knocked someone else over. It was really difficult – almost as tricky as skateboarding down the stairs had been!!

First of all, we had to get our boards securely fastened to our feet. It had been easy when Nick had done it all for me as I'd just stood there and let him do everything – but now it was down to us to do it ourselves.

"Make sure your board is facing *across* the hill," called Suzi, checking we were all in a good position. "We don't want you shooting off without being properly fastened in, do we? Now, put your front foot in while you're standing up. These boards have step-in bindings, so step the toe in first, and push the heel down until you hear a click. Got it?"

A series of clicks from along the line confirmed that we'd all managed it so far.

"Now put on your safety leash," Suzi said. "It goes on your front leg."

"What's it for?" asked Frankie.

"Well, if you fall over – which I'm pretty sure most of you will do – it stops the board from running away," Suzi explained. "OK. All ready?"

We were.

"Now, you always have to sit down to put your back foot in. Make sure there's no snow in the binding or on the bottom of your boot. Step the back foot in just like you did with the front." She waited until she'd heard all of our bindings click in place. "Now comes the fun part," she said with a grin. "Standing up!"

I bet you never thought standing up would be difficult, did you? You have to try this, then! Standing up when your feet are fastened to a bit of wood is reeeeallly tricky!! Take it from someone who knows.

"The main thing to remember is, always put the same weight on both feet," Suzi told us. "Have a go. If you get really stuck, roll over on to your knees and then stand up that way."

Well, one by one we just about managed to get up and stand there in a line on our boards. But then Lyndz started wobbling, made a grab for Rosie – and the pair of them collapsed down face first into the snow! I found myself giggling so much I thought I was going to go the same way and had to clutch at Frankie to keep myself vertical. This was going to be a lot harder than I'd thought!

Once we'd got used to standing up on the boards without wobbling off, we started going down the baby slope – or bunny slope, as Suzi called it. She pushed herself off and showed us how it was done – making it look like the easiest thing in the world, of course!

I went down next. WHHHEEEEEE! It was brilliant!! I stuck my arms out to the sides for balance, gritted my teeth and went down in a dead straight line, all the way to the bottom. As soon as I'd made it safely down, I promptly fell over on my bum. All the others cheered their heads off from the top.

"Way to go, girl!" yelled Frankie, punching the air.

She went next, and was just about to push herself off when Carli gave her a shove from behind...

"Wooooaaahhhhh!" Frankie shouted as she shot down the slope. She recovered her balance a bit, but was going so fast, she had to windmill her arms about to keep herself upright. "Heeeeeeellllp!" she screamed as she wobbled over and then tumbled down the hill. *Bump!* She landed in a heap at the bottom.

"Are you OK?" I called, scrabbling to undo my bindings. I rushed over to her – and heard Molly and Carli sniggering from the top.

Frankie struggled to her feet. "I'm gonna get you for that!" she yelled to Carli. Then she rubbed her bum where she'd landed on it. "Ouch," she moaned. "This snow feels more like rock!"

Suzi rushed over. "All right there?" she asked. "You did very well, considering that blonde girl pushed you like that. If she does that again, she'll have to sit the lesson out."

She looked up at Carli with a frown. "You there," she shouted. "Let's have less of the pushing, or your lesson ends right here. Got that?"

Me and Frankie smirked at each other and pulled horrible faces at Carli behind Suzi's back. Always good to see the enemy getting a ticking off!

Fliss was next. She looked very nervous about the whole thing, and stood there for ages, fiddling about with her bindings as if they were going to pop undone any second.

"Come on! Give it a go!" Suzi called encouragingly.

Fliss looked warily over her shoulder to check Carli and Molly were out of pushing distance. Fliss hates people doing things like that. She either gets dead cross about it or bursts into tears. When she was sure she was safe, she stood up very stiff and straight and pushed herself off, arms rigidly out to the sides, as if she were made of wood.

"Very good," Suzi shouted as Fliss came down the slope. "Try and relax your body a bit!"

Fliss wasn't about to relax anything for fear of toppling over. She came all the way down in the same stiff way, coming neatly to a stop at the bottom. Only then did she allow her arms to relax. She had this tiny chuffed smile and her cheeks were flushed pink.

"That was very good," Suzi said warmly. "Your balance was excellent!"

Fliss went even pinker. "Thank you," she said, struggling to undo her feet from the board. Her eyes were shining. "That was fun!"

Soon we'd all been down a few times and were starting to get a feel for it. Suzi taught us how to come to a clean stop by digging our back foot right into the board and leaning all our weight on to it, and then taught us how to do left and right turns on the slope. It was just so much fun, whizzing down one by one – but then when Suzi told us that our time was almost up, I nearly cried. I couldn't believe the time had flown by so quickly!

"We'll have one more go each, and then that's about it for your first lesson," she said.

"Ohhhh!" I moaned. "Already?"

She smiled at me. "Afraid so. You've done very well though. I think you're a bit of a natural, Kenny!"

I glowed with pride. I was practically radioactive with glowing! A natural!! She thought I was a natural, after one lesson! How cool was that?!

I should have left it there, of course. I should have just accepted the compliment and left it at that. But no. That's not me, is it? Kenny McKenzie always has to go one further – as I was about to prove yet again!

CHAPTER NINE

OK, I admit it. I was showing off.

All right, all right – so I was showing off a lot.

I just couldn't resist it, OK?!

I was about to have my last go down the slope – and who could say when I'd get the chance to do this again? Maybe not for years!! Maybe this was the last time I'd get to snowboard until I was grown up, and that was just *ages* away.

The way I looked at it, it was my last chance to try something a bit... well, a bit adventurous. And there's no need to look at me like that. I bet you'd have done the same.

"Come on, then, Kenny," Suzi said. "Last go. Let's see you make a left turn first, followed by a right turn to finish off with."

"OK," I said.

Do you ever get a voice in your head that urges you to do naughty things? I seem to get it all the time. And this time it was a loud voice. This time it was saying, "Try one of those jumps that Nick told you about!"

The sensible side of me was trying to ignore the naughty voice – but this voice was just *sooooo* persuasive...

"Go on, Kenz," Frankie said. "What are you waiting for?"

"Ooh, Kenny's scared!" Carli mocked, and started making all these chicken noises at me.

Well, if there's one thing I'm not, it's a chicken. No-one could ever call me that!

"Right, Carli," I thought. "I'll show YOU!!!"

I had in mind this thing I'd seen on one of the videos in Nick's shop. I think it's called the corkscrew, but basically it's someone on a snowboard jumping up and whizzing round and round in the air and then landing flat and zooming off again. COOOL!

I was a natural, wasn't I? I reckoned I could have a go at it – and really impress Suzi!

"Watch this!" I said grandly.

I started off down the slope. Then, about a third of the way down, I bent my knees and tried to whizz myself round like I'd seen the guys on the video do. It had all looked so easy for them...

"Kenny, what are you...?" I heard Suzi call anxiously – but suddenly the world had become a blur. With a massive effort, I'd launched myself into the air, spun round and round – and landed flat on my back. YOWCH! I gave a scream as my ankle was wrenched from the snowboard and I rolled all the way down the rest of the slope, my board bumping along after me.

There was this terrible silence. All I could hear was the sound of my own pain roaring all over my body. Every part of me seemed to be throbbing and aching. I lay in a heap, breathing quickly, my heart pounding.

Suzi ran over. "Kenny, what on *earth* were you trying to do?" she shouted, sounding half-cross and half-frightened.

"I'm sorry," I gasped, as dizzy spells came and went in my head. For a second I thought I would faint. "I was trying to do the corkscrew," I said, feeling like an idiot.

"The *corkscrew*?! Kenny, you're a beginner, remember!" she said. "You can't expect to do that kind of trick for months!"

I groaned as she started taking the board off my other foot. "Ouch," I said. "Ow – *please* don't touch my ankle. It's really really sore!"

Frankie snowboarded down to us. "What's up?" she asked breathlessly. "Do you want me to get your dad, Kenz? He's a doctor," she added for Suzi's benefit.

"Yes, that's a good idea," Suzi said. "This ankle's had a nasty twist. It definitely needs some looking at."

Frankie took her board off and charged away. One by one, the others came down the slope and stood around us.

"You idiot, Kenny!" Molly said scornfully.

"It looked good, though," Lyndz said, trying to be kind. "It did look really good, Kenny."

"Yeah, till she went whack on her back!" Carli sniggered. "That just looked stupid, if you ask me!"

"I'm really sorry, Suzi," I said in a small voice.

"Well, it was a very silly thing to do, Kenny, but I've got to confess – I did exactly the same thing on my first lesson," Suzi said, winking at me. "We must be as bad as each other."

"Did you?" I asked, feeling a bit better.

"Yep," she said. "Broke my wrist. It was a good lesson to me, though. It taught me to know my limits."

"Well, this has taught me how painful an ankle can feel," I grumbled. "OW!!"

"Here's Dad," Molly called. "He doesn't look very happy, Kenny."

Dad was picking his way over the snow with the medical bag of tricks that he takes everywhere. "How did I know this was going to happen?" he said gruffly. "And how did I know it was going to happen to you?"

Mum was right behind. "Oh, love, are you all right?" she said sympathetically. "How did you manage that?"

Dad knelt down and took my boot and sock off. My ankle was about the size of a grapefruit and still throbbing.

"Ouch!" I yelled as he pressed it all over. "Careful, Dad!"

"It's not broken," he said at last. "But it's a nasty sprain. We'll have to get that strapped up for you."

Suzi got to her feet. "Well, I'm sorry the lesson had to end this way, everyone," she said. "But you all did very well, and I hope to see you again for another lesson soon. Bye!"

Dad snorted as she walked over to the next group of people. "Not if I've got anything to do with it!" he said. "I don't want my daughters to be crocked before they're even in their teens!"

So that was me out of action for the rest of the day. I couldn't believe that my daredevil ways had got me in trouble AGAIN! That's the last time I do anything like that, I'm telling you.

Well. Until I forget and do it next time, of course...

Dad strapped my ankle up tightly and helped me hobble along. I suddenly felt really tired after all the excitement.

"That was so excellent," Rosie said, skipping along to the pool changing rooms.

"Awesome," Frankie agreed happily, her eyes shining. "I loved doing those turns, didn't you?"

"We'll definitely have to try and come again," Lyndz said. "I want to have a go at the corkscrew too!"

"No, you don't," I said feelingly, wincing with pain as I hobbled along.

"Thanks ever so much for taking us," said Fliss to my mum and dad, going a bit pink. "We did really enjoy it."

"Glad to hear it, Felicity," Mum said, sounding pleased. "Do you think you lot have got enough energy for a swim next?"

"YEEEEAAAHHH!" everyone shouted. Well, everyone except me – old Hop-Along!

I turned to Frankie. "Do you want to give

your mum a ring first?" I asked. "I might as well come with you, seeing as I won't be swimming!"

"Yeah, good idea," she said. "Don't wait for us, everyone – I'll catch up with you all in the changing rooms!"

The two of us slowly made our way to the telephone area, Frankie helping me hobble along. I sat and waited while she spoke to her mum.

When she came off the phone, she looked a thousand times happier. "Oh, guess what! Her blood pressure's getting back to normal – and everything's fine with the baby!"

"Oh, brilliant!" I said, giving her a hug. "That's ace news. Do you feel better?"

"Yeah, tons better," she said, grinning all over her face. "I've just been so looking forward to having a little brother or sister. I wanted it all to be perfect, you know what I mean? I've just been so worried about her – and now it looks like it's all going to be fine. Brilliant!"

"Yeah," I said – and then I paused,

remembering what she'd said to me earlier. "Frankie, did you mean what you said before, about me caring more about Nick than the Sleepover Club?"

She looked a bit sheepish. "Not really," she said. "I was just in a bit of a funny mood."

"Really?" I said.

She nodded. "Really."

"So we're best mates again?" I asked. Well, I had to check, didn't I?

She smiled at me, and helped me to my feet. "Definitely best mates again."

While the others were all swimming and having a good time in the pool, I had to sit in the spectators' area with Mum and Dad. Typical of my luck, eh?! I was really starting to regret being a daredevil – as usual. The only good bit was watching the others grabbing Carli and dunking her in the deep end. I was just gutted I wasn't there to help them!

After they'd all got showered and changed again, we had a quick lunch and then it was time to go home again.

"How's it going, Hop-Along?" Frankie asked me as we headed for reception and the way out.

"Oh, it's OK," I said. "Better to twist your ankle snowboarding than running for a bus, I suppose. At least everyone's going to ask me how I did it, and I can tell them all about today!"

"Oh yes, I did it snowboarding, don't you know?" Rosie said, putting on a posh voice. "What? You've never been? Oh, darling, you're missing out!"

"Yeah, and I can't wait to tell Nick about it all," I said enthusiastically. "I feel like I'll know what he's talking about now – I'll feel like a *real* snowboarder, if you know what I mean."

"Talk of the devil..." Lyndz said, pointing straight ahead. "Why not tell him right now?"

I blinked in surprise. There at the reception desk was... was Nick!!

CHAPTER TEN

I could hardly believe my eyes. Nick! In the flesh! So had it really been him slithering around on the beginner slopes? No... it just *couldn't* have been! He was far too experienced for that! What about all those resorts he said he'd been to? What about everything he'd said to me?

"It must be a massive coincidence," I said in the end, with a frown. "Maybe he's come here to teach a lesson or something."

The others exchanged looks, and Frankie raised one of her eyebrows in disbelief.

I started to feel a bit weird about the whole thing. Just what *was* he doing here, anyway?

We were almost level with him now, and I was just about to tap him on the shoulder when he reached the front of the queue at the reception desk.

"Hi. Could I book another Beginners' lesson for next week, please?" he said. "Yeah, it's Nick Parker..."

I nearly fell over in shock. *Beginners'* lesson? What?? What was going on?

"Did you hear that?" Frankie said. "He's a beginner too!" She burst out laughing. "After all that!"

The others all started to giggle. "What a liar!" Fliss said indignantly. "Pretending he knew all about it!"

Nick obviously heard her because he turned round quickly. When he saw the five of us staring at him accusingly, he flushed a deep red.

"Hi, Kelly," he said weakly. "Fancy seeing you here."

"It's *Kenny*," I said, feeling scornful. "And fancy seeing *you* here – booking a Beginners' lesson!"

He went even redder, right up to the roots of his hair. It looked like a beetroot had been plopped on top of his neck instead of a head. "Well, er... I've got a trip to France planned soon," he said falteringly. "Just brushing up on a few tricks, you know..."

"Oh yeah?" Frankie said disbelievingly, putting her hands on her hips. "You made out to Kenny you were an expert!"

"Well, I..." he said, obviously trying to think of something to say.

The woman at the reception desk tapped her pen loudly. "Excuse me, sir – your ticket?"

Nick grabbed it, looking grateful for the excuse to finish the conversation. "Thanks," he said to her. "Well, you guys, gotta go," he said, not meeting any of us in the eye.

"Yeah, I bet you have," Rosie said loudly.

"What a creep!" Frankie said as he scurried off to the car park.

"And what a liar, coming out with all those

stories!" Fliss said, folding her arms across her chest.

I said nothing. I just couldn't believe that my hero had turned out to be so... so *pathetic*. He was no more experienced at snowboarding than us!

Lyndz slipped an arm in mine. "I bet he's never even *tried* a corkscrew," she said comfortingly. "You're far more daring than him!"

"Yeah! All he can do is work in a shop and make stories up about it," Frankie said. "Sad!!"

"Sad, but quite funny as well," Rosie said. "Did you see his face? He was so gutted!! He's probably terrified you're going to spoil his cool image in the shop now!"

"You should do," Lyndz said. "It would serve him right!"

I knew they were trying to cheer me up but I couldn't help feeling massively disappointed in Nick. I'd built him up in my head to be this total super-cool dude, the kind of person that I really wanted to be. He'd been my role model, coming out with all those stories about the amazing things he'd done all over the world. And then to find out that really he was just a bit sad, as Frankie said... It had made me feel all mixed up. How could I have fallen for all his stories like that?

I felt dead quiet and confused. What a let down!

"Who cares about him, anyway?" Fliss said. "We're proper snowboarders ourselves now. We've got our own stories to tell!"

"Yeah," Frankie said. "And you've even got an injury to show off about, Kenz."

"That's true," I said.

"And you're a natural, remember," Lyndz pointed out. "You'll probably be giving HIM lessons soon!"

"Yeah," I said, brightening up. "That would show him, wouldn't it?"

Then I remembered how this had been a one-off treat that I'd had to beg and plead for. "Mind you, when will we ever get to go again?" I groaned.

"There's always birthdays," Frankie said. "And Christmas coming up..."

"And our parents are soooo generous, they're bound to take us again soon," Molly said, winking at Dad. "Aren't they?"

He laughed. "We'll see," was all he would say.

"Goodbye, snow centre," I said sadly as we got near the exit doors. "Hope to see you again soon, hint hint..."

Then Molly pushed open one of the doors, and we all gasped...

It was snowing outside! Real snow – and lots of it!

Frankie was the first to react. "You know what this means, don't you?" she said, grabbing me excitedly. "Sledging in the park! Almost as good as snowboarding!"

"And it's free!" Lyndz yelled, jumping up and down. "Yippeeee!"

Well, what do you know? Things were looking up already. "I can practise doing the corkscrew on a sledge," I said excitedly, imagining in my head how totally cool it would look.

"Oh, no you don't," Mum said warningly.

"Not until that ankle's better, anyway!"

"We can have a snowball fight with the M&Ms!" Rosie said gleefully.

"We can build snowmen!" Fliss squealed.

"Sledging races down Cuddington Hill!" Lyndz shouted, jumping up and down.

Suddenly the world seemed a much better place as the snowflakes drifted down into our hair. Even Carli and Molly were dancing about in it.

I stuck my tongue out to catch a snowflake. "Yum!" I said as it melted in my mouth.

"You have to make a wish now," Mum said, with a smile. "I wonder what it's going to be?"

I screwed my eyes up tight and crossed all my fingers. Guess what I wished for?!

Well, that's about it from me on our snowboarding story. I'll tell you what, though. When my ankle's better and we sort out another trip, you'll have to come with us. Honestly – it's just the best!! And next time, I'm determined to work out how to do the corkscrew properly, too...

But guess what? In the meantime, I'm boycotting Mega Sports and going back to the old sports shop in Leicester again. Maybe I'll find a new role model there, who knows?

Hang on – the phone's ringing. Just a sec...

"Hi, Kenz – it's Frankie. Just to say that now Mum's OK again, I've been thinking about some more brilliant things the Sleepover Club can do together, and I was wondering if you fancied coming over so we can make some plans together..."

What do you reckon? Of course I fancied it! Now *that's* what I call a happy ending!

Well, looks like that's all from me this time. I'd better go. I said I'd meet her in half an hour. See ya later, alligator!

Happy New Year, Sleepover Club!

HarperCollins *Children's Books*

CHAPTER ONE

Hi there. I know what you're going to say. "Frankie, you're late!"

I'm right aren't I? That's what the others are always saying these days. It always used to be Lyndz who was late, and I was super-dooper organised. Not any more! My house is so manic at the moment it's a wonder I ever get out at all. But I'll tell you all about that in a minute. We really ought to sit down and catch up on all the goss. Fliss is still recovering. Poor Fliss, it all got a bit much for her – and her mum. But Kenny was in seventh heaven because she managed to do her doctor bit at last. And Lyndz and Rosie, well they're still hiccuping and giggling about it whenever anyone even mentions what happened.

Sorry I'm gabbling, but there's just so much to tell you. Come on, let's sit over here and I'll fill you in on all the details. But boy, where do I start? OK, well I guess the beginning's as good a place as any.

It all started before Christmas. No, much sooner than that. It all *really* started months ago when I found out that Mum was pregnant. I'd wanted a little baby brother or sister for as long as I could remember, and when I found out that Mum was expecting one I was totally blown away by the excitement. The others all tried their hardest to put me off by giving me loads of grisly details.

"Babies are just totally embarrassing," warned Lyndz. "Didn't you learn *anything* when we were helping Rosie's sister with her babysitting last time?" (Now that's a story and a half – if you haven't read about it yet, you're in for a real treat!) "Babies are either pooing or being sick. And my older brothers aren't much better."

Poor Lyndz has *four* brothers and she reckons that they make her life a misery.

"At least you'll be a lot older than your brother or sister," reasoned Kenny. "You'll be able to boss it about all the time. How cool is that!"

Her eyes gleamed at the thought. Molly the Monster, as you know, is only a year older than Kenny, but is one major super-witch when it comes to being horrible.

"Yeah, when you're wanting to go out, it'll be pestering you to play!" laughed Rosie. "Tiff always says that I'm a major pain when she's getting glammed up, and she's only four years older than me! But I'm sure that you'll have a lot more patience than her," she added. "And you won't have a boyfriend as ugly as Spud either."

The others all nodded.

"I won't have a boyfriend at all!" I said indignantly.

"Yes you will!" snorted Fliss. "When the

baby is our age, you'll be twenty! Imagine that. You'll probably be at university then. You might even be married!"

We all guffawed.

"No way!" I yelled. "You'll be married to Ryan Scott, more like!"

Fliss just blushed and went all giggly – as usual!

We had loads of conversations like that, and the others always told me horror stories about being a sister. Now don't get me wrong. I was still desperate to have a baby to look after, but the more they told me, the more nervous I got. I mean, it just seemed so long since I'd found out about the baby, and it wasn't even due until January.

"I wish it would hurry up!" I told Mum one day at the beginning of December. "I just want to get on with being a big sister."

"Well, I'm not ready to be a new mum again just yet, thank you very much!" she laughed. "We've still got far too much to do!"

That was true. They still hadn't sorted out where the baby was going to sleep for one thing. At this rate, it would be sharing Pepsi's basket in the kitchen!

"But how will I know if I'll be any good as a sister?" I asked Mum.

"You'll be just great!" she smiled, ruffling my hair. "If you're so worried, you could always practise on something. There are some schools which make students look after a bag of flour as though it's a baby. I know it sounds weird, but it gets them used to having someone else to think about."

"You want me to push a bag of flour about in a pram?" I asked, open-mouthed.

"It doesn't have to be a bag of flour," Mum explained. "You could use one of your old dolls. The important thing is to treat it as though it really is a baby. No dumping it under your bed when you're fed up with it. Just look after it for a day or so and I guarantee it will open your eyes."

Yes, I know, I know – it sounds really wacky, doesn't it? But I thought it might be worth a try. I went up to my room and pulled the box of old dolls out of my cupboard. I hadn't looked at them for absolutely *ages* and it felt really weird holding them again.

"You're way too old for all this, Frankie," I told myself.

But I got them all out anyway and sat them in a line on my bed. I felt kind of funny seeing them like that, because it brought back memories of when I was little. I had this one doll I used to call Diz which I used to take everywhere with me. I picked it up now, and it looked so tiny and shabby. I felt really bad, like I'd abandoned it or something. But I couldn't use that as my baby because it just didn't look right. It was too small for a start and had matted wool hair. The others didn't look much better, to be honest with you.

Then I spotted 'the doll with no name'. A friend of Mum's had given it to me just as I was growing out of my doll phase and I'd never really played with it. But it was about the right size for a baby. It had no hair and it still smelt kind of clean and new.

"Come on then!" I said, picking her up. "You

can be my baby. Are you going to be a good girl?" I cooed, tickling her under the chin.

I was amazed how quickly I got into all the baby stuff. Before long it didn't seem weird at all to be wandering round with a doll. But you know my friends. As soon as they saw me with the doll one Saturday, they thought I'd lost it completely.

"Francesca Thomas, have you gone mad?" screeched Kenny when she saw me carrying Izzy. (I called my doll Isobel, Izzy for short, because that's what I wanted Mum to call the baby if she had a girl.)

"I'm just winding her after her feed!" I explained, patting Izzy's back.

"I'll wind you in a minute!" she yelled. "What are you like?"

No amount of explaining what I was doing would make her shut up. And the others weren't much better. Even Fliss had a go at me.

"You look really silly, Frankie," she hissed. "I wish you'd put that stupid doll down. It's going to be really embarrassing if anyone sees us."

I must admit that I did feel a bit of a dipstick taking it to the shops with us, but a deal is a deal. Mum said that I had to treat the doll just like a real baby. If I had to go to the shops then it would just have to come with me. I couldn't leave Izzy at home, could I?

"Couldn't you ask your mum to babysit?" asked Lyndz. Kenny rolled her eyes.

"I don't think so. I'm supposed to be learning how to be a big sister," I explained. "Mum already knows how to be a mum, so asking her to babysit a doll would be a bit pointless."

"The whole thing's pointless if you ask me," grumbled Kenny. "Well, are we going to the shops or not?"

To start with, I made a sort of sling with my scarf and kept Izzy snuggled under my jacket. The December wind was pretty fierce and I didn't want her to get cold.

"You are sad, sad, sad," chanted Kenny, as I kept fussing beneath my jacket.

"At least no one can see the doll," said Fliss. "You just look fat!"

"Thanks very much!" I said, feeling a bit miffed.

But it soon got uncomfortable having Izzy in one position so I started wriggling and jiggling, trying to move her about. It didn't help that her arms and legs weren't all squidgy like a real baby's. They were rigid plastic and kept digging into me.

"Don't do that, Frankie!" Rosie reprimanded me. "You look as though you've got ants in your pants or something. People are looking at you."

It was true. There were hundreds of people about doing their Christmas shopping, and I could sense that most of them were glancing at me and frowning.

"Maybe I should just show them Izzy," I suggested, unzipping my jacket.

"Don't do that!" the others all yelled together.

"That would be a major embarrassment for all of us," hissed Kenny.

"Hey, what's that poster?" Fliss suddenly shouted at the top of her voice. She was being so OTT, it was obvious that she was trying to divert our attention. She sort of galloped over to the noticeboard at the end of the high street. The rest of us cracked up and galloped after her. It wasn't easy with a doll poking you in the chest with every step, I can tell you.

"It's advertising a Millennium New Year's Eve party at the church hall," explained Fliss, standing in front of the poster. "Do you think we'll be able to go?"

"Not a chance," said Rosie. "My mum's only ever let me stay up to see the New Year in once, and that was because I was sick."

"I'm not sure I'd want to go anyway," Kenny said. "It'll be full of boring old duffers who we don't even know. It'd be much better to have a New Year's Eve party of our own."

"Yes!" we all screamed. "Why don't we? It'd be so cool!"

"We should try to organise a special New Year's Eve sleepover," I suggested. "I mean, we're usually awake till well past midnight when we're together anyway. It would be great to stay up properly. Everyone else'll be up too, because of the year 2000, so who could object?"

We were so excited we started doing a little dance together on the pavement. And that's when Izzy fell out of my jacket and bounced on to the ground.

"Oh no!" I screamed, picking her up. "I've killed her!"

"Erm, earth to Frankie!" hooted Kenny. "It is only a doll, you know!"

"But it's supposed to be my baby sister," I spluttered. "What if I do that to her?"

"Don't be crazy!" shrieked Lyndz. "Do you think your parents would really let us loose in charge of their baby? I don't think so!"

"But even so," I wailed. "I was supposed to take care of Izzy and I haven't. I'm going to be a useless sister!"

Fliss led me over to a nearby bench and we all sat down.

"You're going to be a great sister, Frankie," she reassured me. "That was just an accident when you forgot about the d... I mean, Izzy."

"But what if I forget about the real baby when I'm supposed to be looking after it?" I asked.

"Believe me, you *never* forget when you've got a baby around," Lyndz grinned. "They never stop crying. And they usually smell disgusting too!"

I was rocking Izzy in my arms and the others were all bending over her, just like she was real.

"Well I've seen everything now!" boomed a loud voice.

We looked up quickly, but with sinking hearts we already knew who it was. Why had the M&Ms picked that exact minute to walk past us?

"Aw, has Francesca got a baby? Diddums," said Emma Hughes in a stupid voice.

"Does she like playing with her dolly then?" cooed Emma's sidekick Emily Berryman.

"I always knew you were a big baby, Thomas!" cackled Emma. "I grew out of dolls when I was about four. You lot have never grown up, have you?"

Kenny was seething, I could sense it.

"Frankie's taking part in some scientific research, if you must know," she said in her weariest voice. "Not that you'd understand."

"Oh right, that's the first time I've heard playing with dolls called 'scientific research'," sneered Emily. "Why don't you face it? You're a load of little kids!"

They both screamed with laughter and tottered down the high street on their platform wedges.

"I don't believe that!" Fliss had her head in her hands. "Of all the people to see us with that stupid doll!"

"They'll never let us forget it," moaned Rosie. "It'll be all round the school on Monday!"

"Not if I've got anything to do with it," fumed Kenny through gritted teeth.

And when Kenny spoke like that the rest of us knew that it meant trouble. Trouble with a capital T!

CHAPTER TWO

To be honest with you, seeing those two galumphing gorillas put a real damper on our whole weekend. We didn't even discuss the Millennium New Year sleepover again, so you can tell how bad we were feeling. And Kenny went totally weird. I mean, even weirder than usual. When the rest of us were panicking about the M&Ms, she was like lost in a trance. Then she suddenly leapt up and announced that she had to go to the shop to buy some – get this – JELLY CUBES. I mean, here we were, facing doom and disaster from our biggest rivals, and Kenny's planning a party tea! But she just had this crazy look on her face and kept saying that she needed jelly cubes to make everything all right. I prefer chocolate to cheer myself up actually, but each to their own, as my gran always says.

Anyway, before we said goodbye to each other on Saturday, we arranged to meet outside school on Monday morning. That way we could all face the Gruesome Twosome together.

I had a really bad feeling as I walked to school that morning. Doom and panic whizzed about in my stomach like one of Kenny's disastrous cooking experiments. Fliss and Rosie were already standing together by the wall, and they looked as green as I felt. Only Lyndz seemed as bright and breezy as usual. I swear that if that girl was any more laid back, she'd be permanently asleep!

"Oh come on, we've taken flak from the M&Ms before," she reasoned. "How bad can it be this time?"

Nobody answered.

When we got to the gate we could see the M&Ms in a little huddle with their stupid mate Alana 'Banana' Palmer.

"I wonder where Kenny is? She ought to be here by now," mumbled Fliss. Her teeth were chattering, and I don't think it was because of the cold.

Rosie stuck her tongue out and pulled gruesome faces at the M&Ms – well, at their backs, to be precise. Then she mumbled something no one could understand.

"What?"

Rosie stopped pulling faces. "I said 'I don't know but she seemed really mad on Saturday'!" she explained.

Just before the whistle went, Kenny came flying up to us, holding tightly on to her school bag. She didn't look mad now. In fact, she looked positively perky.

"What's up with you?" I asked her suspiciously.

"You'll see," she grinned. "Just distract the M&Ms for a couple of minutes when we get inside."

"What?" Fliss looked horrified. "But we're trying to stay out of their way!"

"We can't avoid them for ever," Kenny told her calmly. "Better to get all their sarky comments over with at once."

Now it wasn't like her to be so rational, so I knew she had something majorly wicked up her sleeve.

Just then the whistle sounded, so we had no choice but to go into school.

"Remember – distract them!" hissed Kenny as we headed towards the classroom.

As it was December, we were all muffled up in coats and scarves, so we knew that we'd be in the cloakroom with the M&Ms for a few minutes. When we got there, Kenny gave me this big wink, and headed behind the coat rack. The M&Ms were already tugging off their boots. As soon as they saw us they started laughing in a really OTT way.

"Have you got your doll under there then, Frankie?" asked Emma loudly so that everyone could hear.

"We were wondering if you'd like to start

a little dolly crèche in the corner of the classroom," Emily Berryman rasped in her gruff voice.

"Or better still, go back to the nursery class!" guffawed Emma. "Four-year-olds are about on your level, aren't they?"

We just took off our coats and ignored them. I could see Kenny ferreting about in the M&Ms' bags and there was a bit of a weird smell, but I couldn't tell what she was doing. All I did know was that when the M&Ms looked ready to go into the classroom, I had to stall them.

"I was conducting an experiment, that's all!" I blurted out. The others looked horrified.

"You make me laugh Thomas, you really do!" sniffed Emma.

"What kind of experiment?" asked Emily curiously.

I didn't really want to tell them about Mum being pregnant and everything. It felt like if they knew, they'd make fun of that too and it would spoil everything.

As I was trying to think of an answer,

Kenny appeared and said, "She's not going to tell you is she? It's classified information."

"Get real!" snapped Emma, and gathering up their bags, they walked into the classroom.

"What were you doing?" I asked Kenny when they'd gone.

"You'll find out soon enough!" she smiled, and tapped her nose.

At least Mrs Weaver had something exciting to take our mind off the dreadful duo. At the end of the Christmas term, each class performs in a concert. This year Mrs Weaver told us that we would be writing our own play.

"Well it's not a play exactly," she explained. "It's going to be a series of sketches about the twentieth century."

We all looked pretty blank.

"Say someone born in 1900 was still alive," Mrs Weaver continued. "What changes would they have seen?"

"There's more football on the telly now!" Ryan Scott shouted out.

Mrs Weaver flashed him one of her 'you-think-you've-got-the-better-of-me-but-you-haven't-really' smiles.

"I think what you mean, Ryan, is that yes, we do have television now. But there wasn't a broadcasting service at all until 1936."

"Imagine life without *Match of the Day*!" moaned Danny McCloud. "Bummer!"

"That's exactly what I want you to do, Danny! Imagine what life would be like," Mrs Weaver went on. "I want you to think of all the things you take for granted now, and find out when they were invented and how they have developed. Work in your groups, but I don't want any noise. Understood?"

We all nodded, and started chattering away.

"I love doing this kind of thing," I told the others. "You learn about stuff without even realising it."

But Kenny wasn't listening. She was propped up on the desk, eyeballing the M&Ms. "Open your bags," she was muttering under her breath. "Come on!"

"There's almost too much to think about," Lyndz said, doodling on her notebook. "I mean, *loads* of stuff must have happened since 1900."

"Yeah, but what's the most important?" I asked. I looked around the classroom. "I mean, look at computers. They haven't been around for that long, have they? And now everyone's got them."

"And they use them in supermarkets and banks and stuff where you can't even see them," added Rosie.

"My gran thinks supermarkets are really new!" laughed Lyndz. "She says that she used to have to queue up at loads of different shops for her shopping. Imagine that – it would take *ages*!"

Fliss didn't seem to be listening to the rest of us either. She was doing loads of little drawings. Typical Fliss.

"Come on Fliss, we're supposed to be working!" I told her.

"I *am* working!" she snapped, showing me her drawings of fashion designs. "Clothes have changed loads since 1900. Women still wore long dresses then. And Mum said that when girls started wearing mini-skirts in the 1960s, it caused a real stir. There must have been loads of changes in between."

Fliss did have a point.

"Drawing dollies, are we?" Emma Hughes sidled across and peered over Fliss's shoulder.

"No I'm not!" snapped Fliss, and covered her work with her arm.

"What are you doing, Thomas? The development of experiments using dolls?" asked Emily Berryman.

They both giggled in that stupid way they have.

"And what are *you* doing? The history of not doing any work, as usual," Kenny sneered. "You haven't even got anything out of your bags yet."

"We're just going to look at some books!" Emma 'the Queen' Hughes said crossly, and they both stalked past us to the book corner.

We settled down again and made loads of

lists. Nearly everything we could think of that was important in our lives had been invented since 1900. We looked things up in books and on the computer, and the time flashed past. We even talked about the work over break too, which is very unusual for us. Well, the rest of us talked about it – Kenny didn't. She kept trying to see whether the M&Ms had their bags with them. They didn't.

When we got back into the classroom after break, Mrs Weaver said that she wanted some idea of what we would all be contributing to our play. I could see the M&Ms huddled together with their cronies. They kept flashing looks over to our table, then whispering and giggling together.

"Well, what are we going to do?" I asked the others. "Any ideas?"

"Fashion!" Fliss piped up. "Please let's! It'd be dead cool."

"I don't want to get involved in a stupid fashion show again!" grumbled Kenny.

"It won't be a fashion show, it's history. Please, pretty please!" Fliss pleaded.

The rest of us looked at each other.

"Oh all right!" we agreed, but Kenny looked pretty disgusted.

"Right then, who's going to start?" asked Mrs Weaver.

Emma Hughes stuck up her hand and started waving it about. She always has to get noticed. And with Mrs Weaver, it usually works.

"Yes Emma, what have you got planned?"

"Well, we thought we'd trace the history of fashion since 1900," she said, ever so sweetly.

"But that's what *we* were going to do!" squealed Fliss. "That's not fair, she's copied us!"

Poor Fliss was quite red in the face and angry.

"Now Felicity, there are thousands of exciting ideas to cover," soothed Mrs Weaver. "I'll give your group a few more minutes to think of another topic. Well done Emma, that's a splendid idea."

I thought Fliss was going to cry, I really did. Especially when we turned round and saw the stupid M&Ms and their awful cronies grinning at us.

"We'll get you!" Kenny mouthed to them menacingly.

"What should we do?" I whispered to the others.

"What about television and radio – stuff like that?" suggested Rosie.

But just then Ryan Scott announced that they were covering television.

"I don't believe it!" grumbled Rosie.

"What about computers, then?" I suggested.

"OK!" the others agreed, but you could tell that they weren't very enthusiastic.

"We're going to look at the way computers have altered our lives," piped up Kevin Green, who's a real swot.

We all groaned. Mrs Weaver thought that we were being rude about Kevin Green and turned to us crossly.

"Well Francesca, what is your group going to entertain us with?"

My mind went blank. I couldn't think of a thing.

But then Kenny piped up, cool as you like, "We're going to look at medical developments since 1900."

"What?" shrieked Fliss. Blood and gore are just not her thing *at all*.

"It'll be cool, Fliss, trust me!" Kenny grinned.

"Excellent!" smiled Mrs Weaver, clapping her hands. "Books out everyone, it's time to do some maths!"

Kenny nudged me. "Watch this!" she hissed.

Everyone bent down into their bags... and a few seconds later, there was this *terrifying* scream! Emma Hughes ran for the door with awful slime dripping from her hands. Her friend wasn't far behind.

We immediately turned to Kenny.

"Wicked, isn't it? I made up some of our sleepover slime last night," she whispered, grinning madly. "And it was great because it felt just like *snot*. But the best bit is, I added some of Merlin's droppings as well!"

Fliss shuddered. She hates even the *thought* of Kenny's pet rat.

"That's gross!"

"And you poured it into the M&Ms' bags?" squeaked Lyndz. "Fab!"

Mrs Weaver had gone to investigate. When she came back into the classroom, she was mega mad. And so were the M&Ms, who were following behind her.

"I hope that no one in here is responsible for that ridiculous prank," Mrs Weaver barked.

We all looked suitably shocked.

"Because I warn you, I'm going to come down like a ton of bricks if I find anybody engaged in such childish behaviour."

I swear that she looked right at Kenny as she said that. But Kenny just nodded in a really serious way, like she was agreeing with everything Mrs. Weaver said. She's got a nerve, that girl!

When we were finally getting on with our work, Rosie whispered:

"We haven't had a slime-fest like that at our sleepovers for ages. We ought to do it at our next one!"

And then I remembered. We hadn't actually planned our next sleepover. And it was going to be the BIG ONE – our Millennium New Year's Eve sleepover! I couldn't believe that those stupid M&Ms had made us forget about it! I felt all excited at the thought. But of course, I didn't know then just *how* exciting it was going to turn out to be!

CHAPTER THREE

The others went into mega-planning mode when I reminded them about the New Year sleepover.

"I can't believe we actually *forgot* about it!" squealed Lyndz. "We've never forgotten about a sleepover before."

Kenny narrowed her eyes and looked menacingly across the playground. "Those M&Ms have a lot to answer for!"

"Chill out, for goodness sake!" said Rosie, leaping on Kenny's back. "Our sleepover's more important than them. Where are we going to have it? And what are we going to do? We've got to make it really special. Hey, Kenny! *Stop!* Put me down, NOW!"

Kenny had gone racing across the grass outside our classroom with Rosie clinging furiously to her back. The rest of us creased up – they looked hilarious. Only Rosie didn't seem to think so when Kenny finally came back and dumped her on the ground next to us.

"You really are a nutcase!" she fumed. "You could have killed me!"

Rosie can still be a bit too serious sometimes, so there was nothing for it but to tickle her until she begged for mercy. It was class!

"But what are we going to do for the sleepover?" asked Fliss at last. "Can't we do something a bit, I don't know – grown-up? I mean, it is kind of special seeing in the year 2000."

We all agreed that we should do something different, but I knew that we wouldn't be able to agree on anything more than that.

148

"Look, let's ask our parents if we can have a sleepover on New Year's Eve first," I suggested. "Then once we know where we're going, we can decide what we're going to do."

Even as I was saying that, I knew that we wouldn't be having it at my place. I didn't think Mum would mind. But Dad's something else. I mean, ever since he knew that Mum was pregnant, he's been clucking round like a mother hen. He used to be all cool and laid back, then suddenly he went into fusspot overdrive. To hear him talk, you'd think my friends and I were a pack of wild animals out to destroy our house, and scare Mum into the bargain. And he's just got worse and worse. Whenever he starts fussing, Mum just raises her eyes behind his back, and we have a good giggle about it together when he's gone.

Still, I thought I should mention our plan. So that night when I was washing the dishes, I said:

"I don't suppose I could have a sleepover here on New Year's Eve, could I?"

149

"On New Year's Eve?" Dad plopped a few cups into the soapy water. "I don't think so. I'm not sure my nerves could stand seeing in the year 2000 with all your crazy friends."

But he was smiling as he said it. "Sorry champ!" He ruffled my hair. "Maybe next year. We'll see."

"Yes, sorry Frankie," Mum smiled at me sympathetically. "But I think your dad's probably right."

I wasn't really disappointed, because that's exactly what I'd expected him to say. I just hoped that my friends were having better luck.

When the phone rang a bit later, I knew it'd be for me.

"I'll get it!" I yelled.

"Hi Frankie, it's me, Lyndz." She sounded fed up.

"Don't tell me," I said. "You can't have the sleepover at your place."

"How did you know?"

"It didn't exactly take Sherlock Holmes to

suss that one out," I sighed. "You sound really cheesed off. What's up? Why won't they let you have one?"

"Apparently Mum's promised Stuart and Tom that they can have a few of their mates round. I said that was cool because we'd just join in. But Stuart and Tom both said 'No way Jose' and Mum and Dad seemed to agree. Their friends are all stupid morons anyway. I wouldn't want to have a party with them."

Still, poor Lyndz sounded really upset.

"I've had no joy either, because of Mum," I told her. "But don't worry, I'm sure one of the others is having better luck than we are."

"I hope so. See you tomorrow."

I decided to give Kenny a ring to see how she was getting on. Bad move! She was in the middle of a huge row with Molly and her older sister Emma about using the phone. And every time she started to speak to me, the other two started yelling at her.

"I'll ring you back, Frankie," she shouted. Then – silence. The line had gone dead.

"I hope they haven't murdered her," I said, shivering really dramatically when I told Mum and Dad what had happened.

"Her father's probably pulled the phone out of the socket, more like!" Dad laughed. "You do realise that in a few years *we'll* have two people to fight with for the phone?"

He smiled at Mum and patted her stomach and they went all soppy-eyed. They've been doing that a lot lately. I thought I might heave, so I went to my room.

To be honest with you, I didn't give the sleepover much thought that night. I was sure that someone had sorted something out. I kind of hoped that it wasn't Fliss though. She'd make us play stupid games and her mum would make us eat silly little sandwiches. And we wouldn't be able to let our hair down in case we made a mess of her clean and tidy house. I know that sounds awful, but girls just want to have fun sometimes. You know what I mean?

Anyway, as it turned out I needn't have bothered about Fliss, because the next morning she told us that her mum was organising her own party.

"And I don't think she can cope with one of our sleepovers as well," Fliss explained.

Lyndz and I rolled our eyes at each other. I don't think Fliss's mum copes with our sleepovers at the best of times.

"Actually," muttered Fliss in her quietest voice, "I thought I might like to stay at home and join in with Mum's party myself. You wouldn't mind, would you? I mean, not having a sleepover on New Year's Eve after all?"

Rosie had joined Lyndz and me by that time, and we all stared at Fliss open-mouthed.

"Of course we'd mind!" I screeched. "You were as excited as any of us about it! And now that something better has come along, you expect us to drop the idea altogether. Well maybe the rest of us will have our sleepover without you!"

I didn't really mean it, but Fliss winds me up sometimes. She always expects us to alter our plans just to suit her. But it looked like our plans were altering anyway. Rosie hadn't had any joy in persuading her mum to let us have the sleepover at her place either.

"She says she'll see," Rosie told us glumly. "And that usually means she'll pretend to think about it for a fortnight and then tell me the answer's 'no' anyway."

I tried to sound positive. "Let's hope McKenzie comes up with the goods. She usually does."

Typical Kenny. The one morning we were all desperate for her to be early (apart from Fliss, who'd gone off by herself to sulk) was the one morning she was very late. She was so late that Mrs Weaver was about to mark her absent in the register. And Kenny didn't look happy. She didn't look happy at all. In fact, if I didn't know her better, I'd swear that she'd been crying.

We knew by the way that she slammed all her pens on the desk that she was in a bad mood. We were supposed to be finding out about medical developments in the twentieth century for our bit in the play. But Kenny just made loads of doodles in her notebook. And they were all doodles of really gory things, like blood spurting out of hearts and severed legs and stuff. *Awful!*

When break came, I couldn't bear it any longer. As soon as we got outside I tackled her.

"What on earth's the matter with you? Don't tell me – your dad's forbidden you from using the phone ever again?"

"Worse than that. Although he was so angry with us all last night that he did pull the phone out of its socket," Kenny admitted.

I just laughed. "Dad said that's what would have happened."

"Why the long face then?" asked Lyndz.

"I'm not going to be here on New Year's Eve," Kenny blurted out. "We're going up to Scotland to spend it with my grandparents."

What? I just never thought that one of us wouldn't actually be around.

"Well that's it, then. We can't have a New

Year sleepover now, can we?" I couldn't bear to see Kenny so miserable.

"Hang on a minute!" It was Fliss. "When I said that I couldn't come, you said you'd have the sleepover without me. When *she*," she pointed at Kenny, "says she can't come, you say that you can't have a sleepover. That's not fair! You like her better than me, don't you?"

Typical Fliss, only bothered about herself.

"Don't be silly, Fliss. It's different because Kenny really wanted to come and she can't. You told us that you'd rather go to your mum's party," I pointed out. "Besides, we probably wouldn't have had a sleepover without you either."

Fliss smiled weakly.

"I was really looking forward to that sleepover," Kenny mumbled. "I'm sorry that I've let you down."

"Don't be daft. We'll just have to arrange something special for when we're all around." I tried to sound bright, but I was really disappointed too. I'd been convinced that our New Year sleepover was going to be the best yet.

"Still, there is a plus side to all this." Kenny started to grin. "We've got more time to plan our revenge on the M&Ms. I've had a few ideas already..."

We went into a huddle and Kenny outlined her plans to us. And when I say that they were wicked, I mean that in *every* sense of the word. Fliss looked quite pale when she'd heard them.

"I'm not sure about this," she kept whimpering. "I think we might be taking things too far this time. What if we get into trouble?"

Fliss hates the thought of anyone telling her off.

"Look, it's almost the end of term. By the time we put this into practice, there'll only be a couple of days to go. What can anyone do to us then?" reasoned Kenny. "Besides Fliss, they *did* steal your idea for the play. Don't you think that deserves a little revenge?"

157

Fliss thought for a bit.

"Well I guess so," she admitted slowly. "But I don't want to do any of the risky stuff, OK? And I certainly don't want to get messy."

So I guess you want to know what we did to the M&Ms then? It was mega, MEGA, *MEGA* brilliant. But Fliss was right to be worried. It did get a bit out of hand.

CHAPTER FOUR

Now as you know, the M&Ms are the yukkiest things on the planet at the best of times. Well, multiply that by a billion and you'll guess how awful they were as we prepared for our end-of-term play. They got up our noses *big*-time. They swanked about in their costumes, telling everyone how wonderful they were. And what made it worse was that the clothes they were going to wear were really fab. They had spangly dresses with fringes on them, and dresses with sticky-out skirts.

"This is a proper dress from the 1950s." Emily Berryman twirled round in front of the class. "It belongs to my Auntie Sally. She said she'd lend it to me if I promised to look after it."

Rosie made a being-sick face and Danny McCloud shouted out, "We can see your knickers when you do that!"

The rest of the class collapsed into giggles and Emma Hughes told him to "grow up".

Fliss was getting more and more furious.

"It should have been us in all those great clothes!" she spat. "No-one's going to remember our little bit of the play, are they? I mean, 'medical developments since 1900' isn't the most exciting topic in the world, is it?"

Kenny just sighed.

The truth is that none of us were very thrilled when Kenny had suggested our topic for the play. I mean, she wants to be a doctor, so stuff about medical history is fascinating to her. But to the rest of us it was one big YAWWWN. We went round to Kenny's house one night though, and her father told us some really interesting stuff. And he's a doctor, so he knew what he was talking about.

"When you've got a really bad virus, doctors prescribe tablets called antibiotics which fight infection," he told us. "Do you know how their discovery came about?"

Of course, none of us had a clue.

"Well, a man called Alexander Fleming discovered that a particular mould could kill certain nasty germs..."

"A mole? The animal?" asked Rosie.

"No!" he laughed. "A mould, a fungus."

"YUK!" Fliss leapt about ten feet in the air. "Antibiotics aren't made from mould, are they?"

"No Fliss, things have advanced a bit since then!" he grinned. "But back then, that mould led to the discovery of penicillin, which was really the first type of antibiotic. Now antibiotics save millions of lives."

Fliss was still looking a bit green.

"There are lots of other developments

that aren't to do with illnesses," Dr McKenzie went on. Fliss brightened up a bit.

"I bet your mum's had a lot of scans recently, hasn't she Frankie?" Kenny's dad smiled at me.

I nodded. Since Mum's been pregnant, she's always going to hospital and being hooked up to some machine or other.

"Things like ultrasound machines enable doctors to check out what's going on in the body without doing it any harm," said Dr McKenzie. "It means that we can monitor Frankie's mum's baby and make sure everything's normal. That kind of thing would have been unheard of a hundred years ago. And now we're much better equipped to look after babies if they're born early too. Surely that's a good thing?"

Suddenly, medical developments seemed quite a cool thing to talk about. The others seemed to think so too. Apart from Fliss, who still seemed a bit grossed out about the mould thing.

Anyway, after that we had lots of ideas for

our play. The problem was that we were only going to be on stage for five minutes. Ryan Scott and his group were going to be on just before us, with the M&Ms straight after.

"Great!" chortled Kenny when she found out. "It should be easy to put my plan into practice!"

The rest of us looked at each other. The M&Ms certainly deserved what was coming to them, but the end-of-term play was a bit of a risky place to dish it out...

For the next week or so we worked really hard on our performance. We painted loads of boxes so that part of our scenery would look like an old-fashioned laboratory and part of it would look like a high-tech hospital.

Every time the M&Ms saw us rehearsing, they started yawning.

"I bet you'll send everyone to sleep with your bit," they screeched. "But never mind – we'll wake them up with our fashion presentation. Thanks for the idea, Fliss!"

Poor Fliss, I thought she was going to

strangle Emma Hughes with her plaits.

"It won't be your stupid fashion show that wakes them up!" muttered Kenny under her breath. The rest of us smirked.

Of course, no one else knew what we had planned, and Mrs Weaver seemed really pleased with our part of the play. Fliss was our narrator, dressed in a white coat to look like a doctor, and Lyndz was going to be Alexander Fleming. We'd saved all this yukky mould from old cheese and fruit and stuff, because Kenny said she wanted it to look realistic. But it was so *gross* that we made Kenny look after it.

Rosie was playing the part of a patient with a nasty virus. First she was going to die a horrible death to show what it would have been like before antibiotics were invented. Then she was going to pretend to be cured by the new drugs. She liked the dying bit best. It seemed to take longer every time we rehearsed it. If we didn't watch out, our entire five minutes would be taken over by her death scene!

For my bit, I was going to be a pregnant woman having an ultrasound scan. Kenny had this great idea of taping a big pink balloon to my tummy so that it looked just like Mum's enormous stomach. Then she was going to be the doctor and smear jelly stuff on to it and pretend to do the scan, just like they do in hospital. It was well cool!

On the evening of the performance, I was really nervous. All our parents were coming to watch, and that suddenly made it all serious. Fliss and Rosie were already at school by the time I arrived, both jiggling about and looking sicky green.

"Come on, you guys!" I tried to jolly them up. "We're only on stage for five minutes and we know what we're doing, don't we?"

They nodded weakly, and I started to blow up the balloon that was going to be my tummy. I'd just got it nice and big and was trying to tie the knot when Lyndz came flying into me. THUD! I ended up on the floor and the balloon went shooting about in the air, making a really rude noise.

"You're disgusting, Felicity Sidebotham!" Emma Hughes sniffed as she walked past.

The thing was – *she wasn't joking*. She hadn't seen the balloon, and she really thought that Fliss had made that noise!!! I was still on the floor, but I was laughing so much I couldn't get up. The more Rosie and Lyndz tried to pull me up, the more we creased up. And what made it worse was that Fliss was just standing there like a goldfish, opening and closing her mouth!

When I eventually got up, my sides ached.

"Can you believe that?" I spluttered. "I'd better go and find my balloon."

"Hurry up!" Lyndz called out after me. "I've got something to tell you!"

I hadn't really seen where the balloon had ended up and no one else had seen it either, so I had to return empty-handed. Fortunately I'd brought a spare one.

"What's your news then, Lyndz?" I asked when I got back to the others. I found the other balloon and started to blow it up.

"It's great!" Lyndz was hopping from foot

to foot. "But shouldn't we wait until Kenny gets here before I tell you?"

We all looked at each other, then said together, "Nah!", which made us all laugh.

"Well..."

Lyndz was just about to tell us what this great news was when someone thumped me in the back and started shaking a tube of red liquid in front of my face. I nearly swallowed the balloon, which wasn't very funny.

"Don't do that, Kenny!" I yelled, and had to start blowing the balloon up again.

"Look, this is for the operation!" Kenny ignored me and shook the liquid again. "Cool, isn't it?"

"What operation?" I gasped.

"Operation 'Destroy the M&Ms'!" Kenny announced proudly.

"What are you going to do?" shrieked Fliss. "You're not really going to operate on them, are you?"

"Grow up, Fliss!" shrieked Kenny. "It's only for effect!"

"B...but we can't really do anything to

them," Fliss stammered. "Not in front of all these people—"

"Don't be such a wet blanket!" Kenny hissed.

Fliss looked as though she was about to cry.

I had finally blown up my balloon and was knotting its neck. "What was your news?" I asked Lyndz quickly, trying to change the subject.

"Crikey, I almost forgot!" Lyndz shrieked. "A sleepover! Mum says we can have one at my place between Christmas and New Year. Then you'll all be able to come! She said, what about Tuesday 28th? We can pretend it's New Year's Eve if we want and do something special. Well, what do you think?"

We all hugged her.

"That'll be great, Lyndz!"

"Yeah, cool!"

"Hey, mind my balloon!"

"Places everyone!" Mrs Weaver clapped her hands and started getting everyone organised.

"Don't forget about the M&Ms," Kenny whispered as we made our way to the side of the stage. "Remember the plan!"

Well, if Kenny had a plan, we didn't stick to it. But who cares as long as we made fools of the M&Ms? And we certainly did that. To the max!

CHAPTER FIVE

The first part of our class's performance passed in a bit of a blur. We were so busy trying to calm ourselves down that we didn't watch much of it. Kenny kept disappearing too, and we had no idea what she was up to. I had my own problems with my balloon – somehow it just wouldn't stay taped to my stomach, and it almost floated away twice. The M&Ms of course thought that was hysterical.

"Dolls! Balloons! You're a bigger baby than we thought!" Emma Hughes sneered nastily.

She was done up like a dog's dinner in a spangly dress with fringes round the bottom and a feather in her hair. She was practising a stupid dance – 'The Charleston' or something. She said they did it in the 1920s. It looked pretty silly to me, all knocking knees and kicking your legs up. I'd much rather bop along to Steps.

Emily Berryman was still wandering around in her jeans and T-shirt.

"I'm going to wear my Auntie Sally's dress," she growled in her gruff voice. "But I'm not putting it on until the last minute, because I don't want to spoil it. Amanda's keeping an eye on it for me."

"Are you talking about Amanda Porter?" Kenny suddenly reappeared. "I think you'd better go and help her out – she seems to be stuck in her mini-skirt."

The M&Ms twittered off behind the stage.

"Amanda Porter in a mini-skirt! Ugh, gross!" winced Fliss. It wasn't really a pleasant thought.

"I bet they've made her wear a mini-skirt

so that everyone will think how great *they* look," suggested Rosie.

"Amanda's not really stuck, is she?" asked Lyndz suspiciously.

"Yeah!" laughed Kenny. "I accidentally got the zip stuck when I was helping her into her skirt. How else could I tear her away from Berryman's precious dress?"

"What have you done?" I squeaked.

But before she could answer, Mrs Weaver appeared.

"The play's going very well!" She seemed very pleased. "Right Francesca, can your group please get your scenery together? You're on next."

"I feel sick!" Fliss wailed.

"Don't be such a wimp!" Kenny reprimanded her. "It'll be cool, you'll see!"

Fliss looked as white as a sheet, but I was kind of red and flustered. My balloon was causing me real problems.

We grabbed the boxes we'd painted for our scenery and prepared to go on stage. And getting on stage is where the nightmare *really* began.

We heard the applause for Ryan Scott's group, then a familiar sniggering from the side of the stage, then— TOTAL BLACKNESS. Someone had turned the lights off completely, and we couldn't see anything at all. We were all crashing into each other and treading on each other's toes.

"Ouch, mind my foot!" squealed Fliss's voice.

"Sorry," mumbled Danny McCloud.

There was a crunching sound, then...

"Watch it, you clown!" That was definitely Kenny.

And all the time we were getting totally tangled up in our scenery. When the lights finally went back on – thanks to Mrs Weaver – the stage looked like a battlefield. Ryan Scott was lying dazed on the ground, and Fliss was slumped on top of one of our crushed boxes. People were limping, Rosie was clutching a gash in her shin and Kenny was looking furiously at the M&Ms, who'd collapsed in giggles at the side of the stage. Lyndz had unfortunately started to hiccup, but there was no time to do anything about that.

Red in the face, Mrs Weaver stormed on to the stage and started organising everyone. But I think she was so angry that she didn't really notice what she was doing. So instead of having our own scenery of the hospital, we were surrounded by the televisions and video recorders that the previous group had used for their performance.

As soon as Fliss saw what had happened she started to panic. She turned to Mrs Weaver, but Mrs W just snapped:

"Come on Felicity, I think we've wasted enough time already!"

So Fliss stammered, "Th... there... erm, there have been a great many advances in medicine since 1900..." and at that point Lyndz appeared.

To start with, she was OK and pretended to ignore the fact that she looked like she was standing in a television shop rather than in a laboratory. But when it got to the point where she had to make her discovery about penicillin, she realised that she hadn't got the dish of mould. She looked frantically round at the rest of us.

"Fliss, Fliss..." Kenny hissed. She'd been looking after the mould, hadn't she, and was trying to pass the dish to Fliss. Well, Fliss nearly had a fit when she saw it, and screamed. The yukky green stuff fell out of Kenny's hands and right down Fliss's clean white coat and on to the floor. Fliss started flapping about, trying to wipe the mess off her coat, and the more she flapped, the more the mould got trampled into the stage.

She just looked so funny that the rest of us creased up. Lyndz was giggling and hiccuping at the same time and making this terrible noise, and that just made us worse. Fliss looked really mad at us. She hates being laughed at at the best of times, but in front of all those people too – it was like her *worst* nightmare. Especially as most of the audience were starting to splutter as well. I thought that she might run away, but she didn't. She carried on with her narration.

"Before the invention of antibiotics," she went on bravely, "viruses, which are treatable today, could lead to death."

That was Rosie's cue to do her dramatic dying act. She held her head, she gripped her throat, she started to sink to her knees and... *WHOOSH!* She skidded on the patch of mould and fell right off the stage.

I was waiting at the side to come on and do my bit, but as soon as I saw what had happened, I rushed over to Rosie. We all did. The poor thing was all crumpled up on the floor. Fortunately Dr McKenzie had come to watch the play, and he came running over to make sure that she was all right. As he was checking that she hadn't broken anything, Kenny hissed to me:

"The M&Ms are responsible for this! I'm going to fix them *once and for all...*"

"Wait Kenny!" I yelled, but I forgot that I still had a balloon strapped to my tummy. As I spun round, I fell over – and there was the loudest BANG you've ever heard as the balloon exploded. Everyone went silent. And that's when we heard all the commotion at the back of the stage.

All the boxes, which had been our

scenery, cascaded on to the ground. All apart from two. Kenny and Emma were bashing each other about the head with those. It seemed like everyone else saw what was happening as well, because suddenly they were surrounded by the rest of our class.

"Go, Kenny!" shouted Ryan Scott.

"Hit her, Emma!" squealed Emily.

But Emma suddenly couldn't hit anything, because her feather head-dress had fallen right over her eyes and she couldn't see. She raised the box over her head and stumbled into Kenny. Kenny was caught off balance and fell over – right on top of Emily.

"*Just what is going on here?*" demanded Mrs Weaver, wading through the crowd.

"Kenny's, hic, for it now!" muttered Lyndz, who was standing next to me.

Mrs Weaver's face was like thunder. I'd never seen her so mad.

"I am horrified! I have never..." she began – then Emily Berryman let out this ear-splitting scream.

"I'm bleeding!" she shrieked. "Look!"

Blood was dripping down her arms and falling in a pool on the floor. We looked at Kenny. She had a huge bloodstain spreading over her white coat.

"Kenny, are you all right?" I rushed over to her.

"Oh, that!" She couldn't stop laughing. "It's only red paint. We were going to use it in our play, Mrs Weaver, honestly. The tube must have got broken."

Mrs Weaver looked at her suspiciously.

"I don't remember there being any blood in your performance, Laura," she sniffed. "Emily, do try to calm down, dear. Laura says it's only paint. It will wash off."

But Emily Berryman was wailing harder than ever.

"But look at this!" she cried. "My Auntie Sally's dress is *ruined*!"

We all turned to look. As well as splodges of red paint down the front of the dress, sticky brown blobs were encrusted round the neck and the sleeves.

"More of Merlin's droppings!" squealed Rosie, who had hobbled over to join us. "Kenny's done a real job on her this time!"

We thought that Mrs Weaver was going to rip us to shreds, but I guess she thought that wouldn't look too great in front of our parents. Instead she left it for Mrs Poole, the head, to give one of her "I'm-shocked-and disappointed-by-your-behaviour" speeches and to send us all home. And that, of course, is when our parents ripped into us.

"I don't know what to say Francesca, I really don't." Mum shook her head.

"But it wasn't my fault!" I told her indignantly. "It wasn't me bashing people over the head with cardboard boxes, was it?"

"You're not telling us that you knew nothing about all that business, surely?" said Dad sternly.

But I *honestly* didn't know that was going to happen. All Kenny had planned was tripping up the M&Ms when they were going on stage and bringing the curtain down on them mid-performance, which did all seem pretty tame after that night's display.

"I think you and your sleepover pals are getting a bit out of hand," Dad continued. "Lyndz's mum told us tonight about the sleepover you were going to have to celebrate New Year. Well, that's a definite no-no now."

"But…" I started to protest desperately.

"No buts, Frankie. There'll be no more sleepovers until we can all be sure that you know how to behave."

I couldn't believe my ears. Not only had the M&Ms ruined the play, they'd also ruined my Christmas, my New Year – and my *life*!

CHAPTER SIX

Well, after Kenny's antics we were all in deepest darkest doom. The way our parents went on at us, you'd think we'd just committed the worst crime in the world. I mean, come on! Nobody died, did they? It's just that things got a bit out of hand. I sometimes think parents were never young themselves, the way they get het up about the slightest thing.

And they weren't the only ones. Boy, was Mrs Weaver furious when we got into school the next day. You could virtually see the steam coming out of her ears. But at least we weren't the only ones she was mad at. Even Emma Hughes couldn't do anything right, which makes a huge change. She's usually Mrs Weaver's very favourite pet – but not on that day.

"Emma Hughes!" she bawled her out. "When I say sit down and be quiet, I mean *everyone* – and that includes you!"

Normally the rest of us would have spluttered with laughter, but we were too terrified. When Mrs Weaver is mad she turns into this fire-breathing monster – and you wouldn't want to cross her, believe me.

"Thank goodness we've only got one more day at school!" muttered Fliss as we were leaving. "I don't think I could take much more of that."

"But that means only one more day of seeing each other," grumbled Rosie. "The way my mum's talking, we're never going to see each other out of school again."

"I was really looking forward to our sleepover too," admitted Lyndz.

"Just think, we might have had our last sleepover, ever!" whimpered Fliss.

"Rubbish!" Kenny exploded. "I'm sure I can come up with a plan so that we can still have one!"

The rest of us looked at her in amazement.

"Stop right there!" I turned to her. "It's your plans that got us into this mess to start with, remember. All we can do is be extra good over Christmas, and see if we can talk our parents round."

Kenny tutted and sighed and the others all nodded. But to be honest with you, I didn't hold out much hope. We were well and truly in the doghouse this time.

The next day was really sad, because we figured we wouldn't be seeing each other again until the next term.

"Just think, it'll be *next century* before we see each other again!" marvelled Fliss.

"Yeah, ages away!" Lyndz moaned.

We exchanged our presents and gave each other a hug. Our parents had all come to meet us, because you know what it's like at the end of term – you always seem to have so much stuff to take home. They were all huddled together when we got out of school, which wasn't a good sign. But they seemed happy enough when we joined them. I mean they didn't give us any of those "I-can't-believe-you've-let-me-down-like-this" looks, which was a major improvement from the last few days.

It felt really weird knowing I wouldn't be seeing the others all over Christmas. I know it sounds a bit soppy, but I felt kind of lost without them. Still, there was lots of work to be done around the house. As well as all the usual Christmas stuff, Mum had grand plans for finally sorting out the nursery. Dad had decorated it and everything, but it still wasn't ready for the baby.

"There's still a few weeks to go before it's due," Mum grinned, "but I guess they'll fly by. So we should get it sorted out now."

I bet most people don't spend their

Christmas Eve moving boxes around, but that's exactly what we did with ours.

"You won't overdo it, will you Mum?" I asked anxiously. She was kneeling on the floor, putting away books and files.

"You sound just like your father!" she laughed. "I'm fine. The only problem might be getting me upright again!"

Dad brought my old cot down from the attic, and bags and bags of my baby clothes.

"I can't believe you kept all these!" I squealed as I took out the tiniest, cutest little baby-gros. "Look at these weeny bootees!"

"I can't believe we kept them either," admitted Mum, turning them over in her hands. "They're going to need a good wash."

The doorbell chimed and Dad went to answer it.

"This baby is hardly going to be in the height of fashion, is it? Wearing all these old clothes!" Mum was giggling.

"Speaking of fashion," Dad came back in. "I've got just the person here to advise you."

"Fliss!" I yelled getting up to hug her. "It's so nice to see you!"

Fliss went pink.

"Ooh, aren't these beautiful?" She bent down to look at the clothes. "They're so tiny and soft. Your baby's going to look so cute!"

"There you are!" laughed Dad. "If Fliss has given them her seal of approval, those clothes are fashionable enough for any baby! But you didn't come to talk about baby fashion, did you Fliss?"

"No!" Fliss blushed. "Mum sent this invitation for you."

She handed over a pretty invitation with embossed silver lettering.

"It's for a special party on New Year's Eve, and you've just got to come, she's got something exciting to tell everybody, oops, I wasn't supposed to say anything, but you will come, won't you?"

It felt like we'd just been hit by a whirlwind.

"Thank you Felicity, that's very kind," Mum smiled up at her from the floor. "Tell your mum we'd love to come."

Fliss and I danced around.

"The others are all coming too!" she squealed. "Except Kenny of course, she won't be here."

That put kind of a damper on things. But still, at least I had a party to look forward to.

When Fliss had gone, we tidied everything up in the nursery and went downstairs. Mum turned on the radio and we listened to some carols, joining in when we could remember the words. We had Dad's famous pizza as a treat. And it was kind of cool, sitting there with just the glow from the tree lights brightening the darkness.

"Right champ, time for bed, I think." It was quite late when Dad turned on the main light. "Now you do know that if you make any noise, Father Christmas won't come, don't you?"

"Dad!" I rolled my eyes at him.

"Just make sure you hang up that stocking and go to sleep, OK?"

I gave Mum and Dad a kiss and ran upstairs. I love Christmas and I couldn't wait to wake up in the morning and open all my presents!

Did I just say I love Christmas? Well pardon me, that was a mistake. What I should have said was I *used* to love Christmas, but not any more. Uh-uh, no way. If I tell you that this Christmas was the biggest nightmare of my life, it wouldn't be any exaggeration at all. You might well look shocked. Well, sit tight while I tell you all about it.

It started off OK. I was awake at the crack of dawn and dived into the stocking at the end of my bed. There was loads of cool stuff in it, like nail varnish and a really great ring I'd had my eye on for some time. I opened some of the chocolates that were in there too and crept downstairs. It's kind of a tradition in our house that we wait until everyone's there before we open any presents under the tree. So I just had to feel my parcels and try to guess what they were until the oldies finally put in an appearance.

I knew as soon as I saw Mum that

something wasn't right. She looked really grey and was kind of wincing when she moved.

"Are you OK?" I asked her anxiously.

"Sure am!" she tried to joke. "I didn't sleep very well, that's all. The baby thought it was party time and started doing the samba. Oooh!"

She doubled over and slumped into a chair.

I was dead worried, but Dad just reckoned she'd overdone it with the clearing-up the day before.

"She'll be fine, love," he reassured me, but I could tell that he was concerned too.

That kind of took the edge off my presents really. But I got some great stuff. Fliss had bought me a lovely pair of earrings that looked like butterflies, and Lyndz had bought me a set of megatastic fake tattoos. I got a really cool long scarf from Rosie and a fab new purple pencil case from Kenny because mine was dropping to bits. Mum and Dad gave me loads of clothes and, get this – my own CD Discman! How cool is that?!

I was really thrilled, but all the time I was kind of worried about Mum. Every time I asked how she felt, Mum just said "fine".

It was after we'd eaten Dad's famous Christmas nut roast that it was obvious something was very wrong. Mum kept getting these really bad pains every few minutes and was obviously in agony.

"I think the baby's coming!" she gasped. "We'd better get to the hospital."

I have seriously *never* been so scared in my whole life. I mean, the baby wasn't due for a few weeks, so there must have been something really wrong. What if something awful happened? What if Mum lost the baby? Or what if something happened to Mum? I was so scared I couldn't speak. But I tried not to let Mum see how worried I was. I had to be brave for her sake. So I whizzed round gathering stuff into a bag for her to take into hospital. Then we all piled into the car.

It felt weird. Everyone we passed seemed really happy. There were children out on their new bikes and kids on new rollerblades. And I just wanted to yell, "How dare you look so happy when there's something wrong with my mum?"

I don't think it took very long to get to the hospital, but it seemed like a lifetime. Dad helped Mum out of the car and led her into the Maternity unit.

"She will be all right, won't she Dad?" I squeezed his hand as some nurses led Mum away.

"Of course. She's in the right place now!" Dad smiled and gripped my hand tighter.

As we sat in the waiting room, there seemed to be loads of babies crying, which just reminded me about Mum.

"Do you fancy a cup of tea, love?" Dad asked after we'd been sitting staring at the wall for ages.

I nodded. He went down the corridor to a machine and I waited for him. Suddenly a woman in a white coat came into the room.

"Ah, you must be Frankie Thomas. I'm Dr Wilson," she smiled and held out her hand.

I was sure that she was going to tell me something awful, but she just laughed. "Don't look so worried, everything's fine. We've just been running a few tests on your mum and... oh hello, you must be Gwyn?"

Dad had just come through the door with two steaming cups of tea.

"I was just telling Frankie here that Helena's absolutely fine. The baby's doing great too. You can go and see her now if you like."

I started running down the corridor, until I remembered where I was and just made myself walk really fast. I almost threw myself at Mum when I got to her room, I was so pleased to see her.

"Hey, there you are!" she beamed and ruffled my hair. "Sorry I've messed up your Christmas Day, Frankie. I bet you didn't expect to spend it in a hospital, did you?"

I shook my head, and tears started to roll down my face.

"I'm sorry, darling," she said, giving me a big hug.

I wasn't crying because I was feeling sorry for myself. I was crying because I was so relieved.

"I'm just glad you're all right," I sniffed. "And the baby too."

"It was probably a touch of indigestion," confirmed Dr Wilson. "These things can happen in the later stages of pregnancy."

We all looked at Dad.

"OK, OK, no more pizzas or nut roasts!" he laughed, holding up his hands. "I know that you both think my cooking stinks, but this was rather a drastic way of telling me, don't you think? Everything we eat from now until the baby's born will definitely be out of a packet, I promise!"

It felt so good to get out of hospital and back home. It was dark by that time and it felt really strange, like I hadn't had a Christmas Day at all. Mum kept saying that she was sorry and that she'd make it up to me, but all I wanted was for her to be all right. What did it matter if I'd missed Christmas for one year?

CHAPTER SEVEN

Well, it seems that even if *I* wasn't bothered about missing Christmas Day, Mum was bothered for me. She spent most of Boxing Day on the phone and she wouldn't tell me who she was calling.

"Is that Gran?" I asked as I passed her in the hall. She shook her head and wouldn't even tell me who it was when she'd finished. After that, she sneaked into Dad's office to make all her calls. And if the phone rang she shouted, "That's for me!" and lumbered into the office to get it.

"You're acting really weird, Mum," I told her when she finally sat down. "Are you sure they didn't give you any funny medicine when you were at the hospital?"

"Don't be rude!" she smirked. "All will be revealed soon enough."

I was still kind of worried about her, and to tell you the truth I didn't think all this cloak-and-dagger stuff would be doing her any good at all. But Dad didn't seem too worried about it. In fact, he seemed to be joining in. At one stage I could have sworn I heard Lyndz's father's van outside. Dad disappeared and returned about five minutes later saying it was only someone asking for directions. It was all very strange.

On Monday, the day after Boxing Day, my gran came over from Nottingham, which was great. She brought loads of presents with her and fussed around Mum.

"You know you really should have taken it easier," she scolded her. "Having a baby at your age was never going to be easy. I'm not surprised you had a scare like that."

Mum rolled her eyes, and for a moment she looked like a little schoolgirl who'd just been told off.

"So when are you going to be seeing all those nice friends of yours, Francesca?" Gran turned to me. (She can never quite bring herself to call me Frankie.)

"I don't know," I shrugged. "On New Year's Eve, probably."

I saw Mum and Dad look at each other. I figured they'd decided that Fliss's mum's party might be too exciting for Mum after what had just happened.

"It doesn't matter if you don't want to go," I told them quickly. "I'm not bothered about it, honestly. I don't mind not seeing my friends."

Mum and Dad burst out laughing.

"We'll have to tell her now, won't we!" Mum said at last.

"Tell me what?" I asked anxiously. "You are all right, aren't you Mum? You're not going to have to go into hospital again, are you?"

"Hey, calm down!" grinned Dad. "Since

when have you been Miss Frankie Freak-Out? Your mum's fine, aren't you love?"

"'Course I am," Mum reassured me. "You heard what the doctor said – I've just got to avoid your dad's cooking for a while!"

"Thanks!" Dad guffawed. "Anyway, we weren't going to tell you yet but..."

"Your sleepover's back on!" Mum blurted out. "I couldn't bear to think of you missing out on all your celebrations, so I rang everyone up yesterday. You'll be having your early New Year sleepover at Lyndz's tomorrow after all."

I didn't know what to say – I was absolutely *stunned*.

"You're the greatest!" I squealed when I'd found my voice. I grabbed hold of Mum and Dad in a big hug, then grabbed hold of Gran too. She looked totally bewildered by everything.

When I'd finally calmed down, Dad went into his office and came back holding an envelope.

"Lyndz's dad dropped this off for you yesterday. It's an invitation, I think."

I quickly opened it, and as I pulled out the invitation, hundreds of tiny glitter snowflakes fell on to the floor.

Lyndz invites you to a
SPECIAL (EARLY)
MILLENNIUM NEW YEAR'S EVE SLEEPOVER
DRESS TO IMPRESS
AND
BRING EXOTIC AND TEMPTING GOODIES
FOR THE SPECIAL MIDNIGHT FEAST!

Please arrive at 6pm

How cool was that?! She must have made it specially, as soon as she knew that the sleepover was back on again.

"I'll have to decide what to wear!" I shrieked, dashing up to my room.

The invitation said 'Dress to Impress'. Now what on earth did that mean? I was dying to know what the others were going to be wearing, but I didn't want to ring them. I wanted it all to be a big surprise. Usually we have our sleepovers when we've just been at school together. This time I wouldn't have seen the others for over a week, and I reckon that's some kind of record for us. I couldn't wait to see them again. But first I had the little problem of my outfit to sort out!

It's a good thing that Mum and Dad didn't spring this sleepover on me at the last minute – it took me absolutely *ages* to decide what to wear. My bedroom looked as though a hurricane had hit it by the time I'd got my outfit sorted. Mind you, it was worth it! I put on a skinny-rib black top and black mini-skirt, then draped a couple of big chiffon scarves over the top of them, so they sort of floated away from my body as I moved. I had my best spiky-heel shoes on and masses of necklaces. As I twirled in front of the mirror I was well pleased.

"Yep Frankie, you're certainly dressed to impress now, girl!" I told my reflection.

There was a knock at the door.

"Talking to yourself is the first sign of madness, you know," Mum laughed. Then she came into my room.

"Frankie! My goodness, what a tip!"

Poor Mum! You ought to have seen her face.

"I'll tidy it up, don't worry. You go and sit down!" I tried to shoo her away.

"I didn't realise getting dolled up was such a messy business!" Mum sighed. "That must have been where I've been going wrong all these years!"

"Well Mum, you've either got it or you haven't!" I pretended to swank about.

"And you'll have an earful from your dad if you don't clear this room up sharpish!"

I changed out of my party outfit and hung it up carefully. Then Mum and I tackled the rest of my room. When we'd finished Mum said:

"I loved your outfit by the way! You looked really grown-up."

I gave her a big hug. "Thanks Mum."

We had an early tea so that Gran could get

home before it got too late. She doesn't really like driving in the dark, you see. But I think Mum and Dad were relieved when she did leave, because she'd been fussing over Mum ever since she arrived. She kept going on about how she was kind of old to be having another baby and how she hoped that Christmas Day hadn't been a warning. Mum was getting wound up, I could tell, and Dad just kept calling Gran "The Prophet of Doom" to make her shut up. But what she said kind of got to me, and I started to worry about Mum all over again.

In fact, I got myself into such a state that I almost didn't go to the sleepover. On Tuesday evening I'd got dressed and packed my stuff and everything – and then I suddenly thought: what would I do if Mum had to go into hospital again and I didn't know anything about it?

"Relax, Frankie!" Mum said when I told her how I felt. "I have no intention of going into hospital yet. And if anything does happen, anything at all, we'll ring you at Lyndz's."

"You promise?"

"Promise!"

"Why is it women are always late?" Dad stomped into the lounge. "I've been waiting for you in the car for five minutes."

"I wasn't sure that I was going to go to the sleepover," I told him.

"And let the others miss out on seeing you in all your finery? You must be mad!" Dad smiled. "Don't worry about your mum, Frankie, I'll look after her. And we won't let you miss anything, honestly!"

I felt better after they'd reassured me, but a tiny part of me still felt that I shouldn't be going out and leaving them. But you know what? I felt better as soon as I got to Lyndz's.

I was the last to arrive, and when I knocked on the door there was this stampede to open it. And *wow*! You should have seen what the others were wearing!

Lyndz had had the pick of her dressing-up clothes and was wearing this brilliant Spanish dress with millions of flounces down the skirt. She had this totally wicked comb thing in her hair too. Kenny had really excelled herself by wearing a new Leicester City shirt *and* a Leicester City tracksuit top – no surprises there! Rosie was all done up in some of her sister Tiffany's clubbing gear, which looked really wild. She was wearing this leopard-print mini skirt and a sort of rubber bodice thing. But I think she felt a bit uncomfortable in that because she kept trying to tug it down. But the coolest thing was she'd stuck a blue 'jewel' into her tummy button with some special glue and it sort of sparkled whenever she moved. It was *wicked*.

But Fliss took the biscuit. Her mum had actually bought her – yes, *bought* her – a slinky electric-blue evening dress. Her make-up was immaculate, and she looked as though she'd spent the whole day in a beauty parlour.

"I'm really trying it out for Mum's New Year's Eve party!" she smirked when I told her how great she looked. "It was ever so expensive and I wouldn't normally wear it to one of our sleepovers…"

"Charming!" sniffed Lyndz.

"… but," Fliss carried on, "seeing as this is a special sleepover, I thought I might as well. It's the first time I've ever worn it properly, so you're all honoured!"

"Thanks very much, Fliss!" we all laughed sarcastically. But she thought we were being serious and said, "You're welcome!" which made us all laugh even more. Honestly, what is she like?!

It felt really good being with the others again. And I know that the others felt the same, because for a few minutes we just stood there grinning at each other. But Kenny of course was soon keen to see some action. She leapt on to Lyndz's back and yelled at the top of her voice:

"Let the party begin!"

CHAPTER EIGHT

Before we could get on with the fun part of the sleepover, we had to take all our stuff up to Lyndz's room. Now, I don't know if you remember, but Lyndz's house is all higgledy-piggledy. Her dad is always in the middle of doing some major building project or other, so her house is always in a bit of a state. I don't mean that in a nasty way, I just mean that – well, you don't usually find great planks of wood and old doors propped up in the lounge, do you? And I bet your house has carpet on the floor, doesn't it? There are just dirty old floorboards at Lyndz's, which freaks Fliss out big-time!

Lyndz's bedroom is really tiny, and Kenny always jokes that her rat Merlin lives in a bigger *cage*! But Lyndz knows that she's only teasing. Besides, her dad's building her a spanking new room right at the top of the house. She swears that it's going to be ginormous when it's finished. At the moment, when we all pile into her room we're like a row of sardines in a can! She has to take out her bed, just so that we can all fit in. But we don't mind because we always have a really cool time when we're at Lyndz's. And this time was certainly no exception.

"WOW! Look at this!" we gasped as soon as we got into her room. There were banners all over the wall saying HAPPY NEW YEAR! and helium-filled balloons were tied up at each corner. It was wicked!

"We'd already got the banners for Stuart and Tom's party," admitted Lyndz. "I just sort of borrowed them."

"Won't they mind?" asked Fliss anxiously. I think she's a bit scared of Lyndz's older brothers because they're always teasing her.

"Nah, they'll never know!" Lyndz smiled a little nervously. "They never set foot in my room anyway, so I'll just take them down tomorrow and put them back in the bag."

"You naughty thing!" Kenny teased, and started tickling her.

Now tickling and Lyndz mean just one thing. Yep, you've guessed it – hiccups! It was really hysterical because the more she hicced, the more the comb thing on her head moved around. It looked like a bird or something pecking at her head. We doubled up, it just looked so funny. Lyndz didn't know what we were laughing about until we pointed to her reflection in the mirror. And that of course just made things worse. She got redder and redder and tears started streaming down her face.

"We ought to do something!" Fliss was looking quite concerned.

Suddenly there was a knock on the door.

"What's going on in there?" It was Stuart.

"Quick! Don't let him come in!" squealed Lyndz.

We all bustled out of the door.

"Out of the way, Stu!" Lyndz barged past her brother. "We've got a party to get on with!"

Stuart just shook his head as we all bundled downstairs.

"Your hiccups have gone!" whispered Rosie when we were in the lounge.

"It must have been the thought of Stuart coming into my room and seeing those banners!" Lyndz giggled. "He'd have my guts for garters if he knew I'd borrowed them! Right then, anybody fancy a bop?"

She rushed over to the corner and turned on the CD player. This awful thumping sound blasted out so loud, I swear the walls started shaking.

"Aw man, that's dreadful!" Kenny yelled, covering her ears with her hands.

"Sorry about that," Lyndz grimaced when she'd managed to turn it off. "It's some of

Tom's awful techno stuff."

"I'm glad we're not coming to the party here on New Year's Eve if that's what they're going to be listening to," Rosie told her.

"We're going to have great music at our party," Fliss gushed. "Mum went out and bought loads of new CDs. It's going to be brill!"

I looked across at Kenny. We usually pull faces at each other when Fliss goes off on one of her "I-am-wonderful" speeches, but Kenny was looking really miserable. Lyndz must have noticed too, because she put on a CD and turned it up really loud to drown out Fliss. Then she grabbed Kenny's arm and made her dance.

It was cool bopping around. We could have done without Lyndz's little brother Ben joining us, though. He's a right little tearaway, and thought it would be fun to start pelting us with fruit. A satsuma caught Kenny right on the back of the head.

"This means war!" Kenny muttered through gritted teeth, and grabbed a bunch of grapes from the fruit bowl. "Right, young Benjamin, how d'you fancy this lot crushed over your bonce?"

Soon we were all charging round the room armed with handfuls of fruit. Fliss looked very uneasy.

"Ooh, that reminds me, Mum made me an exotic fruit salad for our midnight feast," she suddenly piped up. "It's in my bag and I really should put it in the fridge. I'll just pop up to get it."

"Typical Fliss!" Kenny shouted across to me. "That girl just doesn't know how to have fun!"

A couple of walnuts came flying across the floor and hit me right in the shin.

"Yow! That really hurt!" I stumbled over to the sofa and rubbed my leg.

"Right, that's it Ben, I'm going to tell Mum!" Lyndz stormed out to the kitchen.

The others crowded round me, and *wallop* – a fig landed on Rosie's lap.

"I'm going to get you!" Kenny yelled, narrowing her eyes as she looked at Ben. She

grabbed a really squashy kiwi fruit from the
fruit bowl and aimed it towards him. He
bobbed down behind an armchair and *splat!*
The kiwi fruit hit the wall. As if that wasn't
bad enough, Fliss had just reappeared, and
the sight of a kiwi fruit hurtling towards her
made her stumble. Unfortunately the lid
wasn't securely on her container of fruit
salad and a little bit of the juice slopped
down her dress.

Tom, of course, chose just that moment to
put in an appearance.

"Oh Fliss, you haven't wet yourself, have
you?" he smirked. "That's a pity, you were
looking pretty good too – for one of Lyndz's
friends!"

"That's enough, Tom!" Lyndz's mum came
in. "Benjamin Collins! I hear you're causing a
nuisance." She grabbed his hand and
dragged him out.

"It might be an idea to pick some of that
fruit off the floor, girls," she shouted over her
shoulder. "We wouldn't want any accidents if
you slipped on it!"

I told you that we always have a cool time at Lyndz's! Any other parents would have gone ballistic if they'd found fruit slung all over their lounge. I know that *my* parents would – wouldn't yours?

"We could put some of this in your fruit salad, Fliss," giggled Rosie, scooping up a squashy tangerine. "The dirt might give it a bit of crunch!"

The rest of us cracked up, but Fliss was still upset about her dress.

"The best thing to do is leave it and let it dry naturally," said Lyndz kindly. "I bet if you dance around in it really fast, it'll dry in no time and we won't be able to see the mark at all."

"Do you think so?" asked Fliss.

"Oh yes!" we all nodded confidently.

Well, it was a good excuse for a dance, wasn't it? So when we'd cleaned up all the fruit, we did the routines we knew for Steps and Britney Spears. And then we put on our favourite bopping tunes.

I was pretty exhausted, not to mention

hungry, when Lyndz's mum called us through for supper. She'd laid out a table so it looked like a really swanky dinner party. We had our Coke in proper wine glasses and everything.

After we'd eaten, we watched a video of *Friends*, and then pretended that we were some of the characters. I don't know what time it was when Lyndz suggested we get ready for bed.

"I thought we were going to see in our 'New Year' like this," complained Fliss, smoothing down her dress. "I wouldn't have worn it otherwise."

I was kind of ready to get into my jim-jams, and I figured the others were too.

"Well, you know Fliss, I think you should save that dress for seeing in the *proper* New Year," I reasoned. "It's so beautiful, and you wouldn't want to risk spoiling it again with our midnight feast, would you? You know what a messy eater Kenny can be!"

Kenny pretended to bop me on the head, but at least Fliss agreed to get ready for bed.

I must admit it felt kind of nice to slob out after we'd been so dressed up. After we'd washed and everything, we wriggled into our sleeping bags, then sat up in them so we could see each other. As I told you, the room is so small that it took a while for us all to get comfortable.

"I know! Why don't we tell each other what we want to happen in the New Year?" suggested Fliss.

"Well, I just want the baby to arrive safely," I told the others. "And for it to be healthy and for Mum to be OK."

"I'm sure everything will be fine," Lyndz reassured me. "What about you Kenny, what do you want?"

"I want to finish the M&Ms off once and for all!" she yelled.

"Yes!" We all agreed with that.

"But what else do you want, Kenny?" Rosie asked when we'd all calmed down.

"Leicester City to win the FA Cup," she grinned. We all groaned. "And for me to get into a proper football team and for my skills to be spotted and to play for England and..."

"Yes, we get the picture!" we laughed, bashing her with our pillows.

"Well, what I want more than anything is actually going to happen!" squealed Fliss. Then she added, in that *really* annoying way of hers, "But I can't tell you what it is!"

The rest of us looked at each other.

"That's what you think!" said Kenny menacingly. We all wriggled in our sleeping bags over to Fliss and started to tickle her.

"We have ways of making you talk!" giggled Rosie, tickling Fliss right under her arms.

"Get off!" she squawked. "That's not fair! I'm not telling you. I promised!"

"Promised who? Who did you promise?" demanded Kenny.

"Don't tell me you're going to marry Ryan Scott!" I joked.

By then we were all kind of breathless, so we collapsed back into our sleeping bags. Fliss was looking really chuffed with herself for not giving in to us. But as soon as we mentioned her beloved Ryan's name, she want all pink and peculiar.

"No silly! But oh, I almost forgot... now, where is it?" Fliss was in a real tizzy of excitement, trying to rummage about in her bag.

"Ah here it is!" She pulled out a Christmas card of two robins nestling together on a branch and started wafting it about in front of our faces. "Well, did anyone else get one of these?"

"Yep, I think we can all say that we got plenty of cards, Fliss," Rosie said, pulling a face.

"No, look who it's from!" Fliss squealed and pointed to the signature at the bottom.

Luv Ryan

"You are joking!" I screeched. "Is this for real or is it a joke?"

I looked at the old prankster Kenny, but she looked as mystified as the rest of us. Fliss just blushed and went all soppy. There was going to be absolutely no dealing with her now.

"What about you Rosie, what do you want in the New Year?" I asked.

"Well, I used to wish for my parents to get back together again," she admitted. "But now I know that they're both happier with the way things are. So I guess I'd like the rest of the house to be decorated. You lot don't fancy helping, do you?"

"No way!" laughed Kenny. "Doing your bedroom was bad enough. Talk about hard work!"

"I guess that's what I'd like too," admitted Lyndz. "No, not Rosie's house to be decorated, stupids! I want Dad to finish *my* new room, so that we'll have more space for our sleepovers!"

"That's what we want too!" shouted Kenny. "I'm getting cramp here being squashed in next to you lot!"

We were just going to pile on top of her when we heard something outside Lyndz's door.

"Have you seen the time, girls?" Lyndz's mum called.

"BONG..." Tom and Stuart were pretending to sound like Big Ben.

"It must be midnight!" squealed Rosie.

"BONG…"

"What should we do now?" asked Fliss anxiously.

"BONG…"

"You're supposed to sing some special song, but I don't know the words," I told them.

"BONG…"

"Well, let's all get in a group hug then," suggested Lyndz. "We've got to do *something*."

We all got into a huddle. And when Stuart and Tom had bonged twelve times, we hugged each other extra hard and yelled, *"Happy New Year!"*

Then Lyndz's mum and dad, Stuart and Tom burst through the door. Her mum was carrying a tray with a bottle of lemonade done up like champagne and five posh glasses. They were grinning all over their faces – until Stuart noticed the banners on the walls.

CHAPTER NINE

I really thought all hell was going to break loose when Stuart spotted the decorations.

"Are those *my* banners?" he asked suspiciously.

"Well, erm, yes," stuttered Lyndz. "I'm only borrowing them, I didn't think you'd mind—"

"Of course I mind!" he yelled. "Mum made me use my own money to buy them, and you didn't even *ask* to borrow them!"

"Well, I knew you wouldn't lend them to me if I did!" Lyndz was getting a bit upset, I could tell.

"Too right I wouldn't," Stuart snapped back. "I know you and your wild friends. You're bound to ruin them with your stupid games."

Rosie mumbled "Charming" under her breath, but he didn't seem to hear.

"Well, I'm going to take them down right now!"

Before anyone could stop him, Stuart stormed right into the room. He grabbed one end of a banner and tugged it, but I guess he'd forgotten that there were five sleeping bags on the floor. He certainly hadn't bargained on Fliss being inside hers. She'd snuggled back inside at the first sign of trouble. Anyway, Stuart tripped over her and stumbled. The banner was still in his hand as he fell, and with a SNAP the string broke and the letters spelling out HAPPY NEW YEAR! fell to the floor like autumn leaves.

We just stood there and didn't know what to do. Fliss was squealing and trying to get Stuart's foot out of her hair, Lyndz looked as though she was about to burst into tears and Tom was laughing his head off.

"Well, your New Year's certainly started with a bang!" observed Lyndz's mum, putting the tray with the glasses down on Lyndz's table. "Or should that be a bump?"

"So much for *Lyndz*'s silly games spoiling your banners, Stu," said Mr Collins, helping Stuart up from the floor. Stuart was bright red and looked furious with Lyndz.

"You really should have asked him first though, you know Lyndsey." Lyndz's mum sounded serious, but then she added, "You'd better toast in the 'New Year' before anything else happens!"

When Lyndz's parents, Stuart and Tom had left, us we all looked at each other. Then Kenny cracked up.

"That was class! Did you see Stu fall?"

"*Felt* him, more like!" moaned Fliss, although she was grinning. "Your brother is one big lump, Lyndz!"

That seemed to cheer Lyndz up. She poured out our lemonade and we wished each other a "Happy New Year" as we clinked glasses.

When we finally settled down to sleep, Fliss said, "Your mum was right though. It wasn't a great start to a New Year, was it? Let's hope we have better luck with the real one!"

"Except I won't be there, will I?" mumbled Kenny quietly. "You'll all be starting the New Year together and I'll be in Scotland."

She sounded really miserable.

"But we'll toast you, won't we guys?" I comforted her.

"Sure will!" the others agreed. Kenny seemed kind of thrilled about that, but still a bit sad.

Saying goodbye to each other in the morning was pretty hard because we knew that we'd next see each other at Fliss's party and Kenny wouldn't be there. It didn't seem right, somehow.

Still, I was relieved to get home, just so I could reassure myself that Mum was OK.

"Did you have fun, darling?" she asked.

"Yes, it was wicked!" I told her all about the fruit fight and the lemonade at midnight and Stuart getting mad and falling over.

"And you should have seen Fliss's dress!" I gabbled. "Well, you will, won't you? She'll be wearing it at her mum's party."

"Ah yes, the party of the millennium!" Mum said sarcastically. "Nikki rang last night in a bit of a flap."

"When *isn't* Fliss's mum in a bit of a flap?" I asked.

"Well, she's in a lot of a flap actually," Mum continued. "She was having a major crisis about some napkins, so I said she could borrow some of ours. You wouldn't mind taking them round this afternoon, would you Frankie?"

Now, going round to Fliss's house when her mum's in a tizz is not exactly high on my list of fun things to do. But it didn't really look as though I had much choice. So later that afternoon, armed with a carrier bag full of napkins, I set off.

It was obvious as soon as I got to the door that things were not exactly rosy inside. I could hear a high-pitched squeaking which

223

at first I thought was Fliss, but then Fliss bundled out of the front door all red in the face.

"Are you OK?" I asked.

"Oh Frankie, thank goodness!" Fliss grabbed hold of my arm. "Mum's going off on one. You should hear her!"

"I think I just have," I admitted. I could still hear the squeaking, but it was getting louder. It was coming closer. It was Fliss's mum!

"Don't you dare run away from me, Felicity!" she squeaked. Then she saw me. "Ah Frankie, I don't think I'm going to need those napkins now. I've decided I'm not having a party, it's too much to cope with. Too much food, too many people, too much mess. I wish I'd never told anyone about it. I don't think I can face it, I really don't."

It was amazing. I mean, the woman never stopped to draw breath! And boy, did she look rough! Usually she's dead trendy, but not today. Today she made Godzilla look like Naomi Campbell. I knew something must be really wrong because she hadn't even bothered to put any make-up on. She usually wears enough to supply the cosmetics counter at Boots.

"You can't cancel the party now, Mrs Sidebotham," I told her, alarmed. "Everyone's really looking forward to it."

Fliss's mum's chin began to wobble and she started to sniff. I wasn't sure that I could face seeing her break down in tears. It's bad enough coping with Fliss when she's like that.

"Why don't I make you a cup of tea?" I suggested, as Fliss and I steered her towards the kitchen.

And that was another sign that Fliss's mum wasn't quite right – she actually let me into the house without me taking my shoes off first. And that almost *never* happens. But I wished I hadn't thought about it, because you know how your mind sometimes wanders? Well, mine went on a major expedition! I kept thinking how funny it would be if Mrs Sidebotham made everyone take off their shoes when they came to the party. There'd be a great pile of them by the door and they'd all get muddled up and everyone would end up going home in the wrong pair...

"What's so funny?" demanded Fliss as we got into the kitchen. I hadn't even realised that I was smiling. But fortunately, before I had a chance to explain, Andy and Callum appeared, carrying huge boxes piled high with bags of crisps and things.

"Hiya Frankie, how are you?" Andy beamed at me and dumped his box on the breakfast bar.

"Fine thanks," I smiled back at him. I really like Andy. He's Fliss's mum's boyfriend, but we tend to think of him as Fliss's stepfather because he's been around forever. Even Fliss calls him her stepfather sometimes. Anyway, he's always really bright and cheerful, and I've no idea how he manages that, living with Fliss and her mum – not to mention Callum!

Mrs Sidebotham was slumped on one of the stools next to the breakfast bar, and as Andy and Callum carried in more and more boxes from the car, she started to whimper again.

"Oh, I can't cope with this, I just can't!" she wailed. "We're going to have to call the party off!"

"Now, now, we've been over this," murmured Andy soothingly, putting an arm around her shoulder. "We're having someone in to prepare the food. We've bought all the drinks, the house is clean, the decorations are still up from Christmas, and we're here to help out, aren't we guys?"

Fliss and Callum nodded solemnly.

"So you see, all you have to do is look beautiful, my love." Andy kissed Fliss's mum on the cheek. "And you can't help doing that, can you? This party is definitely going ahead, because I want to show you off!"

Yuk! I thought I was going to throw up, I really did, but at least Mrs Sidebotham was smiling again.

"And besides, Mum, you've got to have the party because you want everyone to know about..." Fliss bent over and whispered something in her mum's ear. I don't know what it was, but Mrs Sidebotham went all giggly and pink.

After that she went back into traditional 'Fliss's mum' mode. You know, twittering about and fussing over where to put things so they wouldn't get broken. That was definitely my cue to leave.

"I'll see you at the party, then?" I called as I left.

"OK sweetie, thanks for the napkins!" Mrs Sidebotham called out from the lounge. It was like she'd totally forgotten all about the state she was in when I first got there.

Fliss came to the door with me.

"Thanks for coming, Frankie. I think Mum's excited, that's all!"

"Yeah, 'course," I nodded. I was just glad that *my* mum didn't go off on one whenever she was excited.

"I wonder what the party's really for?" I asked Mum when I got home. "Fliss's mum's certainly all ga-ga about something, and it's definitely not just New Year's Eve."

"If it's what I think it is, Nikki will want to make it a party to remember!" Mum replied.

Well, let me tell you, none of us will *ever* forget that New Year's Eve party. But I don't think it was exactly what Fliss's mum had in mind!

CHAPTER TEN

When the day of the party finally came round, I was well up for it. I suppose I was excited because it was the first grown-up party I'd ever been to, and I didn't really know what to expect. I just figured it would be sophisticated and glamorous and—

"Boring!"

That's what Dad said, anyway. He reckons that whenever grown-ups get together, all they talk about is how tiring their jobs are and how much money they spend. Great! I was in for a really fun evening, wasn't I?

I didn't take much notice of him actually, because I think he was just trying to put me off. I don't think he and Mum were really looking forward to Fliss's mum's party.

I was kind of hyper as soon as I got up, but I knew that I had a whole day to get through before we went out, so I thought of all the things I could do to calm me down. The first thing on my list was to ring Kenny. I was sure that she said they were going to drive up to her grandparents in Scotland at about ten in the morning of New Year's Eve. But when I rang her at nine, there was no reply.

"They probably set off early," Mum suggested. "It's quite a drive up there."

"They might even have gone up last night," Dad chipped in. "I'm not sure I'd want to drive all that way and be thrown straight into the Hogmanay celebrations. It gets pretty wild up there, I gather."

"Kenny will fit in well then!" I chuckled.

"Ooh, I've just had a vision of Kenny doing the Highland fling!" groaned Dad. "Now that's not a pretty sight at breakfast time!"

"Give over, Dad!" I laughed, and punched him on the arm.

I was a bit miffed that Kenny hadn't rung me before she left, though. But then again, she had been kind of upset knowing that we would all be together on New Year's Eve without her. Perhaps she was still a bit cut up about it.

When the phone rang a little later I pounced on it, expecting it to be Kenny. Wrong! It was Fliss's mum and she was in another tizz. In fact, we are talking Panic City!

"Ooh Frankie, is your mum around, only..."

I held the phone out to Mum and mouthed "Fliss's mum!"

Mum rolled her eyes and took the receiver. "Hello Nikki, are you ready for the party then?"

Stupid question, Mother. Mum was on the phone for *forty minutes,* trying to reassure Fliss's mum that yes, she was sure she had enough food, and no, she didn't think there would be any gatecrashers, and... Well, you get the picture, don't you? Poor Mum looked shattered when she got off the phone.

But if *that* wasn't bad enough, Fliss's mum kept ringing back. When the phone rang for the fifth time, Mum said:

"Will you get that, Frankie? And if she asks for me, tell her I've gone to the doctor's with earache!"

"Mum!" I pretended to look shocked and picked up the receiver.

"Hi Mrs Sidebotham, I'm afraid Mum's had to pop out," I fibbed. "Yes, I'll tell her you rang. See you tonight then, bye."

"My father always told me it was wrong to lie," I said in a sickly-sweet voice when I'd put the phone down.

"Well Frankie, there are nasty big lies and there are little white ones which might just save someone's sanity..."

"... and that was one of those, right?" I asked seriously.

"You bet your life it was. I'm going to lie down, I feel exhausted." Mum pretended to clutch her head and swept dramatically out of the room.

I don't know how I got through the rest of the day without going crazy. I tried on my outfit about a million times (I'd decided to wear what I'd worn to our sleepover), and experimented with loads of different make-up. I picked out one of the fake tattoos Lyndz had bought me, then decided to have a bath before I put it on. And all the time excitement was kind of bubbling inside me.

When it finally got to early evening and Dad was fixing us all something to eat, I could barely contain myself.

"Do you think there'll be dancing? I can't imagine Fliss's mum dancing, can you? Ooh, thanks Dad, veggie bangers, my favourite! Do you think there'll be lots to eat there tonight? I mean, am I going to be too full up if I eat these now?" I babbled on, barely pausing for breath. "Oh, Mrs Sidebotham won't have those silly little sandwiches, will she? What's up Mum, aren't you eating anything? Are you saving yourself for the food later?"

"No, I think I'll just have a piece of bread or something," Mum said quietly. "I've just got a touch of indigestion again. Nothing to worry about."

"Nikki's worn you down with all her fussing hasn't she?" Dad turned to Mum and started rubbing her back. "Never mind – after tonight it'll all be over. We probably won't see Nikki for a month, she'll be in such a state of shock after all those people have trampled through her house!"

"Aw, don't say that, Dad! I'm looking forward to this party, even if no one else is," I told them defiantly. "Do you think you can teach me the words for that song you sing at midnight, 'Old Land Signs' or whatever it's called? I don't want to be the only one who doesn't know the words."

Mum and Dad looked at each other.

"The song's called 'Auld Lang Syne'," Dad explained. "But I don't think you'll be needing the words for that. We're only popping along to the party for a couple of hours, you know. We'll be home well before midnight."

"What?!" I yelled. "What's the point of

going to a New Year's Eve party in 1999 if you don't stay till midnight? This is, like, a new century! A new *millennium*!"

I was really, *really* gutted. I mean, I'd been building up to this party for a week, and they had to choose now, like an hour before we went, to drop the bombshell that we were only "popping along", like it was a tea party or something!

"All the others will be staying. It's not fair!" I knew that I was whining and that I must sound like Fliss. But I didn't care.

"Well, if you're going to behave like a spoilt child, we needn't go at all." Dad was looking at me sternly over the rim of his glasses. "We thought you were more mature than that, Frankie."

I felt *awful*. I didn't know what was worse – being disappointed myself, or disappointing Mum and Dad because of the way I was reacting.

"Sorry," I mumbled, and went up to my room.

I felt kind of hopeless, you know? I mean,

～ what was the point of getting all glammed up to go out, if we were going to be back home as soon as we got there? What made it worse was that Kenny wasn't even going to be there. She can always manage to cheer me up, however gloomy I am.

There was a knock at the door.

"Can I come in?" Mum peeped round the corner, then came in and sat on the bed.

"Sorry you're so disappointed, love, it's just that I'm kind of tired, you know." Mum did look a bit pale, and she still looked to be in pain from her indigestion. I suddenly felt very guilty for being so selfish.

"I'm sorry Mum, I know you really aren't looking forward to going at all," I smiled apologetically. "And I guess I might be fed up of Fliss's 'Isn't-this-a-wonderful-party-and isn't-my-mum-clever?' routine after two hours anyway!"

Mum just laughed. "OK then, you'd better get your glad rags on before your dad decides not to go at all!"

Then Mum noticed the fake tattoo I'd put

round my arm. She stared at it, and I really thought she was going to go ballistic...

Then a big grin spread over her face.

"Is that one of the tattoos Lyndz gave you for Christmas?"

I nodded.

"Will you put that rose one on me, just there?" She pointed to her shoulder. "I can't wait to see Fliss's mum's reaction when she sees it!"

We both collapsed into fits of giggles and went into the bathroom.

I have to say that Mum looked *well* cool when I'd finished with her. Not only did I apply the tattoo for her, but she also let me do her make-up. When we were both dressed, we went downstairs together and Dad whistled really loudly.

"Wowee!" he smirked. "You both look fantastic! You'd better wrap up warm though, it's starting to snow."

He hadn't even *noticed* Mum's tattoo! When she put on a jacket as we went outside, she gave me this big, soppy wink. We couldn't stop giggling all the way to the party, and Dad just couldn't work out what was going on.

"What is it with you two?" he asked. "You're like a couple of monkeys."

That, of course, made us laugh even more.

When we pulled up outside Fliss's house, there seemed to be loads of noise coming from inside.

"It sounds pretty lively!" Dad said.

And I suddenly began to feel really nervous. I knew that the others would be there and Mum and Dad and everything, but I really began to miss Kenny. We're always there to support each other, and I knew that she wouldn't be nervous about going into a big party at all.

We started to walk carefully up the path. The snow was starting to settle, and it was kind of slippery. I gingerly slid one foot in front of the other – and that's when I saw it. A figure. A very familiar figure. A figure wearing a bright Leicester City top. A figure which just *had* to be Kenny!

CHAPTER ELEVEN

"Kenny!" I yelled, tottering up the path as fast as I dared. "What are you doing here?"

Kenny turned to me, beaming all over her face. "Blizzards and 'flu," she said, ever so seriously.

"You what?"

"There are going to be blizzards in Scotland and Granny and Grandpa have gone down with 'flu," Kenny explained. "So here we are!"

We grabbed each other and did one of our silly dances. Well Kenny did – she was wearing her Docs so she was all right in the snow. I just kind of stood there whilst she danced round me.

"You are so childish, do you know that?" moaned a voice from the shadows.

Uh-oh! If Kenny had made it to the party, then so had her cruddy sister, Molly the Monster.

"Molly's in a foul mood because Emma's gone to Stuart and Tom's party, and she wanted to go too. But Mum said she was too young and had to come here with us, worse luck!" Kenny whispered.

"That doesn't mean she'll have to hang around with us, does it?" I asked anxiously.

"No fear!" huffed Kenny dismissively.

Mum and Dad meanwhile were walking up the path with Kenny's parents. They all get on pretty well together, so I was kind of hoping that Mum and Dad might stay at the party a bit longer now that they were here too.

Suddenly the front door opened and the music from inside the house spilled out to meet us.

241

"Oh good, it's you! Do come in and let me take your coats," twittered Fliss's mum, staring very hard at our shoes. Now we all know how fussy she is about us trailing dirt into her house, so we all wiped our feet extra hard before we went in.

She was looking very thin and glamorous in a slinky evening dress, which was just like the one Fliss had worn to Lyndz's sleepover. She had a pinched look on her face and a strange sort of smile, as though she was trying to enjoy herself but hadn't quite cracked it.

"Felicity darling, help me with these, would you?" she called out.

And Fliss appeared, looking like an exact replica of her mum. But a lot younger, obviously. They had the same hairstyle and the same make-up, everything. They even had the same odd expression. It was really weird.

"Hello, let me take those," Fliss said ever so politely.

"Are you all right, Fliss? You look as though you need to go to the toilet or something," said Kenny, barging past her into the hall.

"Kenny!" reprimanded her mother, but she didn't sound very cross.

Mum and I took off our snow-covered jackets and gave them to Mrs Sidebotham. And, well – you should have been there to see the look on her face when she clocked our tattoos! For a few moments she just stared at my arm and Mum's shoulder. Then she huffed a bit, opening her mouth with no sound coming out. Then she went really pink and hurriedly took our jackets into the cloakroom.

Dad looked kind of shocked when he noticed Mum's tattoo. Then he cracked up laughing and Mum had to push him into the lounge. As we were waiting for Andy to give us a drink he whispered, "You are two very wicked women!"

If Mum had known anything about high fives, we'd have done one then!

Lyndz was already there with her parents, so Kenny and I made a beeline for her.

"Have we missed anything?" I asked.

"Nah, only Fliss's mum going off on one because someone had trailed muck on to the carpet."

"Nothing new there then," we all screeched together and spluttered into our Cokes.

"Ryan Scott's not here?" I asked when we'd recovered. "I was sure that Fliss would have invited him after he sent her that card."

"Don't get her started on that!" groaned Lyndz. "She's already told me twenty times how she wanted to invite him but her mum wouldn't let her."

Lyndz then turned to Kenny. "I didn't expect to see you here either."

Whilst Kenny was telling her all about the blizzards and the 'flu, I had a look round. Mum was sitting on the sofa deep in conversation with Lyndz's mum, talking about babies no doubt. Dad, Andy and Dr McKenzie were huddled together by the drinks cabinet. Callum was sitting under a table with a huge bowl of crisps, and Mrs McKenzie looked to be having words with a very sulky Molly. Fliss was nowhere to be seen. I went into the hall to investigate, and saw her wrestling with the front part of Adam's wheelchair, trying to get it up the front step. Rosie and her mum were behind, pushing, and Adam was beaming regally at everyone like a king.

"Here, let me help!" I rushed over to them.

After a few minutes of heaving, Adam was in.

"That was a close one, Adam!" I grinned. "We nearly had to bring the party out to you!"

He nodded and laughed and presented a bunch of flowers to Mrs Sidebotham, who was hovering anxiously behind the door.

"Thank you, that's very kind!" she said very slowly. People always seem to do that with Adam. Just because he has cerebral palsy and finds it difficult to speak himself, it doesn't mean he can't understand you.

Rosie wheeled him through to the lounge and everyone went to say hello.

"Fliss's mum's going to have a fit about

that wheelchair!" whispered Lyndz. "You can't exactly wipe the wheels on the mat, can you?"

I had visions of Mrs Sidebotham flipping completely. But she was being very brave and pretending not to notice the dirty, snowy tyre-marks which had criss-crossed over her cream carpet.

"Hey Rosie, come and join us!" we called over.

Kenny went to fetch her a glass of Coke and the rest of us chatted together. But after about ten minutes there was still no sign of Kenny. I went into the kitchen to look for her, and found Mum tucking into some garlic bread.

"I thought you had indigestion," I said.

"It's not too bad at the moment," she told me. "Besides, I've got to keep my strength up. I'm eating for two, remember?"

"Yeah, right!" I laughed. "Well make sure you leave some food for us, OK!"

I still couldn't see Kenny anywhere. But I could hear raised voices coming from the downstairs loo.

"I never wanted to come to this downbeat party anyway. We'd be having much more fun in Scotland."

"Yeah, well we're not in Scotland, are we, so you'd better start livening up before you depress everybody else, you miserable toad!"

That had to be Kenny and Molly doing their usual sweet sister act.

"Hey guys, come on. Give it a rest, for goodness sake!" I burst in on them. It's a good thing I did too, because Kenny had Molly pinned up against the wall.

I broke them up and they reluctantly followed me back into the kitchen, where Kenny quickly swooped on the food.

"Grub! Great, I'm starving!"

She started piling things on to a plate.

"No wonder you're getting fat, eating like that!" Molly sneered.

"Right, that's it!"

Kenny grabbed a spoon and loaded it with sour cream dip. She took aim, and was about to fire it when...

247

"Hey not so fast!" Andy grabbed her arm and took away the spoon. "We'll have no food fights here, thank you very much. That would definitely finish Fliss's mum off!"

Molly started laughing mockingly at Kenny, who looked absolutely furious.

"What about taking some food in to Adam, Molly?" Andy suggested. "And I thought you two might like to help Fliss and Lyndz sort out the music for dancing. It's about time this party started swinging. What do you say?"

"Cool!" We piled in to the lounge.

All the adults seemed to be standing around talking, but I couldn't see Mum anywhere.

"She's around somewhere," Dad told me. "I've just seen her with a plate full of cheesecake!"

We both laughed and I went to join the others, who were sorting through a stack of CDs.

When we'd got everything sorted, we put the finishing touches to one of our Steps routines. Fliss was wiggling for all she was worth when her mum appeared and started flapping her arms about too. I kind of assumed that she was trying to join in, until I heard her squeaking:

"Can everyone be quiet for a minute?"

But of course nobody heard her. So she tried again. But still everyone carried on chatting.

"Would you like me to get everyone's attention?" asked Kenny.

"Thank you Kenny, that would be very kind," she smiled.

Kenny stood on a chair, put two fingers in her mouth and made the most ear-splitting whistle ever. Then she yelled:

"LISTEN UP EVERYBODY, MRS SIDEBOTHAM WANTS TO SAY SOMETHING!"

Well, that certainly shut everyone up.

"Er thanks Kenny, that's not exactly what I had in mind!" Mrs Sidebotham said lamely, and everyone laughed. "I'd just like to say, er – where's Andy?"

"Is that it?" asked Kenny. "I thought it was something important!"

Everybody screamed with laughter, but Fliss's mum seemed quite anxious to find him. So we all looked round, and then we heard the downstairs toilet flush. We heard a running of water and whistling, and Andy reappeared in the lounge to great guffaws and a huge round of applause. Fliss's mum looked dead embarrassed, but Andy just smirked.

Fliss's mum tried again.

"As you know, Andy and I..."

"Erm, sorry to interrupt you, Nikki..."

It was Dad. I couldn't believe it! Fliss's mum was starting to look really annoyed.

"If you're going to make an important announcement, I'd really like Helena to hear it, and I don't think she's here."

Everyone looked round again. Mum was definitely not there. Where on earth was she?

CHAPTER TWELVE

Now I don't know if you've seen my mum since she's been pregnant, but she is kind of big. She's usually just normal-sized, but expecting the baby had made her balloon into a big fat waddly duck. And to be honest, I was worried that she'd got stuck somewhere.

When we'd all done a thorough search downstairs, Dad whispered that maybe I should check upstairs too.

"You know what she's like when she's had a plateful of cheesecake – BAM – she's out like a light. Just check that she hasn't crashed out on one of the beds," he suggested.

"Like Goldilocks, you mean!" I laughed.

"Yeah, something like that!"

I crept upstairs and tried all the bedrooms. First Fliss's, which was as neat as usual. I looked at her bed, but there was only a row of dolls looking back at me. I peeped inside her mum's bedroom too, but I felt kind of guilty doing that. I know how Mrs Sidebotham hates anyone going in there without her permission. It smelt all perfumed and lovely, like roses.

"Mum? Are you here?" I hissed.

There was no reply, and I could see from the doorway that the only things on the bed were a few frilly cushions.

Next there was Callum's room. I'd never been in there before. It smelt all funny, like little boys tend to do. And it was kind of hard to see where anything was. I crept in a little bit further and BANG – I stumbled into something. Then there was a groan.

"Mum!" I squeaked. "Is that you?"

I fumbled for the light switch and flicked it on.

"Whaddyawant?" a small weary voice murmured. It was Callum, lying on the bed and shielding his eyes from the light.

"Nothing," I whispered. "Sorry to disturb you, go back to sleep!"

I switched off the light and went back on to the landing. There were only two places left to try – the room where Fliss's mum practises her beauty therapy and the bathroom. I figured Mum might have gone to lie down on Mrs Sidebotham's treatment couch. So I was going to try there first, when I heard a noise coming from the bathroom.

"Mum, is that you?" I called out, my face right up to the door.

"Frankie?"

"Are you OK? We were worried about you? Fliss's mum is making an announcement and Dad thought you ought to come down," I told her.

"Actually Frankie, do you think you could get your dad for me?" Mum called back.

253

"You haven't got indigestion again, have you?" I asked. "Dad told me about you eating that cheesecake..."

"No!" she interrupted me, gasping slightly. "I'm sure... the baby's... on its way... this time."

"Hold on Mum! I'll get Dad!" I shouted, and flew downstairs like a mad woman.

"Dad, Dad, quick! Mum says she's having the baby!"

Suddenly everyone seemed to be rushing around like headless chickens.

"Call an ambulance, will you Nikki?" Dad shouted, leaping up the stairs two at a time.

Lyndz's mum hurried after him. She'd been teaching Mum's ante-natal classes, so she was kind of a good person to have around. And then of course there was Kenny's father the doctor too.

"I'll go and get my bag from the car!" He opened the front door and was met by a blizzard of snow. "My goodness me! I thought it was supposed to be Scotland that was going to get all the bad weather," he said, stumbling out into the cold.

I felt really strange, like everything was going on around me but I wasn't part of it.

"Dad, Dad! Can I help?" Kenny rushed over to her father as soon as he came back through the door.

"I'm not sure that Helena would thank me for giving her an inexperienced, under-age midwife!" Dr McKenzie laughed, ruffling Kenny's hair. Then he noticed how disappointed she looked. "But there are lots of important things you can do. Like getting a bed ready for her to lie down on until the ambulance arrives."

"My bed!" whimpered Fliss's mum as Kenny hared upstairs. "My beautiful bedroom!"

Peeping up through the banisters, I could see Dad and Mrs Collins helping Mum into the bedroom. Mum caught sight of me.

"Don't look so worried Frankie, I'm fine." She tried to smile, despite wincing with pain. "And look at all this attention I'm getting. It's better than hospital!"

Yeah, right! Like every woman would

choose to give birth in Fliss's home on New Year's Eve!

"Your mum's right." Lyndz's dad gently led me into the lounge where everyone else was sitting around anxiously. "What Lyndz's mum doesn't know about giving birth you can write on the back of a stamp!"

"I had all my children at home," Mrs McKenzie told me reassuringly. "And Kenny's father assisted at all the births. So your mum really is in good hands. Come on over by the fire, love, you're cold. Fliss, can you rustle up a warm drink for Frankie? I think she's in a bit of shock."

Fliss was looking very pale and in a state of shock herself, but she went into the kitchen and Rosie and Lyndz came over to join me.

"We're not going to forget this party in a hurry, are we?" squeaked Rosie. "And just think, we're all going to be here when your baby brother or sister is born! How cool is that?"

"I think labour sometimes takes quite a

while," Lyndz told us. "The ambulance will probably be here soon, and then they'll take your mum to hospital."

Kenny bounded in, all flushed and excited.

"Dad says we might need some towels, is that all right, Mrs S?"

Fliss's mum shuddered slightly and nodded.

"It's like being in one of those old movies, isn't it?" said Rosie's mum. "You know, they always say 'I'll need lots of towels and plenty of hot water' whenever anyone's about to give birth."

Kenny stopped in the doorway and spun round. "Hey, that's an idea! What about Frankie's mum having the baby in your Jacuzzi bath, Mrs S? A water birth would be so cool!"

"Oh no!" Fliss's mum started sobbing. "I... I... don't think so!"

She seemed to be kind of gasping a bit, so Mrs McKenzie shooed Kenny back upstairs and poured a brandy.

"For the shock!" she murmured, handing it to Fliss's mum.

Rosie's mum had been spluttering with laughter ever since Kenny mentioned her great idea about the Jacuzzi, and she was laughing even harder at the thought of Mrs Sidebotham having to be revived by brandy.

A few minutes later, Andy and Fliss appeared with a big tray of drinks and biscuits for everyone. They both seemed very concerned that Mrs Sidebotham was in such a state. I mean, excuse me, but wasn't it *my* mum who was upstairs having a baby?

"How long did the ambulance say they would be, Nikki?" Dr McKenzie called downstairs.

Fliss's mum leapt up and yelped, like she'd just sat on a wasp or something.

"Oh no, I didn't, I mean… I thought… oh dear!"

We all stared at her.

"You mean, you never even called an ambulance?" Andy asked her sharply.

"No!" she whispered, and started to cry again.

"I'll do it!" he sighed and went into the hall.

"I thought this party was really lame, but it's kind of getting exciting now!" Molly chuckled as she walked past us with a piece of cake stuffed in her mouth.

I would normally have said something, but I couldn't. I was more worried about Mum. I mean, like Gran had said, she wasn't all that young to be having a baby. And to be having it in someone else's house, with no ambulance and a blizzard outside – well, it looked pretty bad.

I wanted to find out what was happening but I couldn't. I tried to stand up, but my legs had turned to jelly and I fell back down again.

"There there, my love!" Kenny's mum helped me to sit down again. And to my horror, I started to cry.

"Will Mum be OK?" I whispered through my sobs.

"I'll go to find out, you just stay here," she told me kindly.

Rosie's mum came over to sit by me and

Adam wheeled himself over. He looked so sad, it made me want to cry all over again. Rosie and Lyndz came to sit by me too, and so did Fliss.

"It'll be all right, Mum's bedroom's ever so clean," she said reassuringly, stroking my arm. "I mean, Mum cleans so much, it's probably even cleaner than the hospital!"

What is she like? It did make us all laugh though, and then Fliss was dead pleased and pretended that she'd said it on purpose.

"They said that everything's a bit delayed because of the snow," Andy told us as he came back into the lounge. "But an ambulance will be here as soon as possible. Hey, what's the rush?"

Kenny had hurtled downstairs and right into him.

"It's so cool Frankie, your mum's doing great, she's going 'whoo, whoo, hee'..." She started puffing and blowing and making all these weird sounds.

"You haven't been watching, have you?" Lyndz sounded really shocked.

"'Course not!" said Kenny indignantly. "But I've been doing stuff for Dad, and I can hear from the landing. Come on Frankie, you should come too!"

She dragged me to my feet. But when we got to the bottom of the steps, I heard the most amazing sound. A baby was crying. I could hear Mum laughing and Dad cooing, "Welcome to the world, little one!" And all the time, there was this newborn crying.

I can't describe how I felt. I was really *really* happy, but I just stood there with tears streaming down my face.

"Congratulations!" The others all rushed over to hug me.

"Hey Frankie!" Dad appeared at the top of the steps. "You'd better come and say hello to your little sister!"

I had a sister! My very own little sister!

I don't know how I got upstairs, my legs were still so wobbly. But just as I got to the landing, I heard chiming. Someone must have turned on the television because that was definitely the sound of Big Ben. I was

261

really confused. I was sure only an hour had passed since we found out about Mum, but it must have been more like three.

"Come on everyone, it's almost midnight!" someone shouted.

I couldn't believe it. It was almost New Year!

CHAPTER THIRTEEN

BONG!

I rushed into the bedroom.

"Mum! Dad! Oh wow!" My little sister was all tiny and bewildered and snuggled up in a towel. She was so beautiful.

BONG!

There was a lot of noise on the landing.

BONG!

"Here we are, guys!" Andy brought in a tray of champagne glasses. He'd even got one for me with a tiny bit of real champagne in the bottom of it. He winked at me.

"If you can't celebrate the birth of your own sister, I don't know what you can celebrate!" he laughed.

I peeped round the bedroom door, and everyone was standing up the stairs and on the landing.

"We thought we should all be together!" Kenny whispered to me. My eyes started filling with tears again. I couldn't ever remember feeling so happy.

BONG!

I'd lost count of the bongs, but that must have been the last one because everybody started hugging each other. Dr McKenzie started singing that song 'Auld Lang Syne' and everybody joined in. They all held hands, even though some of them were on the stairs.

"We should have taught you the words after all!" Mum grinned at me from the bed. She looked kind of hot and sleepy.

"All we need now is a tall dark stranger to let in the New Year!" chirped Fliss's mum, who seemed to have perked up again.

And you're not going to believe this, but

just then the doorbell rang. We all peered over the banisters to get a better view, but all we could hear was Fliss's mum giggling, "Well you're not quite what I expected. But you'll do!"

We all cracked up when she led in a paramedic in his fluorescent green jacket.

"I don't suppose you've got a piece of coal and a bottle of whisky in that bag, have you?" shouted Andy.

"'Fraid not!" he laughed. "Are my patients up here?"

Mrs Sidebotham led him upstairs through the crowd of people, and another paramedic appeared, wheeling in a stretcher. It was only then it started to sink in. *My mum had just had a baby!*

I was still all covered in goosebumps when the paramedics started to carry Mum downstairs on the stretcher. Everybody scooted down into the hall to make way for them.

"Mother and baby are both doing well," Dad announced proudly. "Thanks to Patsy and Jim here!"

Everybody applauded Lyndz's mum and

Kenny's dad. They both looked dead embarrassed.

"I'm going to go to hospital with Helena," Dad told me as he stroked Mum's beaming face.

"And you're going to come home with us, Frankie," said Kenny's mum, smiling at me.

"All *right*!" yelled Kenny, to everyone's amusement.

"But before we go, Nikki," Dad said, "what was that announcement you were trying to make? Before my wife so rudely interrupted you!"

Everyone turned to look at Fliss's mum, who had gone bright pink.

"Erm, well, erm…"

"We're finally taking the plunge and getting married," Andy announced for her.

"Thank you, Andy!" Mrs Sidebotham looked a bit miffed at him for taking away her moment of glory like that. But as soon as everyone started cheering and shouting "Congratulations!" she soon cheered up. In fact, she was soon beaming so much, I thought her face might split. And Fliss looked dead chuffed too.

"We ought to say congratulations to Helena and Gwyn as well," Andy shouted when the noise had died down a little. "Here's to the little one!"

The paramedics seemed kind of keen to get Mum into the ambulance, so I kissed them again and waved to them from the front door. Then I went back inside.

What an evening it had been! I looked at Fliss's mum, and I couldn't help feeling a tiny bit sorry for her. She'd arranged this whole party to announce her engagement and Mum had sort of hijacked it. Still, Mrs Sidebotham had loads of attention now. All the women were cooing over her and asking about the wedding arrangements. And Fliss was in the thick of it, talking about dresses and flowers. Anybody would think it was *her* wedding they were planning! Still, at least I knew now what she'd meant about one of her wishes coming true in the New Year!

"Come on, Frankie! Let's party!" Kenny

dragged me into the lounge where Andy had put on Steps.

I was kind of tired, but it was a *great* night. I mean, that morning I'd expected to be home by ten o'clock. And there I was bopping away at almost one o'clock in the morning! It was as wild as one of our sleepovers!

About half an hour later though, I could feel my energy running out like a battery. I wasn't the only one. Everyone else seemed to be pretty exhausted too. As we left, the only ones still dancing were Fliss's mum and Andy. And I'd been wrong about her – she was a pretty nifty mover!

Of course, going home with Kenny was great, even if it did mean having to listen to Molly the Monster moaning. According to her, it had been the worst party in the world, full of sad old people.

"Ignore her," Kenny whispered. "She's only mad because there weren't any boys there. I thought it was the coolest party ever!"

I grinned. It *had* been pretty amazing.

I crashed out as soon as I got to Kenny's. I slept in Molly's bed, because Emma was staying with a friend so Molly could sleep in Emma's room. Molly nearly freaked because she hadn't had a chance to hide all her things like she does before our sleepovers. But I was too exhausted to look at any of her things anyway. In fact I didn't wake up until about nine o'clock, and only then because Kenny's mum was calling me, saying that Dad was there.

It was great to see him. And even better when he took me straight to hospital to see Mum and my baby sister. It was just so cool, sitting there holding this tiny thing who was my new sister. I couldn't really get my head round it, it felt so weird. Weird in a very nice way, though.

Mum was only in hospital for a couple of days. I think she'd been kind of worried that they'd keep the baby in because she was born early. But the doctors said that she was doing really well, so she came home too. I'd made a big banner saying:

Welcome home Mum and ...

But Mum and Dad hadn't agreed on a name yet, so I just drew a slightly wonky baby instead. I hung it in the hall so it was the first thing they saw. I loved carrying my sister round and showing her everything. Mum said that she was too young to focus on anything properly, but I knew that she was taking it all in.

Best of all was introducing her to my sleepover friends. They all cooed over her and went completely mushy. Even Kenny, but don't tell her I told you so! Fliss of course is too full of her mum's wedding plans to think about anything else. And she has this romantic idea of inviting Ryan Scott as her guest.

"Get real, Fliss!" hooted Kenny. "Guys hate mushy stuff. That will put him off you for life!"

"Besides, your mum's wedding is ages away," Rosie reminded her. "We've got loads of other stuff to do before then."

"Yeah. Like destroying the M&Ms for a start!" Kenny reminded us. "I bet they're still mad with us about all that Christmas play stuff."

"We ought to get a plan together," suggested Lyndz. "You know, just so we're ready for them when they do something awful to us."

"Yeah, let's do something really gross!" I suggested. "It was one of our New Year's resolutions, after all!"

So that's what we're meeting up to do now. The others have probably hatched a plan already, seeing as I'm so late. I keep telling them that it's worth it. I'm only late because I have to help out with my baby sister and she is sort of a new member of the Sleepover Club after all!

Oh no! Did you hear a scream? Either Kenny's acting out a wicked plan for the M&Ms, or she's strangling Fliss because she's sick of her going on about the wedding! I'd better go and sort them out. Come on, before it's too late!

Merry Christmas
Sleepover Club!

HarperCollins *Children's Books*

CHAPTER ONE

Merry Christmas! Hello, it's Rosie here of the Sleepover Club – and I'm just about to hang up my stocking as it's Christmas Eve. Excellent!!

I just *lurrrrrrve* Christmas, don't you? It's my absolute favourite time of the year. Summer is great because there's no school and you can stay out late at night, but December has got to be THE most exciting month of the year. You're just waiting and waiting for the 25th, and everyone's buying secret presents for each other, and we do lots of cool stuff at school to celebrate. Sometimes there's even snow, which is awesome!

Now, you know me – the most down-to-earth person you'll ever meet. But even *I* think there's something just a teeny bit magical about Christmas. Do you know what I mean? It just feels like the one time in the year where ANYTHING could happen, when your wishes really might come true!

I was talking to the others about Christmas wishes the other day, and we were all saying what we'd want for Christmas, if we were each granted one wish. If you've never met the other four in the Sleepover Club, I thought it would be a cool way to introduce them, so here goes.

Frankie didn't have to think twice about her wish. "I wish I could go to Mars!" she shouted straight away. Frankie's nuts about space and sci-fi stuff, you see. We used to call her Spaceman for a while because she went completely nerdy about the whole thing – reading loads of books about outer space, building a model rocket launch in her bedroom, borrowing all the *Star Trek* films from the video shop... She even wrote to NASA in America asking if she could go on the next space mission! Yep, she's pretty hooked, all right!

Mind you, if any one of us five was ever going to be something amazing like a rocket scientist or astronaut, it would definitely be Frankie. She's really brainy, and she's also got this knack of coming up with totally cool ideas and plans for us to do. I can honestly say I've never met anyone like her in my life! As my mum says, "That girl's an original!"

Lyndz next. Well, the first wish she came up with was, "I'd love a horse!" as she's completely and utterly crazy about animals. She goes riding at a stables not far from Cuddington, where we all live, but has always wanted her own horse, ever since she was tiny. But then, as soon as she'd said that, she wanted to make another wish. "I wish all the animals in the world were happy, and none of them would suffer or be frightened ever again!"

If you hadn't guessed, Lyndz is a teeny bit soppy! But I'm glad about that, because if she wasn't, I might never have joined the Sleepover Club. You see, it was kind-hearted

Lyndz who took pity on me when I'd just joined Cuddington Primary School and didn't know a soul. She asked me to come along to a sleepover at Frankie's one night and that's how I met the others. So I've got a lot to thank her for!

Lyndz is one of the nicest, kindest people you'll ever meet, who'd do anything for anyone. Sometimes I wish I could be more like her, as I'm a bit sarcastic and impatient at times. You know when you just can't help saying something horrible and you want to bite your tongue off straight after you say it? I do that ALL the time – but Lyndz NEVER says anything mean. Still, I'm not saying she's a goody-goody or anything.

Fliss took a bit of time thinking about her wish. "We can wish for anything?" she said cautiously.

"Fliss, it's only a game," Frankie said impatiently. "Your fairy godmother isn't really going to come along and wave a wand, you know!"

"I know, I know!" Fliss said crossly. "I was only asking!"

"So what's it going to be then, Flissy?" I asked. "Nose job? Modelling assignment?" (See? I told you I could be a bit sarky, didn't I?)

"A fairytale wedding with Ryan Scott, puke puke?" Kenny suggested, pulling a sick face.

Fliss tossed her long blonde hair back, looking a bit annoyed. "What do you mean, *nose job*?" she asked me. "What's wrong with my nose?"

"Er... nothing, nothing!" I said hastily. Fliss is a bit vain, you see, and doesn't take kindly to any criticism of the way she looks!

"I think I'd wish for £100 to spend on clothes," she said, her eyes lighting up at the thought. "No, wait – £1,000!" she said. Then she thought about it a bit more. "I wish I had a MILLION pounds to go on the most amazing shopping spree ever!"

She was positively beaming by now, whereas we were all staring at her, horrified at such a boring wish.

"Oh, I'd buy you all something too, of course!" she said, waving a hand casually.

"Wow, thanks, Fliss," Kenny said sarcastically. "Only if you're sure you can spare it, of course! You can't buy much with a million pounds these days, can you?"

Fliss looked annoyed. "Well, if you're going to be like that, I won't buy you *anything!*" she snapped. "I'll keep it all myself!"

Frankie rolled her eyes. "It's not a REAL wish, Fliss," she reminded her. "You don't really get to have your million pounds, you know!"

That's Fliss for you, anyway. Madly in love with clothes, make-up... and mirrors! She's the girliest one of us five and she sometimes gets on my nerves by being a bit wet and sappy, but she's also quite a laugh because you can wind her up a treat before she realises you're teasing her.

Kenny's turn next. "Well, my wish would be to wish for a billion other wishes!" she said craftily. "That way I can have whatever I want – whenever I want it!"

"You can't do that!" Fliss shouted at once. I think she was just gutted she hadn't thought of it first.

"It's my wish, I can ask for anything I like!" Kenny said, sticking her tongue out at her.

"Just 'cos YOU wasted yours on boring shopping and boring clothes – DERRRR!"

Fliss scowled.

"No, seriously, though," Frankie said. "What would be the one thing you'd like most of all?"

Kenny's next answer was a tad predictable, really.

"I wish I could play for Leicester City and score the winning goal for them in the Cup Final," she sighed longingly. "That would just be *sooooo* cool!"

"Er, Kenz – you're a girl, mate," Frankie pointed out.

"I know, I know," Kenny said. "But that's part of the wish – that the team spot me playing footy in the park and realise I'm so mega-talented they'll have to bend the rules to let me play for them."

"Sounds a bit like Babe the pig where the farmer let Babe be in the sheepdog trials because he was so good," Lyndz said thoughtfully.

"Lyndz, if you're calling me a pig, I'll..." Kenny said warningly.

Lyndz giggled and put her hand up to her

281

mouth. "I wasn't!" she said. "Honest! But it wouldn't have been an insult anyway – pigs are lovely!"

In answer to that, Kenny started making piggy squeals and grunts and chased Lyndz around the room, until Lyndz collapsed in a giggling fit. Then "the pig" got down on all fours, still squealing, and starting nudging Lyndz with her head.

"S-s-s-stop it!" Lyndz panted, weakly trying to push her away. "P-p-pack it in, piggy!"

Anyway, yeah, so Kenny is mad on sport, especially football and swimming. She's captain of our netball team at school, but was really miffed when she couldn't play cricket with the boys. She even went to the head teacher about it, saying it was unfair and sexist! I think she really wishes she was actually a boy sometimes.

Kenny has energy and enthusiasm like you've never seen before. Sometimes we call her "the power station" because she's like a one-woman generator! Her and Frankie are a good match in that way. They both hate sitting still and prefer to be bouncing around somewhere outside. No wonder they're both so skinny.

The other thing you should know about Kenny is that she's a complete gore-hound. She just loves blood and guts and gross stuff like that. She wants to be a doctor when she's older, like her dad. Already, she knows lots of amazing things about the way things work in your body, and loves telling us all the yuckiest stuff to try and gross us out. Fliss usually kicks up a fuss before too long as she's mega-squeamish, and even the word "blood" makes her feel sick (so she says). I think that just encourages Kenny to find even more horrible things to tell us about, though.

I was the last one to make my wish. I just couldn't decide. Part of me wished we had a nicer house to live in. Ours is a complete dump, ever since my dad moved out before he'd had a chance to do it up. I used to get a bit embarrassed about letting the others come round because it was so scruffy, and there's still loads that needs doing to it even now – I mean, we still haven't got carpets in some rooms. Me and the gang ended up decorating my room last year because I got so sick of just having bare plaster walls in there. Dad was originally going to paint my room for me, but... I guess he had other things on his mind.

"Come on, Rosie!" Lyndz was saying, elbowing me. "You've had ages to think about it now!"

"Yeah, what's your gut instinct?" Kenny asked. "What was the first thing that popped into your head?"

"I wish Adam could walk," I said straight out. Adam's my brother and he's in a wheelchair. He's a really lovely brother (apart from when he takes the mickey out of me, of course) and he's never been able to walk or talk properly. Sometimes I catch sight of his face if I'm going off on my bike, and he just has this sad look in his eyes which makes me feel really *guilty* that my legs work OK and I don't even think about them. Or sometimes he'll be watching sport on telly, and I just know that he's thinking about how he'll never be able to play football or rugby or... You know. I mean, I've grown up with him, so I'm used to it, and obviously he is, too – but it's still sad.

The others were a bit quiet when I said my wish. Kenny's great with Adam, she just treats him like a normal boy and has a laugh with him about stuff, but I know the others feel a bit awkward around him. Fliss, especially – I think she's a bit scared of Adam, to be honest. I suppose if you're not used to being around someone who's disabled, you don't quite know how to react at first.

"That's a nice wish," Lyndz said in the end. "That would be lovely if it came true."

"Yeah," I said. I felt a bit bad that everyone had gone so quiet and thoughtful because of me. "But I also wish my mum would find a new bloke now! A nice new boyfriend for the new year, that would be wicked. Especially if he was rich!"

"Ooh, that would be good," said Fliss thoughtfully. She likes anything to do with what she calls "affairs of the heart". "Your mum's quite pretty – I'm sure she'd be able to find someone nice."

"Do we know anyone we could fix her up with?" Frankie joked, raising an eyebrow at me.

"Not Dishy Dave again, after the Brown Owl disaster!" Lyndz said with a shudder. "That was awful!"

We all giggled, remembering our terrible attempt to fix up Brown Owl with Dave, the school caretaker. It had gone about as wrong as it could have!

"I'm definitely not putting my mum through that!" I said firmly. "In fact, I totally intend to stay OUT of her love life, so don't you lot get any ideas!"

Frankie's face fell, and I could tell she'd been half-serious about plotting to fix my mum up. "Well, if you're sure..." she said reluctantly. "We do have quite a hunky next-door neighbour who's just moved in – no girlfriend, either!"

"No, thanks!" I said, shaking my head. "End of discussion, Frankie!"

Anyway, you've hopefully got a good idea of what we're all like now. We're all best friends and do lots of stuff together. We have a sleepover once a week, on a Friday or Saturday, and take it in turns to host it. Wherever we have the sleepover, it's always an excellent laugh. There's not much sleep involved though, what with all the games we play and sweets we munch!

What I like most of all, though, is having four really close friends who I can have a laugh with, be myself with and trust with all my secrets. I've never had that before, and it's absolutely ACE! Sure, we sometimes bicker and fall out about stupid things, but at the end of the day, I don't know how I'd get along without them. Well, that's the Sleepover Club for you!

CHAPTER TWO

I'd better get on with the story, now you've met everyone.

I suppose it all started in the last week of November, when Mrs Weaver came into the classroom and announced that our class and Mr Nicholls' class would be putting on a Christmas pantomime of Cinderella for the parents and the rest of the school.

There was this big excited OOOOH! from all of us. Excellent! Normally we only ever do a boring nativity play and a carol concert. I don't know about you, but singing *Little Donkey* is NOT my idea of a good time. But Mrs Weaver went on to say that Miss

Middleton, the new infant teacher who'd come to our school in September, was a bit of a creative sort. Not only had she written the pantomime, but she'd also agreed to organise the whole thing. COO-ELL!

Us five grinned and made thumbs-up signs at each other. Miss Middleton was really young and pretty and funny. This could turn out to be an ace Sleepover Club event!

The classroom was buzzing as everyone started whispering things to each other in excitement. Mrs Weaver banged on her desk with a ruler. "Quieten down!" she called. "Do you want me to tell you how to audition for the panto, or not?!"

Instantly, everyone was as quiet as mice.

Mrs Weaver smiled. "Oh, that got your attention, didn't it?" she said. "Seeing as I obviously have a class of budding actors and actresses, I'd better tell you that there's a meeting in the hall at lunchtime today, for everyone interested in taking part. And for those of you who AREN'T interested in being on the stage, let me remind you that we'll need lots of scenery painters, costume designers, prop makers and people to help out with the lighting, too! So if you want to sign up for anything, come along to the hall at one o'clock sharp."

We all grinned at each other. This was going to be wicked!

Fliss put her hand up, blushing slightly. "Er, Mrs Weaver, who gets to be Cinderella?" she asked, tossing her long hair.

Kenny rolled her eyes. "Let me guess – you think it should be YOU!" she muttered.

Mrs Weaver frowned at Kenny, and then turned her attention to Fliss. "Well, Felicity, that's why we're having auditions," she said. "Miss Middleton will tell us more about it at lunchtime, but basically, anyone who's interested in being Cinderella will have to do an audition next week. For the audition, you'll have to read out some of Cinderella's lines and maybe sing a song, too, so we can see who has a good voice, and who can speak nice and clearly."

Fliss bit her lip. "But Cinderella IS blonde, isn't she?" she said, frowning. "I thought—"

"The Cinderella in the Disney cartoon is

blonde, yes," Mrs Weaver said firmly. "But we're not going to choose our Cinderella on hair colour, Felicity – just talent!"

"Oh, of course," Fliss said, sounding a bit dejected. I knew – and the whole class knew – that Fliss had thought she'd get the part on looks alone!

"She's got no chance, then, if they're going for talent!" whispered Emily Berryman loudly. Snidey cow!!

If you didn't know, her and her snotty sidekick Emma Hughes are big enemies of the Sleepover Club. We call them the M&Ms, but that's certainly not because they're as nice as the chocolate M&Ms. They're the sort of girls who'll pull your ponytail really hard, or nick your nicest pen when they think you're not looking. I'm sure there's a couple like them in your class, too, worse luck!

That morning seemed to go really *really* slo-o-ow. I swear time stood still and we were trapped in the classroom for about a week. Mrs Weaver was teaching us this complicated thing about fractions which I just couldn't understand. Every time I looked down at my maths book, the same thought popped into my head. *Cinderella! Cinderella! Cinderella!*

I was dying for lunchtime to come, so we could go to Miss Middleton's meeting and hear all about the panto. How could anyone concentrate on boring fractions at a time like this?

I *love* the story of Cinderella. OK, so the ending's a bit sloppy with Prince Charming and all that yucky lovey-dovey stuff, but I just adore the bit where the fairy godmother turns the pumpkin into a magnificent carriage, and the four mice into beautiful white horses. Wouldn't that be awesome, having a real-life fairy godmother who came into your bedroom and magicked everything up for you? But how on earth was Miss Middleton going to make that happen on stage? Unless she—

"Rosie Cartwright! Are you with us?" came Mrs Weaver's voice. "Have you lost the power of your ears, suddenly?"

I went bright red. Oops! Caught daydreaming! "Sorry," I said, staring down at my page again.

"We were talking about expressing the

fraction two-thirds as a decimal," Mrs Weaver said, still not finished with me. "Would you care to share your thoughts on that with us?"

"Er..." I said, hoping a flash of inspiration would strike. But wouldn't you know, it didn't. I'm TERRIBLE at maths! "Er... I don't know, Miss," I said in the end, feeling a bit of an idiot.

"You don't know, Miss," repeated Mrs Weaver. "I see. You don't know the answer, even though I've just spent ten minutes explaining it to the rest of the class who WERE listening. Now if I was feeling really mean, I'd tell you to stay in at lunchtime for some extra work on fractions..."

I stared at her in horror. She couldn't be so evil, surely?

"... but luckily for you, I'll let you off – provided you pay attention for the rest of the lesson. Do we have ourselves a deal?"

"Deal," I gulped gratefully, vowing to be a model pupil for the rest of the morning. There was no way I wanted to miss that lunchtime meeting!

"Good," said Mrs Weaver. "So who CAN tell me the answer, then?"

Smug keen-bean Emma Hughes stuck her hand straight up. Surprise, surprise! Couldn't resist a chance to make one of the Sleepover Club look bad in front of the teacher, as usual.

Wouldn't you know it, the morning went even *slower* now I actually had to pay attention and do some work. About three years later, it was lunchtime. We wolfed down our sandwiches in the dining hall, then charged along to the pantomime meeting in the main hall – along with practically everyone else in our year! The joint was JUMPING, as Frankie would say.

Miss Middleton stood at the front with a clipboard. Mrs Weaver, Mr Nicholls and Mrs Somersby were also standing around, holding pieces of paper with lists printed on them.

"Hello, everyone," Miss Middleton said, when we'd all quietened down. "What a great turn-out! I'm delighted so many of you are interested in helping out on this year's pantomime. As your teachers have no doubt told you, we're going to be putting on two performances of Cinderella. There's plenty of work for everyone to get involved with, so we'll need lots of helping hands."

She cleared her throat, and then looked serious.

"Now, this is going to be the first meeting of many, between now and Christmas. There are going to be LOTS of rehearsals, too, so if you're already busy with things like football or swimming clubs, please make sure you're not taking on too much. We don't want anyone collapsing with exhaustion right before Christmas, do we?"

I saw Kenny look a bit thoughtful at that. She's in the Cuddington Swimming Club and trains twice a week and sometimes on Saturday mornings, too. Still, as Kenny didn't seem to know the meaning of the word "exhaustion", I guessed she would probably manage to combine that with the panto quite easily!

"Now, like I said, taking on a part in the play will mean a lot of work, but it's also going to be a lot of fun," Miss Middleton said, smiling around at everyone. "Does everyone know the story of Cinderella? Good. Well, what we'll do next is try and organise everyone into groups.

Mr Nicholls has kindly agreed to be in charge of props, scenery and lighting, and Mrs Somersby is going to be sorting out all the costumes and make-up. Last but not least, Mrs Weaver and I will be running the auditions and coaching the rehearsals. Got that?"

"Yes!" everyone chorused.

"Excellent!" said Miss Middleton. "If you're interested in helping with props and scenery, go and stand in that corner with Mr Nicholls. If you want to help with costumes and make-up, go and stand in THAT corner with Mrs Somersby. And if you'd like an acting, singing or dancing part, stay where you are."

There was bedlam as lots of people got up and started making their way to different parts of the hall.

The five of us looked at each other.

"I quite fancy a go at making props..." said Kenny.

"I wouldn't mind doing make-up," Frankie said thoughtfully. "I can do some wicked designs, I've been practising!"

"Oh, let's stick together!" Lyndz said. "It'll be much more fun if we're *all* acting in it!"

"Yeah, Lyndz is right," I said. "Why don't we all go in for the auditions? It would be a right laugh!"

"What do you think, Fliss?" Kenny asked. "Don't you fancy having a go on the lighting or carpentry?"

Fliss shuddered, and the rest of us laughed. Not likely! Fliss thinks anything technical is "man's work" – and anyway, she might break a nail doing something like that.

"No, thanks!" she said, feelingly. Then she smiled serenely. "Anyway, I'm going to be Cinderella. I just know I'm going to get the part!"

"Ooh, very modest of you to say so, Fliss," Frankie joked. "Should I ask for your autograph now, or when you're REALLY famous?!"

"Fliss, EVERYONE's going to be going for Cinderella," Lyndz said tactfully. "You don't know for sure you'll get the part, do you?"

Fliss tossed her hair back, looking a bit peeved. "Don't tell me *you're* going for the part as well, then?" she asked.

Lyndz shook her head. "Nah," she admitted. "Actually, there's another part I'd rather play..."

"What?" I asked in interest. I hadn't had Lyndz down as the dramatic type before.

She went a bit pink. "Well... you know that bit where the fairy godmother magicks everything so Cinderella can go to the ball?" she said.

"Ye-e-e-es," we said.

"Ahh, you want to be the fairy godmother?" Kenny asked.

"No," Lyndz said.

"The pumpkin?" Fliss said – rather cattily, actually, as Lyndz is a teeny bit plump.

"No, one of the horses!" Lyndz said, looking a bit embarrassed. "Oh, don't laugh, it's what I want to be!"

Too late – we all started roaring with laughter! Of all the things to wish to be in the pantomime!

"Don't worry, I'm sure there won't be much competition to be a horse," I spluttered.

"No, it's not like it's the MANE part or anything!" Kenny giggled.

Luckily for Lyndz, Miss Middleton clapped her hands for quiet just then and we all had to bite our lips to stop ourselves laughing any more.

There were still a lot of people left in the hall, even when Mr Nicholls and Mrs Somersby had taken their volunteers off to different rooms. It looked like *everyone* wanted to be treading the boards this Christmas.

"First of all, I'm going to tell you the cast list of the pantomime, so you can start thinking about what you'd like to go for," Miss Middleton said, when everyone was listening. "Here goes – Cinderella, her stepmother Wicked Wilma, the two Ugly Sisters Grizzle and Moana, Buttons, Prince Charming, Angelica the fairy godmother, and a narrator. They're the main characters, and auditions will be held for those parts on Monday lunchtime in my classroom."

Emma Hughes smirked at Fliss. "Ever thought about trying out for one of the Ugly Sisters?" she said. "I reckon you'd get it easily!"

Fliss looked as if she was about to burst into tears, but Kenny, as ever, was straight in there.

"Shame there aren't any DOGS in Cinderella," she said, eyes glittering. "You and your poochy mate might actually get picked to do something then!"

"Girls, please!" called Miss Middleton. "We've a lot to get through today. Right, so those are the main parts. We'll also need dancers for the ball scene, a chorus, Prince Charming's butler, and some people to be Cinderella's horses and coachman. And there'll be an open audition for those parts on Tuesday lunchtime, in my classroom."

Fliss stuck her hand in the air. "Please, Miss, what will we have to do at the auditions?" she asked.

"Good question," said Miss Middleton. "I'll give you a page from the script and we'll practise acting it out in pairs. Anyone who wants to be Cinderella or the fairy godmother must have a good singing voice as there will be a couple of songs for you in the show. I think that's it for now. See you all next week, I hope!"

The hall broke out into an excited chatter. It all sounded like it was going to be excellent fun!

"I can't wait for next Monday!" said Fliss, with her serene smile again. Honestly, I'd never known Fliss to be so confident about anything before!

"First things first," I said. "We've got to have a Cinderella sleepover to practise for the audition, and talk about what parts we all want to do."

"Deffo!" Kenny said. "How about at mine? We haven't been there for ages."

"Agreed!" said Frankie. "I'll bring my greasepaint along so we can look the part!"

"And I'll bring some of the dressing-up clothes!" Lyndz promised.

"Cool!" Kenny said. "It's a date!"

CHAPTER THREE

There's nothing like a good sleepover to start the weekend with a bang! Everyone was really looking forward to this one, too. I mean, sleepovers are always excellent, but when we've got something really special coming up, like the pantomime, it makes it even more fun.

By the end of Friday afternoon, none of us could think about doing any work – we were all too excited about the evening ahead. Luckily, on Friday afternoons, Mrs Weaver always reads to us, so you don't have to concentrate too hard. This time she took out a copy of *Matilda* by Roald

Dahl, so we all got to sit and listen to that. It was such a good story, I actually managed to STOP thinking about Cinderella and sleepovers for a while – but only just!

Then all of a sudden it was three-thirty and time to go. Yippeeee! Me and Fliss were going straight back to Kenny's house with her, while Lyndz and Frankie were going to go home and pick up their bags of goodies first, then come over a bit later. Kenny doesn't live far from the school, so we all walked back – stopping at the sweet shop first, of course.

We don't seem to have that many sleepovers at Kenny's, partly because of her horrid older sister, Molly Moany-guts, who Kenny shares a room with. Whenever we have a sleepover, Molly has to move in with Emma, their oldest sister, for the night. And boy, does Molly kick up a stink about it! She makes a real fuss if we so much as TOUCH any of her stuff, so I'm always a bit worried about breaking something of hers, especially when Kenny sets up one of her famous assault courses round the bedroom.

This time, we'd just left the sweet shop

when we heard a familiar horrible voice.

"Ahh, look! It's the Bedtime Club for little girly-wirlies!"

You guessed it – Molly and her equally horrible friend, Carli, sniggering so hard they looked as if they were about to wet their pants.

Fliss looked a bit rattled. She hates scenes, especially in public, where someone might see her. "Ignore them, Kenny," she hissed. "Come on, let's go."

Ignore them? Fat chance! Kenny doesn't know the meaning of the word "ignore" when it comes to miserable Molly. She turned round at once, eyes sparkling, ready for battle.

"Ahh, look! Battersea Dogs' Home have let some strays loose because they were so hideous, nobody wanted them!" she said sweetly. "Here, doggies! Come here!"

Molly took a step forward. BIG mistake!

"Oh, look, they're so obedient, they even come when I call them!" Kenny cooed in delight. "Good doggy!"

Molly glared at her younger sister and folded her arms across her chest. "You think you're so clever, don't you, LAURA?" she said, using Kenny's real (hated) name, the name that only teachers and parents are allowed to use.

"I think, therefore I am," Kenny shot back. "Shame YOU haven't learned how to think yet, big mouth!"

"You've had it!" Molly snapped. "C'mon, Carli – let's get 'em!"

"Run!!" yelled Kenny as they both came charging towards us.

Fliss and I didn't need telling twice, and we sprinted off at once. Luckily, all three of us are pretty fast, and after a couple of minutes, Molly and Carli gave up the chase and just shouted a few horrible things after us up the street.

"What did you have to do that for, Kenny?" grumbled Fliss, patting her hair anxiously. Fliss is actually quite good at running because she's got long legs, but she hates getting hot and bothered because it messes her hair up.

"For fun, of course!" grinned Kenny. "Didn't I ever tell you our family motto? It's *Meanus Sisteris.*"

"What does that mean?" Fliss asked, looking puzzled.

"Be mean to your sisters," Kenny said solemnly. "So I try my hardest, whenever I can."

"Really?" Fliss asked. "That's a bit weird!"

Kenny and I rolled our eyes at each other, trying not to giggle. Fliss was just TOO easy to wind up sometimes!

"Of course, there's also the other family motto – *Fibius Flisseratum*," Kenny said, biting her lip. "Did I ever tell you that one?"

"No," said Fliss, all wide-eyed. "What does that mean?"

I could hardly watch! Fliss was just SO gullible, it was untrue!

"It means, tell lies to people called Fliss," Kenny said, trying to keep a straight face.

It was no good – I started giggling helplessly. Kenny is such an excellent wind-up merchant!

Fliss looked puzzled. "You mean..." she started – and then she finally clocked what was going on. "Kenny!" she said, swinging her bag at her indignantly. "Did you just make that up? Did you?"

There was no reply. Me and Kenny were both snorting with laughter, leaning against someone's garden wall.

"You did, didn't you?" Fliss said crossly. "Well! Of all the—"

"It was only a joke," Kenny spluttered weakly. "I couldn't resist... *Fibius Flisseratum* – I'll have to remember that!"

We were nearly at Kenny's house now, and we'd spent so long messing around and giggling that Molly and Carli had caught up with us.

"Oh, look who it isn't," Kenny muttered under her breath.

"Is Carli sleeping over tonight as well?" I asked. It was going to be a pretty full house, if so!

Kenny pulled one of her sickest faces. "Afraid so," she said. "You know Molly. Can't bear to be left out of anything, even having friends round. Luckily Emma's staying over with one of HER friends, so Molly and Carli are both in Emma's bedroom tonight." She lowered her voice. "I THINK Molly's just got a boyfriend, believe it or not, so hopefully they'll be chatting about that all night and they won't be bugging us!"

"That would be a first," Fliss said gloomily.

"Well, it IS, as far as I know," Kenny said, deadpan. "No-one's ever asked her out before!"

"What about Edward Marsh?" I asked. "I thought she was dead keen on him for a while."

"Nah, they were just mates," Kenny smirked. "Like he would really fancy that monster, anyway!"

Edward Marsh was this horrible, annoying boy who'd ganged up with Molly against us on our circus skills course at half-term. (Now there's a Sleepover story to look out for!)

Kenny leaped on to Fliss's back as we were coming up the path. "Giddy-up, horsey!" she told her.

Just then, Kenny's mum opened the front door. "Hello, girls!" she smiled. Kenny's mum is VERY smiley and gentle – totally unlike her youngest daughter! "Laura, what on earth are you doing to Felicity? The neighbours must think the circus is back in town!"

"Yeah, with Molly as the talking chimp this time," Kenny said quietly – but loud enough for her mum to hear.

"That'll do!" Mrs McKenzie said, half-sternly, half-smiling. "Now come in, it's freezing! I'll make you some hot chocolate."

We'd just polished off a load of hot chocolate and Jaffa Cakes when Frankie and Lyndz turned up with big carrier bags of stuff. So then we had to have a load more hot chocolate and Jaffa Cakes, just to keep them company, of course. Once we were all feeling completely stuffed, we went up to Kenny's room to get away from Molly Monster-Features and creepy Carli. As usual, there was a handwritten note on Molly's side of the room:

LAURA: Don't touch my stuff – don't even look at it! Molly

"Yeah, yeah, like we're scared!" Kenny said casually, ripping the note up and tossing it into the bin.

"Let's get down to business!" Frankie said.

"I've brought along lots of groovy make-up so we can do ourselves up as our characters."

"And I've got a load of clothes here as well," Lyndz said, dumping two huge bags on Kenny's bed. "But I couldn't find a horse costume for me – just these brown jodhpurs and a brown jumper."

"I can make your face up to look like a horse!" Frankie said at once.

"Right, well, I'll be Cinderella, then," Fliss said decisively.

"Hang on a minute," I said, feeling my cheeks going a bit red. "I wouldn't mind being Cinderella either, so—"

"YOU?" Fliss said, sounding astonished. "But you haven't even got long hair!"

Well, she'd got me on that one. I've got quite short, brown hair in a bob and a stubby nose and freckles, so I suppose I didn't exactly look the part. But I'd been thinking about it all week and I'd decided I was going to go for Cinderella as well. Why not? Reach for the moon, as my mum always tells me.

Kenny groaned. "Fliss, being Cinderella isn't just about having long hair, you know," she said. "Remember what Mrs Weaver said? They'll be going on talent, not looks. And anyway, Rosie could always wear a wig if she got the part!"

"Oh, so you think Rosie's going to get the part, do you?" Fliss said. She sounded all sniffy, as if she was going to cry. "Charming!"

"Kenny, what part are you going to go for?" Frankie said, changing the subject. I shot her a grateful look. There was no way Fliss was going to stop me going for Cinderella just because SHE wanted to be it. And if she thought she could give me a guilt trip about it, she had another think coming!

"One of the Ugly Sisters, maybe," Kenny said, and we all laughed. "No, seriously!" she said. "It's probably going to be quite a funny part, right? And I don't want anything serious or soppy to do. I'd prefer to make everyone laugh."

As she was saying this, I could just imagine Kenny in a horrible outfit and wig, clowning around on stage and making the audience laugh, just like she had done on our circus course. She'd be perfect in the part!

311

"How about you, Frank?" I asked. "No aliens in Cinderella for you to play!"

"Shame," she said, sounding serious. "I wouldn't mind being an Ugly Sister, too – but what I'd REALLY like to be is Wicked Wilma, the evil old stepmother. Then I'd get to boss the Ugly Sisters around and make Cinderella cry!"

I laughed at that but Fliss looked a bit fearful.

"That's not very nice!" she pouted.

"THAT's the point, derr-brain!" Frankie said. "I'm meant to be horrible, aren't I?"

"This is going to be such a laugh," Lyndz said happily. "I'm so glad they picked a pantomime that has horses in it! I've already asked Miss Middleton if I could be one of the horses, and she said that would be fine. Isn't that cool?!"

"Awesome," I said, trying not to smile. "So shall we practise for our auditions or what?"

"Oh, good idea!" said Fliss, jumping up. "I've prepared something already, actually." She raised her eyebrows at me, as if to say, *Bet you haven't*!

She pulled a piece of paper out of her bag, and was about to start when she fixed me with a hard stare. "Maybe Rosie shouldn't be in the room while I do this," she said. "I don't want her copying the way I do my audition piece."

Kenny threw a Curly Wurly at her. "Get a grip, Fliss!" she said. "Stop being a prima donna and get on with it!"

"I'm nothing like Madonna!" Fliss snapped back at her, tossing her hair over her shoulders.

"No, she meant... Oh, never mind," said Frankie wearily. "Just dazzle us with your talent!"

Fliss cleared her throat. "Now, obviously, I don't have a proper page from the pantomime script, like we will in the audition," she said primly. "So I've just written a few lines that Cinderella might say, OK? It's the bit where Cinders is at home while the Ugly Sisters have gone off to the ball, just before the fairy—"

"Yeah, yeah!" Kenny said impatiently. "Let's hear it, then!"

Fliss knelt down on the floor, tossed her hair back again and put one hand in front of her, almost as if she was begging.

"Oh, woe!" she began. "Woe is me! Here all alone on the night of the ball, when handsome Prince Charming will choose a bride!"

She paused dramatically and Lyndz started clapping. Fliss glared at her. "I haven't finished yet!" she snapped.

"Oops! Sorry!" said Lyndz. "It's very good, though!"

Fliss had a quick look at her piece of paper then continued, flourishing her hand theatrically. "Oh, woe! It's all dark, and there are horrible rats scratching around me! And I must do all this cleaning while those mean sisters of mine are dancing around in their best dresses! Oh, woe! If only I had a fairy godmother!"

She collapsed on the floor, one hand still outstretched, and was motionless. The four of us looked at each other, trying not to giggle. Was that the end yet? Dared we clap this time?

After about twenty seconds, Fliss sat up gracefully and bowed.

"That was really good, Fliss," Lyndz said warmly.

"Yes, Rosie must be dead worried after seeing that audition piece," Kenny said sarcastically.

"Oh, I am," I assured her, crossing my fingers behind my back.

Fliss looked pleased with herself. "Thank you," she said modestly. "I did practise it a LOT last night, to be honest, that's probably why it's so good."

"Mmm, probably," Frankie said, looking at the floor. "What about a song, though? What are you going to sing?"

"I thought I'd sing that song from *Titanic*, you know, by Celine Dion," Fliss said.

"What, *My Fart Will Go On*?" Kenny asked. "Always reminds me of my dad, that one..."

"Kenny!" Fliss giggled. "It's *My* HEART *Will Go On*! Anyway, what do you think?"

And with that, she launched into the chorus at top volume. Omigosh – ever heard a cat yowl when you tread on its tail by mistake? Fliss sounded even more pained than that! It was terrible!! To shut her up, Kenny waited until Fliss was singing a really long high note, with her mouth wide open, and then threw a marshmallow straight in there. Glug! That brought her to a stop!

"Well, like you said, you really are NOTHING like Madonna," Frankie mused. She meant it teasingly of course, but said it in a nice voice, so Fliss just looked confused.

"Thanks," she said uncertainly. Then she looked around at the rest of us. "Well?" she demanded. "What do you think? Am I going to be Cinderella, or what?"

"Mmmm... Maybe... Fingers crossed," everyone said politely, including me. But inside I was feeling a bit smug. There was NO WAY Fliss was going to be Cinderella – not with a voice like that!

CHAPTER FOUR

After Fliss's eye-opening performance, the rest of us took turns to dress up and try out different stuff for our audition pieces. No-one else had rehearsed or written anything like Fliss had – we all did it off the cuff. I hadn't done much drama before at school, but found I was really enjoying myself, both watching the others and taking part.

Kenny did a wickedly funny skit as an Ugly Sister who was getting ready for the ball. She had us all rolling about laughing as she primped up the big purple wig Lyndz had brought along, put face powder on her warts and pouted at herself in the mirror. The more we laughed, the funnier Kenny became. It was as if she instinctively knew how to play to the audience.

"I feel pretty, oh so pretty!" she sang into the mirror, in this horrible croak. She was excellent!

Then Frankie took a turn as the wicked stepmother, having a go at Cinders for not cleaning the kitchen floor properly. She made her face up to look like an old granny, put curlers and a headscarf on her head, and pulled herself up to her full height, so as to look as scary and mean as possible.

Then she pursed up her mouth and let rip, and I nearly jumped out of my skin! Frankie's never normally in a bad mood, so it was quite scary, seeing her being so aggressive and nasty.

"Cinders, you lazy good-for-nothing hussy!" she yelled, glaring ferociously at us. "If I wanted something useless in my kitchen, I'd get an ornament! But you – YOU – are meant to clean this place! Do you know what clean means? I said, *do you know what clean means*?"

Frankie was yelling right into Fliss's face, who flinched. "Er... n-n-n-o," she stammered.

"Ha!" sneered Frankie. "You DO surprise me! Here, watch this!"

At that point, Frankie started flinging her arms around in the air.

"What's that?" Kenny asked.

"I'm throwing bags of rice all over the floor, just to be mean," Frankie said in her normal voice. Then Wicked Wilma's voice came back. "See that? That's a mess, that is. And when I come back, I want it all cleaned up, you hear? Clean, clean, CLEAN!"

Frankie threw herself on the bed as we all clapped.

"You are one wicked stepmother," I told her, admiringly.

"You are a cow!" Kenny agreed, sounding respectful. "No wonder Cinders cuts all her hair off in despair!"

Fliss looked anxious at that. "Does she? I don't remember that bit."

"Yeah!" Kenny said, straight-faced. "She gives herself a skinhead, trying to disguise herself as the bald chef, don't you remember?"

"No!" Fliss said, shaking her head. She was looking REALLY anxious now, at the thought of being a skinhead Cinderella!

"Fliss, she's only messing about," Lyndz said.

"AGAIN!" Kenny grinned. "Fliss, you're making it too easy for me tonight."

Fliss pulled a face and nibbled on a Loveheart. "We haven't seen Rosie's piece yet," she said, giving me a challenging look. Blimey, she was feeling competitive! Obviously it had really narked her that I'd decided to go for the part of Cinderella as well as her.

"OK, here's my song," I said. I'd decided to sing one of my mum's favourite old songs, *That Old Devil Called Love*. Not because it has anything to do with Cinderella, but just because it's kind of sad and slow, and I'd thought it might suit the mood.

"It's that old devil called love again..." I sang. I haven't got a fantastic singing voice or anything, but I can hold a note at least and our music teacher at school says I have good pitch, whatever that means. I felt a bit embarrassed at first, singing in front of the

others, but it's such a great song, I closed my
eyes and just got into it. When I finished, the
others all clapped and cheered me.

"Girl, you can SING!" Frankie said in an
American accent. "That was brilliant, Rosie!"

"Not bad," Fliss sniffed critically. Oh well – I
was never expecting any praise from HER!

Then I did my audition piece. I was dreading
it a bit, after seeing such a flop from Fliss, then
two such hilarious ones from Frankie and
Kenny. I decided to just play it straight, and do
a scene where Cinderella is confiding in
Buttons.

"Those sisters, they're not just ugly, they're
so horrible as well!" I started. "The other day I
caught Grizzle putting itching powder in my
knicker drawer, and when I confronted her, do
you know what she said?"

"No!" called out Lyndz, getting into it.

"She told me it was talcum powder to make
my clothes smell nice! Well, of course, I didn't
believe a word of it! So do you know what I did,
then?"

"NO!" the others all called out.

"Well, I waited until she'd gone out

321

shopping with Moana, then I swapped all our knickers around so that if it WAS itching powder, THEY'D get it! You should have seen them the next day, Buttons – ants in the pants, or what? They were rolling around, scratching away like you've never seen before!"

I'd only just got going when Fliss interrupted me.

"Rosie, don't you think it's a bit VULGAR to talk about knickers in your audition piece?" she said disapprovingly.

"I'll be reading from the script in the audition, won't I, you derr-bo?" I said scathingly. "I won't REALLY be saying all this!"

"Knickers are more interesting than 'woe is me' anyway," said Kenny. "At least Rosie's Cinderella had a bit of life in her, she wasn't just flopping about on the stage like a dying fish!"

Fliss went bright red and shut her mouth tightly. "That's what YOU think, Kenny," she started. "Let me tell you—"

"Aaaaaand... moving on, let's change the subject," Lyndz said swiftly. "Shall we have a game of something?"

"Yeah, good idea," Frankie said. "That was great, by the way, Rosie."

"Thanks," I said, feeling a bit cross with Fliss for interrupting me like that. Talk about spoiled brat. She just couldn't handle it if she wasn't getting her own way!

"Well, I think we're all set for the auditions," Kenny said, catching my eye. I could tell she knew how I was feeling. "And I say, just like in football, all's fair in love and war!"

"What?" said Fliss, frowning at her.

"I mean, Fliss," Kenny said, speaking extra-slowly, "may the best man – or girl – win! And let's not have any sulking or bad feelings because that's just boring."

"How about Hide and Seek?" Lyndz said diplomatically, as Fliss's chin wobbled a bit.

No bad feelings, indeed! I thought to myself. If Fliss didn't get her precious part, there would be a LOT of bad feeling, directed at whoever got to be Cinderella!

"How about Spy On Molly And Find Out Who The Unlucky Boyfriend Is?" Kenny suggested, eyes gleaming at the thought. "Go on, let's! I'm dying to find out. Just think how

323

much teasing material I'll have once I know which loser she's got her sticky mitts on!"

Once Kenny's got her mind set on something, it's difficult to talk her out of it. Anyway, it sounded like fun to me. One of my favourite hobbies at home is earwigging on my big sister Tiffany's phone calls, especially when boys are involved. Some of those conversations are just hilarious!

Under Kenny's strict instructions, we all tiptoed along the corridor and stood in a huddle outside Molly's room. Kenny had brought along her Walkman, and, holding it up to the door, she pressed the Record button and gave us all a big happy wink. There was nothing Kenny liked more than getting one over on Molly.

Sure enough, Molly and Carli were deep in conversation.

"... And then he kissed me, right, and..."

"Ooh! What was it like?"

"Well, it was kind of soft and nice but... well, I didn't really know what to do, so I just sort of put my arms around him, on his back..."

"Really?"

"Yeah – ooh, he has a lovely back! Dead muscly!"

"And how long did you kiss for?"

"Only a few minutes – then you'll never guess what, Mr Graham came round the back of the science lab and caught us!"

"No!"

"I swear!"

"Nightmare!"

"Tell me about it!"

Kenny pulled a face at us, shaking her head. "Bor-ring!" she mouthed.

"So then Andrew said he had to go..."

We all looked at each other and grinned. Andrew, eh?!

"So has he asked you out, properly, like?"

"Yeah! That's the best bit! We're going to the pictures tomorrow afternoon!"

Kenny raised her eyebrows at that, and looked pleased with herself. That was good information to have up her sleeve!

"Ooh, are you going to sit in the back row?"

"Too right we are!"

Unable to resist keeping quiet any longer, Kenny suddenly sang out, "Molly and Andrew sitting in a tree, K-I-S-S-I-N-G!" Then she put on this silly high voice. "Ooh, he has EVER such a muscly back, you know!"

And then we all pegged it back to Kenny's room, quick as anything, giggling our heads off.

"You nosey BRATS!" Molly yelled, storming in the room after us. "You'd better not tell Mum about that!"

"What's it worth?" Kenny asked, smiling sweetly.

"Well, I WON'T kick your head in, if you don't say anything, put it like that!" Molly growled.

"Ooh, I hope you don't speak to Andy-Pandy loverboy like that," Kenny said, solemnly. "Not very feminine, is it, Mols?"

"Just zip it, all right?" Molly snapped, poking Kenny in the ribs. "And don't spy on us again, you losers! Don't you have better things to do?"

With that, she flung herself out of the room, slamming the door behind her. The rest of us looked nervously at Kenny, who hadn't turned a hair.

"She's really mad," Lyndz said in a low voice.

"Oh, she'll get over it," Kenny said easily. "She loves it, really, you know. Anyway, how about a game of Bed Frisbee?"

Bed Frisbee is one of Kenny's inventions, surprise surprise. One person bounces on the bed, while another throws a frisbee at them which the bed-person has to catch, still bouncing. It's really difficult, and you get so out of breath, it's dead hard to control what you're doing and catch the frisbee each time. It always ends with us collapsing in giggles on the bed, feeling all weak and silly.

To make it even harder, Kenny said we had to be in character for the game – so we each had to act as our pantomime character while we bounced up and down! It was just about impossible to keep a straight face, watching Fliss doing her woe-is-me routine in mid-air – even she got the giggles after a while. That became our sort of catchphrase for the evening, so each time someone missed the frisbee, everyone chorused, "Woe is YOU!" It's the sort of thing that Fliss could have got a bit stroppy about. After all, she does hate being teased by us, but she ended up having as much of a laugh as the rest of us did.

After we'd had our tea and watched a bit of TV, we all cleaned our teeth and got into our sleeping bags in a long line on the floor. As usual, we started discussing the pantomime.

"Who do you think will be Prince Charming?" Lyndz asked sleepily.

"Oh, I hope it's Ryan!" Fliss said at once. "That would be *soooo* wonderful!"

If you didn't know, Fliss has got a real crush on Ryan Scott at school. She's convinced she's going to marry him and everything, it's totally bizarre.

"Wouldn't it be romantic?" she continued. "Me as Cinderella, Ryan as Prince Charming! Oh, I hope I get to kiss him on stage!"

"*Fliss!*" Kenny said, laughing. "You're starting to sound like Molly!"

Just as she said the word "Molly", there was a soft popping sound from somewhere in the darkness.

"What was that?" I asked, and then one whiff of air told me. "Ugh! Gross!" It was a *stink bomb!*

"Poo! Eeeeurrggggh!" we all said. "Quick, open the window!"

"I think I'm going to be sick!" Fliss groaned dramatically. "Ugh, that is totally disgusting!"

Kenny flung open the door and I pushed open her window, and we all breathed in the fresh air thankfully.

"Molly the Monster strikes again!" Kenny said grimly. "She's such a pig! Talk about Ugly Sisters – I know exactly who to imitate when I go for the audition!"

Fliss was hanging her head out of the window. "I hate your sister, Kenny," she moaned. "AND it's freezing out here!"

"It must be a warning from her, about not telling your mum and dad about her boyfriend," Lyndz said, holding her nose.

"Pah! It'll take more than a stink bomb to shut me up," Kenny said scornfully. "I've got plans for Saturday afternoon now, and her date with Mr Andy Pandy. Sabotage plans!"

CHAPTER FIVE

We didn't get to hear about Kenny's "sabotage plans" until Monday morning at school – but it was worth the wait.

Not only did she follow Molly into town on Saturday afternoon, but she hung around until Molly met Andrew ("who's a right nerd, by the way"), then snuck into the cinema after them and sat right behind them. Kenny told us that as soon as Andrew's arm started creeping around Molly's shoulders, Kenny tapped him on the shoulder.

"Excuse me, but as my sister's chaperone, I'd like to ask you to remove your arm from her," she whispered to him. "No hanky-panky on the first date!"

Well apparently, if looks could kill, Kenny would be six feet under by now. Molly went purple, tried to strangle Kenny – and then all three of them got chucked out of the cinema for fighting.

"You are *sooooo* evil!" Frankie said respectfully. "I'm totally glad I don't have a sister like you!"

"Serves her right for nearly suffocating us with that stink bomb," Kenny said airily. "I just WISH I'd thought to play that tape I made of Molly telling Carli about kissing him! Can you imagine how embarrassing THAT would have been?"

We all shook our heads at her. Kenny could be so horrible sometimes!

"Remind me never to get on the wrong side of you, Kenny," Lyndz said with a shudder.

"Anyway," Kenny continued, "they went off towards McDonald's after that – I tried to follow them but they gave me the slip. But Molly only went and told Mum what I'd done, and Mum went ballistic at me. She's stopped my pocket money for two weeks now."

"Gutted," I said sympathetically.

Kenny shrugged. "Oh, it was worth it!" she said. "I'd do it again for a month without pocket money, just to see the look on their faces! It was *soooo* funny!"

We were laughing so loudly, we didn't hear Mrs Weaver come in to do the register. She was carrying an armful of holly, which she started putting up around the classroom – a couple of sprigs above the blackboard and on the tops of the windows.

"There! Is everyone feeling Christmassy?" she said. "I hope so, because I've got some news for you. As well as the pantomime, we're going to be holding a Christmas bazaar this year to raise money for homeless people. Christmas isn't just about GETTING things, remember – it's about giving, too."

The classroom was silent as everyone listened closely.

"So in the next few weeks, we'll be making lots of things to sell at the bazaar, like calendars and Christmas stockings, and we're also asking parents to bake cakes and donate bric-a-brac for the stalls. And we'll be making a collection of food that we can give directly to the new homeless shelter in Leicester, so we're asking you to bring in tins of food, please – anything you can spare, so that some homeless people can have a nice Christmas dinner. Does everyone think that's a good idea?"

"Yes!" we all shouted.

"Good! Let's start this morning by making some calendars for the new year!" Mrs Weaver said. "There are lots of pieces of coloured card in the art cupboard plus glitter, paint, felt scraps – anything you like, to make it colourful and pretty. Just remember to leave a space at the bottom for your actual calendar, which is this big." She held one up to show everyone. "Other than that, you can let your imaginations go wild!"

I love making things at school. Mrs Weaver is quite arty-farty, so she always has wicked ideas for things we can do. We all got stuck into our calendars, and the morning flew by. Before we knew it, it was lunchtime – time for the auditions! EEEEK!!

Lyndz was the only one of us five not to go along to Miss Middleton's classroom. She said there wasn't much point in her being there as she wouldn't have to audition to be a horse. It seemed like everyone else we knew was there, though. The M&Ms, Alana Banana, loads of boys from our class (including Ryan Scott, much to Fliss's delight). I suddenly started to feel a little bit nervous. Having to sing in front of all these people was going to be pretty scary!

Then I got a grip of myself. If I couldn't even sing in front of a few people from school, there was no way I'd EVER be able to sing in front of a huge audience, so it was just going to be a case of put up or shut up.

I took a few deep breaths and tried to think calming thoughts. The others all looked as petrified as me, apart from Kenny, who was doodling a fake Leicester City tattoo on her hand. Fliss was as white as a sheet.

"Thanks for coming, everyone," Miss Middleton said, clapping her hands for quiet. "This is the order we're going to do the auditions. Cinderella, Prince Charming,

Wicked Wilma, Angelica, the narrator, Grizzle and Moana, and finally Buttons. When you audition for one part, you'll be considered for all the others, so you only need to give us one audition piece. We might think you're better suited to playing Angelica than Cinderella, for example, or Buttons rather than Prince Charming, so do have an open mind!"

Mrs Weaver stood up next. "As we're so short on space in here, once you've auditioned for a part, you're free to leave and go out into the playground with everyone else," she said. "Right! Can we have the Cinderellas first, please? Everyone else, sit back and be very quiet. And I'm sure I don't need to say this, but just in case – we don't want anyone sniggering or making silly remarks. Anyone who does so will have to leave the auditions, OK?"

"Yes," everyone muttered. I was secretly glad she'd said that, though. Imagine if you did your piece and the boys started making stupid comments. Embarrassing or WHAT?!

About fifteen of us went up to try out for the Cinderella role. My legs were starting to feel wobbly and my throat was all dry with nerves. I crossed my fingers, praying I wasn't about to make a great big chump of myself. I couldn't think of anything worse.

Miss Middleton passed around some sheets of the script. It was a scene between Cinderella and Prince Charming, and I scanned through it quickly, looking for any words I didn't know how to pronounce. It all looked quite easy, though.

"I feel sick," Fliss whispered to me. I gave her hand a squeeze, not wanting to admit how sick I was feeling, too.

"I'll read the part of Prince Charming," Miss Middleton said. "OK, who wants to go first? Felicity?"

Fliss stared at her, horrified. She looked like one of the rabbits you sometimes see on the road late at night, staring at car headlamps as if they're in a trance.

I gave her a nudge. "Break a leg!" I whispered.

She looked as if she'd been stung, and just stood there, still transfixed.

"Good luck!" I said, pushing her forward.

Fliss stood opposite Miss Middleton at the front of the classroom. I could see that her hands were shaking terribly. Poor Fliss! Suddenly I felt really sorry for her, having to go first. This could be a bit painful to watch...

"Would you care for another dance?" said Miss Middleton, reading from the script.

There was a pause.

"I... I..." stammered Fliss, staring at the paper as if the script was written in a foreign language.

Someone tittered from the back of the classroom – it sounded like one of the M&Ms, but I couldn't be sure.

"OK, take a deep breath, let's start again," Miss Middleton said kindly. "Would you care for another dance?"

"I-I-I have to go," Fliss said in a tiny little voice. Her face had gone bright red. "I-i-i-it's almost m-m-m-midnight."

"But you still haven't told me your name!" Miss Middleton said.

"It's Fliss!" Fliss said in surprise. Hadn't Miss Middleton just called her Felicity a moment ago? Had she forgotten already?

There were a couple of laughs at that, and Fliss went even more red. "Oh, sorry," she said, looking down at the script, all flustered. Then she bit her lip. "I can't do this!" she wailed and ran out of the classroom.

The door banged shut behind her and everyone looked at each other.

"I can't do this!" Simon Graham said in a silly high voice, and all the boys started laughing their heads off.

"Any more noise from you lot and you'll be out on your ears!" Mrs Weaver said crossly. "Oh dear. We seem to have lost our first Cinderella. Lisa, would you like to read next?"

Lisa Warren stepped up opposite Miss Middleton. She'd only started at our school in September, and we didn't really know her as she was in Mr Nicholls' class. She was very pretty with long blonde hair, and as soon as she started reading, my heart did a sickening kind of lurch. She was good. No, she was better than good. She was REALLY good. She had a clear, confident speaking voice and seemed quite at ease in front of the classroom of people. Straight away, you believed in her, you believed she was really Cinderella.

Her singing voice was even better, I'm mega jealous to say. Miss Middleton asked her to sing *The First Noel*, and she sounded great. Got every high note, stayed in tune, the lot. By the time she'd finished, I knew I had a lot to live up to! Hmmm...

Emily Berryman went next. Her acting wasn't bad but her singing was terrible. She sang in a really high voice that wobbled all over the place, and she put on this yucky simpering expression as she sang. I mentally crossed her off the list. No way, José!

Then it was me. Gulp! I saw Frankie and Kenny giving me thumbs-up signs and big grins which made me feel a bit better, but my legs still wobbled a bit as I went up in front of everyone.

By now, I knew the scene pretty well, so at least I wasn't coming to it completely cold. I tried to speak as clearly as I could, but still managed to fluff a couple of words. I kept trying to imagine just what Cinderella would be feeling as the Prince begged her to stay for another dance. She would be feeling all happy

339

and excited that the Prince seemed to like her, yet worried that if the clock struck midnight before she got home, her beautiful dress would turn into rags again, and her secret would be out.

It was all over before I knew it, and suddenly it was just me, Rosie, in the classroom again. And now I had to sing in front of everyone! I've never been keen on *The First Noel*, either. There are lots of really high bits and some quite low bits, too, so it's a real test of the old vocal chords. I was a bit shaky to begin with, but once I'd warmed up, I didn't think I'd done too badly. And that was it. Game over!

"Thank you, Rosie," said Mrs Weaver, smiling at me. "You can go off for your lunch now."

I was a bit gutted to have to leave so soon – I'd been hoping to see all the other auditions. I gave Frankie and Kenny a wave, just as Emma Hughes stepped up for her turn. Well, I'd given it my best shot, anyway. Let's hope the teachers thought it was OK, too!

I met up with Fliss and Lyndz in the

playground, and then Frankie and Kenny joined us as soon as they'd finished.

"You missed a treat!" Kenny said gloatingly. "Emma Hughes really bodged it up in there! She was so hammy, it was hilarious! And her voice! What a croak! Oh, I wish you'd been there to see it. Me and Frankie were wetting ourselves!"

Fliss went pale. "Is everyone saying things like that about me?" she asked, practically in a whisper.

"Of course not!" Frankie said kindly. "It must have been horrible, having to go up there first, I would have hated it!"

Fliss scuffed her shoe on the ground. "It was Rosie's fault, anyway," she said in a cross little voice.

"Me? But why? What did I do?" I asked indignantly.

"You told me to break my leg!" she said accusingly. "I thought you were my friend, and then to tell me to break my leg just before I did my bit – I was very hurt!"

Kenny burst out laughing. "Fliss, what are you like?" she groaned.

"It's an expression they use in the theatre!" I said, losing my patience with Fliss. "It means good luck!"

"Never mind, Fliss," Lyndz said comfortingly. "Why don't you ask if you can be one of the horses with me?"

"No, thanks!" Fliss said rudely. "Who wants to be a smelly old horse?" And she stomped off in a huff.

"There's no pleasing some people," I said. "Let her stew. I'd feel a bit of an idiot, too, if I'd rushed out of there like she did."

"How were your auditions anyway?" Lyndz asked Frankie and Kenny.

"Pretty good!" Frankie said. "So many people went for Cinderella, there was only me and Alana Banana who went for the part of Wicked Wilma. And Alana went bright red and muttered all her words in this sort of monotone, so I don't think she stands much of a chance!"

"Likewise," said Kenny. "Can you believe, I was the only one who went for an Ugly Sister part?! Everyone else must be far too vain to want a part like that! And I made Mrs Weaver laugh at my reading, too, so..."

"Excellent!" I said. I was starting to worry that maybe I'd pushed my luck, going for such a major part. What if I wound up with big fat nothing?

Just then, a shout went up around the playground. "The cast list is up! The list is up!"

The four of us looked at each other.

"Already?" I said, feeling a bit faint. "That was quick!"

"Oh, per-leeeeze let me be an Ug!" Kenny said, breaking into a run towards the school hall. "Come on, let's check it out!"

CHAPTER SIX

As we ran back into school, I could feel my heart pounding. Please, please, let me be *something*, I wished inside my head. Even if it meant being an Ugly Sister, I was dying to have some part or other. Maybe it was horrible of me to feel glad about it, but I was relieved that at least I knew Fliss wouldn't be Cinderella. That was one less person in the running for it, anyway – and she would have been totally unbearable if she HAD got the part, more to the point!

There was quite a crowd around the noticeboard in the school hall. We pushed our way forward, trying to spot our names on the printed piece of paper. I looked desperately for mine next to the part of Cinderella, but then my shoulders slumped as I read the name. Lisa Warren. Well, she HAD been good – better than me, anyway. Still, it didn't make me feel any less disappointed.

"Yes!! Wicked Wilma – Frankie Thomas!" Frankie read aloud, punching the air and whooping. "RESULT!! Excellent, fantastic, I'm in the pantomime!"

Kenny had pushed her way right to the front. "So am I!" she yelled excitedly. "I'm down to play Grizzle! COOL!! I'm an Ug!"

I chuckled as I saw who was playing Moana. "Have you seen who they cast you with?" I asked, pointing at the name. "Look!"

Kenny read the paper eagerly, and then her face fell. "I don't believe it! Emma Hughes! Great – me and my bezzy mate, I don't think!" Then she paused. "Hey, actually, that's really funny, because she didn't even audition for that, did she? She auditioned for Cinderella! Ha ha!! She's going to be so mad when she sees that!"

Kenny scoured the hall for Emma. Ahh,

there she was, rushing forward expectantly to see if she'd been given a part. Had she ever!

"Yoo-hoo!" Kenny yelled, waving madly at her. "Emma! You and me, mate! We're the Uglies!"

"Ha ha, very funny," Emma sneered, turning away from her and going up to the noticeboard.

"Oh dear, look at that, she doesn't even believe me!" Kenny sniggered. "Get used to the idea – it's me and you as the Ugly Twins!"

Emma clapped a hand over her mouth and looked really upset as she saw the truth for herself. For a moment, I actually felt sorry for her. Talk about a public humiliation!

I sighed, still feeling disappointed that I hadn't been picked. But there were only a handful of main parts after all, and maybe I could be in the chorus or something...

Then Lyndz was tugging my sleeve. "Hey, look, Rosie, here's your name!" she shouted. "You're Buttons!"

Buttons! I had a part! I stared at the cast list, unable to believe it was true. But there, in black and white, it said, "Buttons – Rosie

Cartwright." So it WAS true!

"Yes!!" I screamed, jumping up and down in excitement. "I got a part!" I was SOOOO happy, I can't tell you! So I hadn't been picked for Cinderella, big deal! The teachers still thought I was good enough to be in the pantomime!

The full cast list went like this:

```
Cinderella — Lisa Warren
Prince Charming — Neil Watson
Narrator — Simon Graham
Wicked Wilma — Frankie Thomas
Angelica — Sarah King
Grizzle / Moana — Laura McKenzie
                     / Emma Hughes
Buttons — Rosie Cartwright
```

Wow! I was *soooo* excited!

"It's a fix," I heard Emily Berryman muttering spitefully. "The crummy Sleep-tight Club have got THREE of the main parts. It's a total fix, if you ask me!"

"Judging will be on talent, not looks, as Mrs

Weaver said," Kenny told her sweetly. "Otherwise YOU probably would have got the part of Grizzle, not me!"

THAT shut her up!

There was a note at the bottom of the list:

```
Anyone   interested   in   dancing,
singing   or   other   non-speaking
parts,   please   come   along   to   a
meeting   in   Miss   Middleton's
classroom,  Tuesday  lunchtime.
First    rehearsal    —    Thursday
lunchtime in the hall.
```

Thursday lunchtime! I could hardly wait!

I told my family about the whole thing over tea that night. My mum gave me a big hug and kiss. She's not normally the soppy type, but she kept telling me how proud of me she was. "My little girl on the stage, I can't believe it!" she kept saying.

"MU-U-U-UM!" I kept saying back.

"Well, we'll *all* be there in the audience!" she

said, ruffling my hair. "Fancy that, my little girl, eh!"

"You're in a good mood, Mum," Tiffany said. "Did you get a pay-rise at work or something?"

"Oh, that'll be the day," she said. "No, work's just... really good fun at the moment."

Me, Tiffany and Adam all stared at her in disbelief. Work – fun? Mum had never given us the impression that her office job was anything other than Dullsville Central. Even stranger than that, she started going a bit pink.

"Oh, you know, there's a good team of us at the moment, that's all," she said breezily. "Now eat your dinner before it gets cold!"

Tiffany raised her eyebrows and smirked. "I see!" she said. "And does this team have anything to do with that Richard guy you were talking to Auntie Zoë about?"

Mum blushed. I swear, my mum blushed like a teenager! Then she gave this mysterious smile. "You shouldn't listen to other people's conversations!" she said to Tiffany, wagging a finger at her. "You never know what trouble it's going to get you into!"

Tiffany gave her a knowing look, and I watched open-mouthed. Was Tiff saying what I thought she was? Was something going on with Mum and this Richard guy? For all my saying I wished Mum had a new boyfriend, I suddenly felt a bit worried about it. How did I know this Richard bloke would be good enough for her? What if he upset her, like Dad had done? Worst of all, what if WE didn't like him?

"Rosie, eat your mash, it's getting cold," Mum said. "And don't look so worried! Tiffany might think she knows everything, but she doesn't." She gave me a big wink and I felt a bit better. Still, I couldn't help wondering...

That week at school was really fun. Lyndz and Fliss went along to the auditions on Tuesday, and Lyndz duly got to be a horse, while Fliss got a part as a dancer in the ball scene, which she was really pleased about. "At least I don't have to say anything!" she said, smiling in relief. "AND I'll get to wear a nice dress!"

Emily Berryman still hadn't forgiven us for getting good parts when all she had got was a place in the choir – goodness only knows why, when her voice was so terrible. She was definitely miffed with us, AND with Lisa for getting the part of Cinderella.

"Everyone knows her dad's in prison," Emily said spitefully. "I can't believe a jailbird's daughter is going to be Cinderella. She's only been at this school for five minutes, too, it's not fair! And do you know what? Her family live on the council estate, too, you know that really horrible one, on Cuddington Road? Yeah, there! Don't go near her – she's probably got fleas!"

This all made me really mad. For starters, I used to live on a council estate a few years ago, and there was nothing wrong with it. Just because Emily lived in one of the big posh detached houses near Cuddington Park!

"You are such a snob, Berryman," I said. "AND you're jealous, just because Lisa was miles better than you in the audition! Don't spread lies about people when you don't know what you're talking about!"

"Ooh, since when did you become Lisa Warren's bodyguard?" Emily sneered. "Can't she stick up for herself?"

"I'm sure she can, but she's not here right now, is she?" I retaliated. "You're such a coward! You don't have the guts to say any of your nasty little remarks to her face, so you have to say it all behind her back!"

"Hear, hear," said Kenny. "So do us all a favour and shut up, Berry-head! Go and practise your crummy songs while WE learn our lines!"

Emily's lips were clamped shut so tightly, you couldn't have slid a piece of paper between them. She looked seriously hacked off now. Good, she deserved it!

Meanwhile, we carried on making things for the Christmas bazaar in lesson time, and people started bringing in bagloads of bric-a-brac to sell, plus food for the homeless shelter. Mrs Poole, the head teacher, set up a table in the hall to display all the food people had brought in, and the collection grew and grew. Soft-hearted Lyndz even brought in her chocolate Advent calendar to give to a homeless child. I told you she was the kindest person in the world, didn't I?

Then came the first rehearsal for the pantomime! I'd been looking forward to it all week. I wasn't even quite sure how much Buttons had to say, so I was really dying to get a good look at the script so I could start thinking about how I'd say all my lines. I still couldn't believe that I, Rosie Cartwright, was going to be up on the stage in costume, acting in front of a big audience of parents and teachers and children. Every time I thought about it, I got butterflies. Scary!

The first thing Miss Middleton handed around was a rehearsal schedule. This gave the dates and times of each rehearsal, plus who had to be there for each one. Obviously Lisa, as Cinderella, had to go to nearly every one of them, as she was in most scenes. Frankie, Kenny and Emma also had quite a busy schedule. Mine wasn't too bad. I was in about four scenes by the look of it, so I wouldn't have to go to every single rehearsal. There were also separate rehearsals for all the dancers, and separate ones for the chorus. It was quite complicated, and I started to think that Miss Middleton deserved a medal for organising the whole thing!

Next, Miss Middleton handed round copies of the script to everyone who had speaking parts. At last! A chance to see what we would actually be saying! There were song sheets for the chorus to be passed round, too, and a more general scene-by-scene breakdown so people like Lyndz could see what scenes they were in. Soon, everyone was busily reading away with great interest.

Miss Middleton rapped on the desk after a minute or so. "OK!" she said. "I know you're all dying to read the scripts but there'll be plenty of time for that later. You'll notice that lots of rehearsals for the actors are after school, so please make sure your parents know where you are, and please also make sure you can get home safely afterwards. If anyone is really stuck for a lift, come and tell me or Mrs Weaver.

"Dancers and singers, you'll be rehearsing at lunchtimes mostly, although obviously there will be a few after-school rehearsals nearer the actual shows where everyone will rehearse together. If you go off with Mrs

Weaver now, she'll tell you a bit more about it."

There was lots of kerfuffle as the dancers and singers all went off into the next classroom, Fliss included.

"Now, we don't have time to do very much today," Miss Middleton said to the rest of us, "but I thought we could begin by reading through the script together, just so you can start getting used to it. You don't have to stand up, just follow the script and read your lines out when you have them. So if you could all turn to the first scene, Simon, the narrator speaks first. When you're ready – let's go!"

Simon cleared his throat. "It was a cold December morning, and the De Vere family were eating breakfast together. Little did they know the postman was about to bring a letter that would change all of their lives."

Lisa spoke next, with Cinderella's first lines. "More coffee, madam? Can I get anyone some more toast?"

"This coffee is disgusting!" Frankie said, as Wicked Wilma. She said it so furiously, a couple of people giggled. "Honestly, Cinderella, is it too much to ask you to make a

355

half-decent breakfast for your own stepmother?"

"AND the toast's cold," Kenny said as Grizzle, leering horribly. "Mama, Cinderella's just too lazy to make it properly!"

Then it was me! "The post has arrived, madam!" I said, and pretended to pass a bundle of letters to Frankie. "There's one letter with the royal crest on it!"

I felt myself go bright red after I'd spoken. Had I said it too fast? I glanced anxiously at Miss Middleton, who gave me a little wink.

"The royal crest? OOOH, I say!" said Frankie. More titters. I could tell she was really getting into the part!

"What is it, Mama?" said Emma, as Moana.

"Quick, open it, Mama!" said Kenny.

Frankie mimed tearing an envelope open and reading a letter. "Ooh, girls!" she said, fanning herself with her hand. "Ooh, you'll never guess! We've been invited to a BALL! Yes, a ball – with none other than Prince Charming himself there!"

"Prince Charming?" said Cinderella.

Wicked Wilma gave a horrible frown. "Yes,

Cinderella, Prince Charming," she said. "Although why you're interested, I really don't know! YOU'RE certainly not invited to the ball! You'll be staying at home and cleaning out the kitchen cupboards!"

Miss Middleton clapped her hands. "Very good!" she said. "We're going to have to finish there, I'm afraid, as it's nearly time for lessons."

"Oh-h-h-h!" everyone said in disappointment. The time had flown by!

Miss Middleton smiled. "So take your scripts home and read through your lines over the weekend, won't you? First rehearsal proper is Monday night. Please make a note of all the rehearsals you're meant to be at, won't you? And I'll see some of you then!"

As everyone reluctantly left the room, the four of us grinned at each other.

"This is going to be FUN!" said Frankie happily.

I couldn't have put it better myself!

CHAPTER SEVEN

I couldn't believe it was Friday again already. It really is true that time flies when you're having fun. Already, there were only three weeks left until the end of term, and then it was Christmas itself!

Lyndz had organised the sleepover at hers for that night. She was calling it an early Christmas sleepover, and said she and her mum had made a load of mince pies for us to scoff. Yummo!

However, the spirit of giving and receiving didn't seem to have affected everyone at school. It seemed like someone had the spirit of TAKING instead.

It was sharp-eyed Kenny who noticed something was wrong. Every Friday morning, different classes take it in turns to give a morning assembly in the hall on whatever topic they've been learning about recently. And after this week's, an incredibly boring one by Mrs Burgess's class about bears, we were just about to go to our classroom when Kenny pointed to the "food for the homeless" table.

"Look!" she said. "The Advent calendar you brought in has gone, Lyndz!"

We all stared. Sure enough, it had!

"It must be there SOMEWHERE," Lyndz said, scanning all the goodies that were piled up on the table. "It can't have just disappeared!"

"Unless someone's nicked it," I said thoughtfully. "Is everything else there?"

We went over to have a quick look.

"The stuff I brought in is all still there," Frankie said. "No, wait! Those chocolate biscuits Mum made me bring in have gone! And they were definitely on the table yesterday, because I remember being really gutted that she'd given them away."

"The tins of chickpeas I brought in are still there," Fliss said.

"You surprise me!" Kenny said sarcastically. "I'd have thought they would be the first things to be nicked!"

Fliss laughed. "I was glad to see them go, actually," she confessed. "They don't half make me... well, you know!"

"Beans, beans, good for your heart," I said. "The more you eat, you more you..."

"FART!" everyone joined in.

"Yes, exactly," Fliss said, blushing.

"So if anyone nicks the chickpeas, at least we know to look out for someone with a terrible wind problem," Frankie joked.

"I just can't believe someone is stealing stuff at all!" Lyndz said, as we went back to our classroom. "Stealing food that's meant to go to homeless people – I mean, how out of order can you get?"

"That sounds serious!" came Mrs Weaver's voice, who'd fallen into step behind us. "Stealing food? Who's been stealing food?"

"We don't know," I said. "But we just noticed that a couple of things we'd brought in for the homeless aren't on the table any more."

"Really?" Her face darkened. "Well, that IS serious. Thank you for telling me, girls."

Once in the classroom, we sat down at our desks, and Mrs Weaver rapped on the desk with a ruler to get everyone's attention. "Listen, please! I've just been informed that some of the food that was donated for the homeless shelter has disappeared," she said, frowning. "Obviously, if someone is stealing the food, this is a terrible thing to do. Every child at this school has a roof over their heads and is well fed. To think that someone could be taking food that is meant to go to people who have nowhere to live... Well, it's extremely disappointing to think that someone could do such a thing."

Everyone looked at their desks in silence. Mrs Weaver has this way of making you feel bad about something even if you haven't done anything wrong.

"I bet you it's Lisa Warren," Emily Berryman said in a loud whisper.

"Emily, do you have something to say to the class?" Mrs Weaver asked in an icy voice.

Emily looked crestfallen. "No, Miss," she muttered.

"Good," said Mrs Weaver. "Because stealing food is one thing. Spreading rumours about who's responsible for it is almost as despicable. So if I find out that anyone is gossiping or making allegations, I will be extremely angry – especially if that someone is in my class!"

I snuck a quick look at Emily, who looked utterly embarrassed. Good! I thought. She was asking for it, coming out with comments like that about Lisa.

Unfortunately, the M&Ms don't give up that easily with their nastiness. By playtime, it was all over the school that Lisa and her little brother Michael had been taking the food because their family couldn't afford to buy any. You know what it's like when a rumour starts at school. It was all anyone could talk about – Cinderella the thief!

I felt really sorry for Lisa. Well, we all did. No-one deserved to be judged like that, without any proof. Whatever happened to "innocent until proven guilty", anyway?

The five of us went over to Lisa, who was sitting on a wall, all on her own. She looked really miserable.

"Just ignore what everyone's saying," Lyndz said hotly, putting an arm around her. "WE know it wasn't you that nicked the food."

"Everyone's just jealous because you're going to be a great Cinderella," Frankie said. "Stupid idiots! Lyndz is right."

Lisa's eyes were red as she forced a smile. "I know you're right," she said, "but it's horrible to have the whole school talking about you. And until they find out who's REALLY taking the food..." She shrugged miserably, and didn't bother to finish her sentence.

I caught Kenny's eye. "Maybe we should try and catch the thief," I suggested. "Then we could get you off the hook, and everyone would leave you alone."

"Mmm," said Lisa, although she didn't sound convinced. "Thanks, you lot. I need all the friends I can get right now."

"You just leave it to us," Kenny said confidently. "We'll sort it out! Sleepover Club to the rescue!"

*   *   *

That night at the sleepover, we started wondering if we'd been a bit rash, promising to clear Lisa's name like that.

"It's a good idea, but HOW are we going to catch the thief?" I said, racking my brains.

"And are we sure Lisa *didn't* take the food, anyway?" Fliss sniffed. "After all, she *is* poor, isn't she?"

We all stared at her, horrified.

"Fliss!" Kenny said fiercely. "I didn't think YOU were like all the others! Don't be so horrible!"

"I can't believe you just said that, Fliss," Lyndz said, looking really shocked. "Being poor doesn't make someone a thief. Look at all those rich businessmen and politicians who swindle thousands of pounds out of other people!"

"And so what if her family IS a bit hard up, anyway?" I said. "You can't judge a person on their *money!*"

Fliss looked a bit shaken at our angry words. "S-sorry," she stammered in the end. "I just..."

"You've got a problem with her, just because she's Cinderella," Frankie said sharply. "Well, get over it!"

There was a bit of an awkward silence. Lyndz handed round the plate of mince pies and we all munched away. Honestly, Fliss doesn't half come out with stupid comments sometimes.

"Maybe we should set a trap for the thief," Fliss suggested in the end. You could tell she was trying to make up for what she'd said about Lisa. "Maybe we could rig up a booby trap or something..."

"My brother's got some of this marking powder that looks invisible, but when you touch something with the powder on, it turns your hands black," Lyndz said excitedly. "We could cover all the food with the powder, and then just keep an eye on everyone's hands! It takes days for the colour to fade!"

"What if the powder poisons the food?" I pointed out. "Besides, there's loads and loads of food to cover with this powder, we'd need tons of it."

"And there's new stuff going on the table

every day," Kenny added. "It would be a nightmare, trying to keep track of what we'd powdered and what we hadn't."

Lyndz's face fell in disappointment.

"Good idea, though," Frankie said kindly.

We all thought a bit more.

"How about putting a banana skin under the table so that the thief skids on it, falls over, bashes their head on the edge of the table and knocks themselves out?" Kenny joked.

"Yeah, or build a trap door under the table that they'd fall through, straight into a steel cage?" I said, giggling.

"Or one of us could hide under the table and grab their legs and rugby-tackle them when they came up to nick something!" Frankie said. "Biff! Gotcha, my son!"

We all started thinking of more and more ridiculous ideas to catch the thief until we were all weak with giggles. Lyndz had just come up with a plan to rig up CCTV so that we could monitor the table at all times, when Kenny whistled excitedly.

"Hey! WE could be the CCTV!" she said.

We all stared at her blankly.

"More, please," Frankie ordered. "We don't understand Kenny language!"

"We don't need CCTV to keep watch on the table, *we* can do it!" she laughed. "It's so simple, I can't believe we didn't think of it before! You know the music cupboard at the back of the hall where all the instruments are kept?"

"Ye-e-e-e-s," we chorused.

"Remember Mrs Weaver sent me and Alana Banana to put away the musical instruments last week?" she said, eyes sparkling. "Well, I just so happened to notice that the lock was broken. You can't tell from looking at it, but you don't need the key to open the door. So unless Dishy Dave has got round to fixing it super-quickly..."

"We can hide in the cupboard and spy out on the table!" I finished for her.

"Exactly!" she beamed. "What do you think?"

"We're not allowed inside at breaktimes," Fliss reminded us, shaking her head doubtfully.

Frankie rolled her eyes. "And? Your point

367

is?" she demanded. "Since when have a few rules stopped the Sleepover Club?"

"It's definitely worth a try," Lyndz said. "The only thing is, for us to catch the thief, they have to nick stuff at breaktimes. I mean, I don't really want to be hanging around *after* school in the music cupboard..."

"Think about it!" Kenny said. "There'll be all the pantomime rehearsals and stuff after school anyway, so the hall's going to be out of bounds for the thief then. So if they're going to nick anything else, they'll have to do it before school starts or at lunchtime or playtime. And we'll make sure that WE'RE there to catch them when they next try it!"

"Kenny, you're a genius," I told her. "What would we do without you?"

"Oh, get very bored and miserable, I should think!" Kenny said, grinning. "So are we all agreed, then?"

"Agreed!" we all said together. Even Fliss!

Back at home, my mum's mysterious behaviour was continuing. She hummed whenever she was in the kitchen, smiled at herself when she passed any mirrors and spent AGES on the phone to my Auntie Zoë. Something was *definitely* up! The question was, WHAT?

That Saturday, she took me into Leicester for some Christmas shopping. Tiffany was out at a friend's house and Adam was over at my dad's, so it was just me and Mum for a change. I hardly ever get her to myself, so it always feels like a real treat when the two of us spend a bit of time together. Once again, she seemed really happy and kept laughing and joking about things, even when we were stuck in mile-long queues at the till. What was it all about?

In the end, the suspense was just way too much for me. I waited until we were having a cup of tea in a café, and then came straight out with it.

"Mum, something's going on, isn't it?" I said. No beating about the bush from Rosie!

She took a sip of her coffee. "What do you mean?" she asked.

"It's just... well, you seem different," I said, not quite sure how to put it into words.

369

"Happier. I keep wondering about what Tiffany said the other day about Richard, your friend at work. I mean... is something going on?"

She put down her cup. "Well..." she said thoughtfully, "something MIGHT be about to go on. I really like Richard. He's been a very good friend to me. But my family are what's most important to me – you, Adam and Tiff. I'd only let anything happen with Richard if you three were OK with the idea. I mean, after your dad leaving us and everything..."

She shrugged, and then gazed down into her coffee. I slurped my Coke while I tried to work out how I felt about it. Sure, I'd hoped for ages that she and Dad would get back together. Who wouldn't? But Dad had his new family to think about, and deep down in my heart, I knew that he probably wouldn't be coming back to us.

"Go for it, Mum!" I said in the end. "I think you should just go for it with Richard! If he makes you happy, why not?"

She leaned over the table and hugged me. She looked all excited and girlish at the thought. "If you're sure you're OK with it?" she said again. "Only he's asked me to go to dinner with him next week and I said I'd ask you three first, so..."

"So go!" I said, smiling at her. I felt as if I was the parent suddenly, giving her permission to go out. "Cinderella, you SHALL go to the ball!"

CHAPTER EIGHT

The next week, pantomime rehearsals started in earnest. They were so much fun! As Buttons, I didn't have too many lines to learn, so I was quite relaxed about the whole thing and could sit back and enjoy watching the others.

Everyone else was having a good time, too. Kenny really got into her role as Grizzle and hammed it up a treat every time she was in a scene. She was determined to get more laughs than Emma's Moana, so she worked dead hard to make herself extra funny. Kenny's got one of those really mobile faces and is excellent at pulling comic expressions. After a while, she would have the whole cast roaring with laughter with the twitch of an eyebrow, or just by rolling her eyes up to the heavens.

Frankie was also loving it. Frankie's got an amazing brain for detail, and she'd memorised all her lines by the first rehearsal, so Miss Middleton was dead impressed with that. Frankie and Kenny played well off each other, too, so when they were both in the same scene, everyone would be chuckling away at them, even Miss Middleton and Mrs Weaver! Like Kenny, Frankie was a bit of a star in the making.

Right from the first rehearsal, though, it was Lisa who shone out as having a real acting talent. I actually began to feel glad that she'd got the part of Cinderella, and not me. She was head and shoulders above everyone else who was there, and I was chuffed for her, after all the horrible rumours that had been going around. Often after she'd rehearsed a scene, or one of her songs, I caught Miss Middleton and Mrs Weaver smiling away at each other, both looking dead pleased with their Cinders.

The only character who didn't seem that brilliant was Sarah King, the fairy godmother. She spoke clearly enough, but she was having terrible trouble learning her lines, even the most simple sentences.

I'm not saying I've got a fantastic memory or anything, but after hearing a scene rehearsed once or twice through, I found that even *I* knew her words, without even trying. It was *painful* to watch Sarah biting her lip, trying to think of what she had to say next.

"But Cinderella, you must promise me one thing," she was supposed to say in her first scene. "You must be back by the last stroke of midnight – for that's when the magic will vanish, and so will your dress, coach and horses!"

Sarah kept saying, "Cinderella, you must TELL me one thing" by mistake, which changed the meaning of the sentence completely. She just couldn't remember the word "promise" for the life of her.

"From the top," Miss Middleton called out patiently, and Lisa and Sarah began the scene again.

"Don't look so..." Sarah started, then bit her lip anxiously. "Don't look so..."

"Frightened," I said, and then jumped at the sound of my own voice. Oops! I hadn't meant to say anything, it had just popped out of my mouth!

Sarah shot me a thankful look, and started again. "Don't look so frightened," she said, sounding more confident. "I'm your fairy godmother – and I'm here to help you, Cinderella!"

The next few lines went OK, with Lisa giving a faultless reading of Cinderella and Sarah managing to remember all her words. Then it came to the "promise" line, and...

"Cinderella, you must tell me one thing," Sarah said.

"Promise me," I said. Again, I just couldn't stop myself saying it! I didn't want to butt in or anything, but I couldn't help feeling a bit sorry for Sarah struggling up there on the stage.

She smiled gratefully at me again. "Cinderella, you must PROMISE me one thing," she said, turning back to Lisa. "You must be back by the last stroke of midnight..."

The Sleepover Club

I was a bit worried that Miss Middleton might think I was poking my nose in where it wasn't wanted. And sure enough, at the end of that night's rehearsal, she and Mrs Weaver called me over to them. Uh-oh! I was going to get told to keep my mouth shut when I wasn't involved in rehearsals!

"There's no need to look like that, you're not in trouble!" Mrs Weaver laughed as I came over. "Dear me, you look like a wet weekend, Rosie!"

I smiled weakly at her, wondering what this could be all about. "I'm sorry I told Sarah her lines," I said quickly, thinking that if I could get an apology in first, they might not be cross with me.

"That's what we wanted to talk to you about," Miss Middleton said. "We realised what's missing from our rehearsals – a couple of prompts! Obviously we'll be busy directing the actors so won't always have a script to hand..."

".... But as you seem to be picking the lines up pretty quickly, we wondered if you'd like to sit in as one of the prompts, when you're not

376

rehearsing your scenes?" Mrs Weaver asked.

"What's a prompt?" I asked, feeling a bit stupid. Well, I didn't know!

"A prompt basically does what you did tonight," Miss Middleton said. "They sit by the side of the stage and when someone forgets their lines, the prompt reminds them of the next couple of words. Think you could do that?"

I grinned from ear to ear. "Yes! Oh, yes, definitely! I'm sure I could!" I said, feeling utterly delighted. Anything to get more involved in the play!

"It would mean coming to more rehearsals," Mrs Weaver said. "Would that be a problem?"

"No! No! That's fine!" I said happily. Buttons AND a prompt! This was getting better and better.

"Good!" smiled Miss Middleton. "Thank you very much, Rosie! That will be a big help to us. Alex McKay will be our other prompt, so between you, I'm sure you'll do a great job."

Of the other two, Lyndz was enjoying being a horse, even though she didn't have to do very much. Still, that suited her, she said. No problem! It just meant she had more time to be off riding and mucking out REAL horses, in fact.

Fliss was getting into the dancing thing, too, and kept showing us her moves in the playground, twirling around all over the place until the rest of us were in fits of giggles.

"Wait until you see my dress!" she boasted. "It's really beautiful! Mrs Somersby said she's designing it especially for me, you know!"

"Funnily enough, she's designing MY costume especially for ME!" Frankie said dryly. "Strange that, isn't it, seeing as it's going to be me who's wearing it!"

"Oh, you know what I mean!" Fliss said, tossing her hair. "She said she wanted to make the most of my colouring and that. So there!"

The only thing Fliss DIDN'T like was when me, Frankie and Kenny talked about our rehearsals – or worse still, talked about how good Lisa was.

"When she sang that song today, I honestly got a lump in my throat," I told the others. "She really has got a fab voice!"

"And I love that first scene I do with her," Frankie said. "The one where I'm telling her she can't go to the ball and she's all miserable about it. Do you know, the other night, I was actually worried I'd really upset her because she seemed so gutted. But it was only because she was acting so brilliantly!"

"Oh, anyone can act if they want to," Fliss would sniff, turning her nose up a bit. "The thing is, who can be bothered? I'd much rather be a model any day."

"Proudlove, the green-eyed monster..." Kenny would sing under her breath to the tune of *Rudolf the Red-Nosed Reindeer*, or one of us would start humming the tune when Fliss started on her jealous routine. It wasn't worth falling out about, but it did get a bit annoying. I REALLY had to bite my tongue to stop myself reminding her about her audition disaster!

As well as the pantomime, we also made a start on Operation Food Nicker, as Frankie called it. Who had been helping themselves to the donated food – and why were they doing such a mean thing?

379

To be honest, it was pretty boring at first, especially as we'd half expected to catch the thief straight away and be done with it. I'd thought it might be quite an adventure, playing detective – but boy, was I wrong about THAT.

We took it in turns to hide in the cupboard in twos at lunchtimes and breaktimes, spying out on the food table. The first time I did it with Lyndz, it actually WAS quite exciting, as we were both convinced we would catch someone. Every time we saw someone walk anywhere near the table, we'd hold our breath and clutch each other, watching carefully to see if they'd stash anything in a bag or their pockets.

"OK, here we go," one of us would say. "Get ready to pounce!"

But no! It was just one false alarm after another. The nearest thing we got to a thief was when a woman we didn't recognise strolled right up to the table and started picking up tins and looking at them. Lyndz and I stared wide-eyed at each other. Talk about blatant! This was one confident thief, all right!

But just as we were about to go out and make an accusation, who should walk up at that moment but Mrs Poole! "Yes, this is our collection of food for the homeless," she started saying to the mysterious woman.

Lyndz put a hand over her mouth to try and stop herself giggling. "You know who that is, don't you?" she spluttered.

"No," I said blankly.

"It's the new supply teacher!" she said. "And we were just about to...!"

So apart from that little near miss, the whole thing was a bit tedious. But the rumours were still flying about Lisa and Michael, and whenever I saw Lisa's anxious, pale face or heard the M&Ms gossiping loudly about her, I knew we had to do SOMETHING, however boring Operation Food Nicker was turning out to be.

Kenny insisted on it, anyway. "If someone's desperate enough to steal food, a warning from Mrs Poole won't stop them, will it?" she pointed out. "Whose turn is it this playtime? Me and you, Fliss, isn't it? Right! Come on, then!" And so we carried on with our mission...

Meanwhile, back at home, Mum had broken the news about this Richard guy to Tiffany and Adam, and they were both pleased for her. The date was on!

"The only trouble is," she confided in me and Tiff, "I've got absolutely nothing nice to wear."

It was true. Ever since Dad left, money's been a bit tight in our house, and what with Christmas coming up, Mum had no spare cash to buy a new outfit. Tiffany and I had a look through her wardrobe with her, but it was no good. Everything was old and faded and had been worn a hundred times before.

"I wonder if you could fit into anything of mine?" Tiff said to her in the end. "I mean, we're both about the same size, aren't we?"

Mum laughed. "Thanks, love, but I don't think I've got the legs for any of your little skirts these days," she said. "No, I'll just wear this black dress. It's the best of the bunch, isn't it?"

Well, it WAS the best of them, but it still looked pretty ancient, if you asked me. You know after you wash a pair of black trousers so many times, the black starts to look a bit grey? Well, this dress was grey, dowdy, and looked a hundred years old.

"Mum," I said tentatively, "I could ask Fliss's mum if you can borrow one of her dresses if you like. She's got loads."

My mum frowned at that. She's dead proud, and hates the idea of having to take anything from other people. "We're not a charity, Rosie," she said lightly, but I could tell she hated my offer. "No, the black dress will be fine!"

I felt bad for suggesting it, then, and sloped off to my room. I couldn't help thinking about Cinderella. What Mum really needed was a fairy godmother of her very own, to wave a magic wand and produce a gorgeous outfit out of thin air. But there was no such thing as fairy godmothers. Or was there?

I waited until Mum was in the bath that night, and Tiff and Adam were both watching telly. Then I picked up the phone and started dialling. You never knew – maybe I could work a bit of Christmas magic myself!

CHAPTER NINE

The next exciting thing to happen at school was that we caught the thief red-handed! Another storming success for the Sleepover sleuths!

The only thing was, it wasn't quite the triumph we'd all been expecting. I'd been convinced that the thief had to be someone really horrible and mean – I was even wondering if it was the M&Ms, trying to frame Lisa, to be honest.

Me and Frankie were keeping watch that breaktime. Well, I say "keeping watch", but we were so bored, we were actually playing noughts and crosses in the dust on the top of the piano. Frankie was sitting nearest the door, keeping half an eye out on the hall. I was too interested in the game to be paying any attention to the hall, or listening out for footsteps.

It was quite lucky that we caught him, all in all! Frankie had just trounced me, and leaned back to peep through the glass – and then nearly fell over in shock. She put a finger to her lips and motioned me to come forward. Then she pointed towards the food table.

There was a small figure, quickly tucking things into a small satchel for all he was worth. Frankie crashed through the door and sprinted over to him.

"Got you!" she yelled, grabbing hold of him.

I raced behind her, only to see that it was Andy Mitchell, one of the little Year Threes, looking absolutely petrified.

"Right – straight to Mrs Poole's with YOU!" Frankie said, marching him along by the scruff of his neck. "I think you've got some explaining to do, mate!"

Andy started to cry great snivelling sobs. "Please don't tell her," he wailed. "Please don't tell Mrs Poole!" He looked really scared at the mention of her name.

"But that food was for homeless people!" I said. "It's wrong to take it! That was supposed to be for their Christmas dinner!"

"I know," he blubbed. "I'm sorry. But..." He wiped his nose on his sleeve and we couldn't catch the rest of what he was trying to say, as his voice went all choky.

I have to say, I was starting to feel a teeny bit sorry for him. He was only a little kid, after all. Still, thieving was thieving, wasn't it?

"Oh dear," said Mrs Poole, when we walked into her office, Frankie and me on either side of Andy. "What have we here? What's going on?"

"We caught HIM stealing THIS," Frankie said triumphantly, holding the satchel of food up in the air. "He was at the food table, helping himself!"

"Is this true, Andy?" Mrs Poole said gently.

Andy nodded, keeping his eyes on the floor.

Mrs Poole handed him a tissue. "Blow your nose," she told him. "Now, what's all this about, then?"

Andy blew his nose with trembling hands. "I know the food was meant for homeless people, Miss," he said, "but I was only trying to help my dad. He's lost his job and my mum says..." The rest of his sentence was lost in a new burst of sobs. "I'm s-s-so s-s-sorry," he wailed, blowing his nose again.

Frankie and I looked at each other. Suddenly I felt awkward. I wished the thief was an out-and-out villain that we could have despised. The fact that it was this poor little kid whose family were probably going to have a rotten Christmas... I didn't quite know how to feel about it any more.

Mrs Poole told Andy to sit down, then looked up at us two. "You can go," she said quietly. "Thank you for bringing this to my attention. I'd appreciate it if this could go no further."

"Yes, Miss," I said, anxious to get out of there.

"But what about Lisa and Michael?" Frankie blurted out. "Everyone's saying it's them!"

Mrs Poole thought for a few seconds. "I'll make sure everyone knows they had nothing to do with this," she said. "Thank you, girls."

Boy, was I glad to get out of that office. We rushed off to find the others straight away. Sure, Mrs Poole had said not to tell anyone, but we just HAD to tell the rest of the Sleepover Club, didn't we?

Kenny was jubilant. "What did I say? I just knew we had to stick at it!" she crowed. "Another result for us!"

"So who was it, anyway?" Lyndz said.

"Well..." I started, feeling a bit miserable about the whole thing. "It was this little lad Andy in Year Three. Turns out his dad's just lost his job. I think he was just trying to help out, you know."

Lyndz looked sympathetic, but Fliss wasn't. "Well! He can't just go around stealing like that, can he?" she said, sounding outraged.

"He's only about seven," Frankie pointed out. "And he was really sorry about it, wasn't he, Rosie?"

"Yeah," I said, thinking back to his tear-stained face. "He was crying his eyes out. I don't reckon HIS family are going to have a very nice Christmas this year."

We all went a bit quiet. We should have been feeling dead pleased with ourselves for catching him stealing, but none of us were.

"At least Lisa's off the hook," Kenny said brightly.

"Yeah," said Frankie. "That's true. Mrs Poole wants us to keep schtum about Andy, but she said she'd make sure everyone knew it WASN'T Lisa. So everyone keep their mouths shut, yeah?"

"Yeah," we all agreed. "Definitely."

Mrs Poole was as good as her word. The very next day at assembly, she stood up to make an announcement.

"I just want to say a big thank you to everyone who has brought in food for our homeless table," she started. "You've all been very generous, and I know the homeless centre will really appreciate what you've done for them. Thank you!"

Then she paused and looked serious. "Now, I'm sure you've all heard that some of the food was going missing, which we were very concerned about," she said. "And if this has made you think twice about bringing any

The Sleepover Club

donations in, then you'll be pleased to hear that the person responsible has been caught."

Lots of people started whispering to each other at this news. Mrs Poole clapped her hands for quiet.

"Listen, please!" she called. "Now, it's been brought to my attention that a couple of people have been spreading very nasty rumours about who the thief could be. I was very disappointed to hear this, as I had hoped all the children at my school would be fairer and more open-minded than that."

I shot a quick look at the M&Ms. They had both gone purple with embarrassment.

"Now, when someone's spreading rumours about you, it can be very hurtful and upsetting," Mrs Poole continued. "Obviously I'm not going to tell you all who the thief was, but I would like to make it clear that it was NOT Lisa Warren or her brother Michael – and anyone who has been saying otherwise should be very ashamed of themselves. I think a few people in this room owe Lisa and Michael an apology, don't you?"

Everyone was craning their necks to look at

390

Lisa and Michael. Lisa was bright red, too, but she was also looking relieved, and holding her head high as everyone stared.

"And finally," Mrs Poole went on, "a reminder that the Christmas bazaar is this Saturday, so I hope to see lots of you there. There are some fantastic prizes in the raffle so make sure you get tickets from your class teacher or, of course, at the bazaar itself."

"Oh, I hope I win the raffle!" Fliss said fervently, crossing her fingers. "There's this gorgeous nail varnish collection that I would die for!"

Mrs Burgess started playing *All Things Bright and Beautiful* on the piano just then so we had to stop talking and start singing. And suddenly... I know it sounds corny, but I was feeling really bright and beautiful myself. We'd cleared Lisa's name, the bazaar and pantomime were coming up, my mum was in lurve, and best of all, it was almost Christmas. Could life get any better?

Life DID suddenly get a lot better for my mum that week. My Auntie Zoë came round with a bag of goodies for her, as we'd arranged on the phone. Yes, this was Mum's real-life fairy godmother, come to the rescue on an emergency clothes mission!

I'd told Zoë the whole story about Mum not having anything nice to wear for her date with Richard, and she'd promised to try and help. The thing was, I'd told her she'd have to be really subtle about it. If Mum got a whiff of "charity", she'd refuse to take anything off her, and we'd be back to square one.

True to her word, Zoë arrived with a bulging carrier bag and a bottle of white wine. "Sandra next door is having a bit of a clear-out," she told Mum with a beaming smile. "So I've nabbed a whole load of stuff for us, Karen! I thought we could fight for it all over a few glasses of vino, what do you think?"

Tiffany immediately wandered over. "Ooh, can have second dibs on that lot, Auntie Zoë?" she asked, trying to peer in the bag. "I need something nice for my Christmas party at school."

"Oh no you don't!" Mum said at once. She took out two wine glasses and plonked them down on the table. "Zoë, you're an angel!" she said, smiling. Then a thought struck her. "Ooh – there might even be something in here that I can wear for my date with Richard!"

Zoë gave me the tiniest of winks as Mum started rummaging excitedly through the bag of clothes. "Oh, so that's all definitely going ahead then, is it?" Zoë asked casually. "Where's he taking you?"

"A new French restaurant in Leicester," Mum said happily.

You know, when my mum smiles and stops looking worried for five seconds, she actually looks really pretty. And just at that moment, she looked gorgeous! If this Richard guy had any sense, he'd fall head over heels in love with her – and one of my Christmas wishes would come true!

I grinned to myself as I left them to it. Yippee! It looked like fairy godmother Zoë was going to work her magic, just as I'd hoped she would.

Sure enough, when I casually wandered back into the living room an hour later, Mum and Zoë were sitting there in completely different outfits, giggling like schoolgirls about something or other, with about two centimetres of wine left in the bottle.

"Wow, Mum, you look nice!" I said. "Stand up, let's have a look!"

She stood up – a bit wobbly on her feet – and did a twirl for me. Good old Zoë had come up trumps. Mum had on another black dress, but it was a far cry from the old one she usually wore. This one looked almost new, and fitted her perfectly. The material was a soft jersey, so it clung in all the right places. She looked so good, even Fliss would have approved.

"Mum, that's gorgeous!" I said in delight. "You look really lovely!"

"Doesn't she?" Zoë agreed. "You're going to knock this new fella for six, Karen!"

Mum looked all embarrassed. "Stop it, you two!" she said, but I could tell she was pleased, really. "I must pop in and thank Sandra next time I'm over at yours, Zoë," she said. "Fancy wanting to get rid of this lovely dress!"

As Mum went out to make coffee, I moved

closer to Zoë. "Where did it really come from?" I asked in a low voice.

"From the seconds shop in Cuddington Road," she whispered back, tapping her nose. "But that's just between you and me. Mum's the word, eh?"

"Well, you'd better stop her nipping round to thank Sandra, then, hadn't you?" I said, giving her a hug. "Thank you!"

Mum came back in with a tray of coffee just then, followed by Adam in his wheelchair. I sniggered to see Adam's eyes goggling as he caught sight of Mum in her new dress.

He tried to wolf-whistle, but he's got this computerised voice box because of his cerebral palsy and his whistle came out as a sort of bleeping noise instead. Bleep-BLEEP! That just set me off giggling even more. It was such a funny noise, even Mum and Zoë joined in. Adam grinned and made the noise again and again until we were all roaring with laughter. Bleep-BLEEP! It made me feel all tingly inside with happiness. This was turning out to be a great month!

CHAPTER TEN

So that was my mum sorted, anyway! It was brilliant to see her so happy. If your parents are together, then you probably don't worry about them much, but if your parents are separated, like mine, you can't help it sometimes.

I don't want to sound like an old misery-guts and do a "woe is me" routine, especially just before Christmas, but it makes such a difference to your own life if your folks aren't happy. So now, every time I heard Mum singing in the shower, I felt this lovely warm feeling in my tummy. The magic of Christmas again!

While Mum went on her date on Saturday night, I was busy at the school bazaar. Mrs Weaver had asked for volunteers to help run the stalls – so of course the Sleepover Club wanted to get involved somewhere or other. Lyndz wanted to help out on the cake stall (she's got a real sweet tooth!) but Fliss was worried about putting on weight before Christmas and ruled it out. So we got to help out on the raffle instead.

Of course, the worst thing about doing that was that we had to sit staring at loads of fantastic prizes all night. A few local companies had donated stuff – so there was Fliss's beloved nail varnish collection donated by a cosmetics firm, a food hamper from one of the department stores in town, a lawnmower and some gift vouchers from the big DIY centre outside Leicester – and best of all, a mountain bike from Sports Warehouse. There were lots of other smaller prizes, too, like bottles of wine and chocolates, and even a voucher for a free facial at Curlers Beauty Parlour!

Every now and then, a couple of teachers

would come and relieve us so that we could go round the bazaar ourselves. It was excellent! Frankie won a wonky-eyed teddy on the hoopla, Fliss snapped up a beaded handbag for 20p on the white elephant stall, me and Lyndz splashed out on a couple of chocolate brownies each (well, selling raffle tickets was hungry work) and then Kenny went in for the netball challenge and won... a pair of sports socks!

At the end of the night, Mrs Poole started up the PA system and did the draw for the prizes. Fliss had bought so many tickets, her new handbag was practically full of them.

"And the winner of the Beauty Parlour facial is... number 280," Mrs Poole began.

We all looked around to see who'd won it. Simon Graham! He was so embarrassed, he tried to get his mum to go up and claim the prize for him, but she was laughing so much that he had to do it. Gutted!! Of course, we all wolf-whistled at him like mad!

After all her finger-crossing and ticket-buying, Fliss didn't win the nail varnish. "Number 530," Mrs Poole called out. Fliss's face when she hadn't got the ticket was a *picture*. She actually stamped her foot in temper!

But the person who DID have number 530 was Lisa – which I thought was really nice. Fliss wasn't so impressed, though.

"Typical!" she moaned. "First she steals my part in the pantomime, then she gets her mitts on my nail varnish!"

I was crossing my fingers like anything for the mountain bike. The bike I've got at the moment is a right old cronk, and I'd love to get a brand new one. Well, I didn't get it, but you'll never guess who won it instead! Little Andy Mitchell had the winning ticket – and you should have seen his face!

I caught Frankie's eye. "All's well that ends well," I said softly. It was amazing how this raffle was working out so perfectly.

None of us five won anything after all that, but I didn't really mind. The M&Ms would only have accused us of rigging it, anyway.

At the end of the night, Mrs Poole switched the PA system on again and took the microphone.

"Ladies and gentlemen, may I just have your attention for a few moments," she said. "Obviously we haven't done a final count-up of tonight's takings, but we've estimated the money you've all helped us to raise – and it looks like it'll be about five hundred pounds!"

A huge cheer went around the hall. Five hundred pounds! That was awesome!

"Thank you so much for your generosity," she went on. "This money will really make a difference to a lot of people this Christmas. Well done, everyone!"

When I got home that night, Mum still wasn't back, so the babysitter let me in. Me and Tiffany sat up late, pretending to write Christmas cards, but really so we could find out how Mum had got on when she came home.

It was just after midnight when we heard a car pull up outside. "Just like Cinderella!" I said, grinning. Tiff crossed her fingers excitedly as we heard the key turn in the lock.

"See you on Monday! Thanks for a lovely evening! Bye!" we heard Mum calling.

She took one look at our faces as she came in the room and started laughing. "What's this, my welcoming committee?" she said. "Or just two nosey daughters, wanting to hear the gossip? It's way past your bedtimes – both of you!"

She didn't sound too cross, though. In fact, she looked happier than I'd seen her in ages. She even ended up letting us have a last cup of hot chocolate with marshmallows in before we went to bed. It seemed like Richard was going to turn out to be a GOOD THING!

Enough about my mum's love life anyway. Sorry! It's probably a bit boring for you but it was dead exciting for me. Let me get back to the main story and tell you about the pantomime instead.

Well, after all the gazillions of rehearsals we'd been having, it was starting to look really ace. Everyone knew their lines now – even Sarah King! – and the dancers and singers knew their songs and dances. The first test for us was on the last Monday afternoon of term – a dress rehearsal in front of the rest of the school!

Of course, like all good dress rehearsals, there were a few disasters. When it came to the ball scene, Fliss somehow managed to tread on the hem of her ballgown and there was this great ripping noise as a big piece of material came away from her waistband. She went purple with embarrassment – especially as Ryan Scott was in the same scene as her – but like a true professional, kept dancing and smiling as if nothing had happened.

Then the other thing to go wrong was LYNDZ's fault! The Sleepover Club were certainly making their mark on this dress rehearsal... She and Matthew Silver, the two horses, crashed into each other by mistake and Lyndz went sprawling across the stage. Luckily, the audience seemed to think it was part of the show, and just cheered and laughed!

So that was the dress rehearsal over and done with pretty painlessly. Next, it was going to be the real McCoy, performing in front of all our mums and dads the following evening. Doing the pantomime in front of all the infants and juniors had been nerve-racking enough, but this was serious now. People had actually paid money to come and see the show... Gulp!

By the time Tuesday evening came around, it seemed like everyone backstage was feeling the same. People were putting their costumes on with shaky fingers, looking as pale as anything. It was a good job Mrs Somersby was on hand to put lots of make-up on everyone. At least she could make us look a bit less terrified.

Then I caught Lisa throwing up in the toilets, looking white as a sheet. Blimey, she must be REALLY nervous, I thought.

"Are you OK?" I asked, anxiously. She looked awful!

She wiped her mouth with some toilet paper. "I've got this terrible tummy ache," she said weakly.

"You'll be fine," I told her. "It's probably just nerves."

She shook her head. "I don't think so," she said. "You'd better get Miss Middleton – quick!" And with that, she was promptly sick all over again.

Miss Middleton came rushing into the

toilets at once when I told her. "Are you OK? Are you going to be able to do the show?" she asked, putting a hand to Lisa's forehead. "No, you won't – you're burning up!" she said. "I don't think you're fit to go on, Lisa!"

Lisa started to cry. "I really don't feel very well," she said miserably.

I felt so sorry for her, I almost cried myself. Our brilliant Cinderella, the star of our show... whatever were we going to do?

"Will we have to cancel the play?" I asked fearfully.

"No, don't worry," Miss Middleton said, frowning. Then she stared at me, with this thoughtful look on her face. "You know the script pretty well, don't you, Rosie?" she said.

"Well... yes," I said. "But—"

"How would you feel about playing Cinderella tonight, then?" she said briskly. "Lisa needs to go and lie down in the sick room. She certainly can't go on like this. And you've got a nice singing voice, so..."

"Wh-wh-what about Buttons?" I asked, feeling faint.

"I'll ask Alex McKay," she said. "As our other

prompt, he knows the lines as well as you. I'm sure he'll be fine."

"But..." I said, still not able to take all of this in.

"Come on, Lisa," Miss Middleton said, helping her to her feet. "Let's find you somewhere to lie down. Rosie – you'd better get yourself into make-up! You can do it, I know you can!"

Talk about knock me down with a feather! I was so stunned, I could barely walk back to the dressing rooms. "Lisa's ill – I've got to be Cinderella," I managed to mumble to the others.

"WHAT?" they all screeched. "No way!"

"Congratulations!" Lyndz yelled, half in her horse costume. She gave me a huge hug. "That's fantastic news!"

I grinned nervously. "Is it?" I asked. It was either fantastic news or the worst news I'd ever heard, I couldn't decide which.

"Brilliant!" Kenny said, punching me lightly on the arm. "You'll knock 'em dead, mate!"

"Break your neck!" Fliss said solemnly, looking beautiful in her (mended) dress.

"Break A LEG!" we all groaned at her.

"Ten minutes to go, everyone!" Mrs Weaver called from the next room. "Ten minutes! Please get your costumes on if you haven't already!"

We all looked at each other. Now I really WAS feeling nervous. The five of us had a big hug together. "We'll be great," Frankie told us. "We're all gonna be GREAT!"

It was the quickest ten minutes of my life – because before I knew it, Miss Middleton was calling for us to get in our places for the first scene. Then she made an announcement to the audience. "Ladies and gentlemen, we have a change in tonight's cast list," she said. "Tonight, Cinderella will be played by Rosie Cartwright, and Buttons will be played by Alex McKay."

AAAARRRGGHH! Now my heart was *really* thumping away! What would my mum be thinking about THAT?! I was just so glad that Frankie and Kenny were both in the first scene with me. We all squeezed hands before the curtain went up. This was it! I caught Alex's eye and he grinned at me. Fancy both of us humble prompts getting better parts at the last minute!

I know this will sound mad, but I honestly can't remember that much about the first few scenes. It all seems like a blur now. When I first started speaking Cinderella's lines, I kept trying to think about how Lisa had said them in all the rehearsals. My voice was a bit wobbly to begin with, but as the first scene finished, I remember thinking to myself, "This is going to be OK. We can do it!"

And do you know, as the show went on, I started to really enjoy myself. I'd been especially nervous about singing the songs, but when the moment came, I just went for it and got a huge cheer afterwards. And it was such fun doing scenes with Frankie and Kenny! I felt so relaxed with them, it really helped calm my nerves. In fact, as we got to the bit where I was trying on the glass slipper with Prince Charming, I was starting to wish the night would never end. I was enjoying myself far too much!

Mind you, the best bit was yet to come. The pantomime finished and then there was this huge ROAR of applause! Oh, it was *soooo* wicked, seeing everyone clapping like mad – it just sent a shiver down my spine. I'd never heard such a thunder of clapping! All for us!!!

We all bowed and went off stage, but the audience were still clapping and cheering, so Miss Middleton told us to go on stage and bow all over again. I caught my mum's eye and she gave me a huge wink. She looked as proud as anything, standing up, clapping fit to bust.

Wow! If this was what it was like to be an actress, give me more! I thought. It was a moment I was never going to forget!

As soon as the curtains came across, everyone started hugging each other and jumping up and down. Miss Middleton ran right over to me, picked me up and swung me round in the air! "You were great, Rosie!" she said. "Well done!"

"Thanks, Miss!" I said feeling dazed.

"Everyone was wonderful!" she said. "Alex – fantastic job as Buttons. Frankie – you were superb. Sarah – well done, word-perfect!"

I've got to say, it was one of the happiest moments in my entire life. Even Fliss was hugging me and telling me how good I was. And that's when I knew what my REAL Christmas wish was – to be an actress when I grow up! Now I'd had a taste of it, I wanted more – much more!

Well... that's about the end of the story, really. The next night Lisa was feeling better so she got to be Cinderella again, and I was back to being Buttons. I didn't mind too much, though. I'd had my moment of glory already, and knew that after all her hard work in rehearsals, Lisa really deserved a big round of applause, too. Christmas spirit and all that, eh?

I'll just have to wait for next year's pantomime now. You never know – I could be first choice for the starring role next time!

This is Rosie Maria Cartwright saying Merry Christmas and a very Happy New Year from all of us in the Sleepover Club. Have a great time – I know I will!

MEGA
EDITION!

Mega Sleepover Club ①

In *The Sleepover Club at Frankie's*, the gang decides to set up Brown Owl with Dishy Dave the school caretaker. But playing Cupid isn't as easy as they think... It's Lyndz's birthday in *The Sleepover Club at Lyndsey's*, and the gang plan a spooky video night. Only the spooks suddenly seem for real... And in *The Sleepover Club at Felicity's*, Fliss goes diet-crazy. But sleepovers and food go hand in hand, and the girls must find emergency supplies!

Three fantastic Sleepover Club stories in one!

www.harpercollinschildrensbooks.co.uk

Mega Sleepover Club ②

Fliss is desperate for a pet in *The Sleepover Club at Rosie's*, and volunteers to look after the school hamster for the weekend. Oh-oh... Kenny's horrible sister is out to make trouble in *The Sleepover Club at Kenny's* – have the Sleepover Club met their match? And in *Starring the Sleepover Club*, it's all fun and games with Fliss's mum's camcorder. Will the Sleepover Club discover screen stardom, or will their film be a flop?

Three fantastic Sleepover Club stories in one!

www.harpercollinschildrensbooks.co.uk

Mega Sleepover Club ③

The gang decides to form a pop group in *The Sleepover Girls go Spice*, except their secret rehearsal in the attic doesn't quite go to plan... *The 24-Hour Sleepover Club* sees the mates at loggerheads with their dreaded rivals, the M&Ms – and they soon find that revenge can be sickly sweet! And make way for chaos in *The Sleepover Club Sleeps Out*, when a school trip overnight to a local Egyptian museum provides a perfect excuse for terrifying the M&Ms...

Three fantastic Sleepover Club stories in one!

Mega
Sleepover Club ④

In *Happy Birthday Sleepover Club*, the gang realises that they've had exactly TEN sleepovers. It's time for a birthday party! Horse-mad Lyndz gets the Sleepover Club together to help save Mrs McAllister's stables in *Sleepover Girls on Horseback*. And in *Sleepover in Spain*, five crazy Spanish girls threaten to spoil all the Sleepover Club fun...

Three fantastic Sleepover Club stories in one!

www.harpercollinschildrensbooks.co.uk

Mega Sleepover Club 5

The next sleepover is guaranteed to get spooky in Sleepover Club on Friday 13th – but then things get really out of control... In Sleepover Girls go Camping, the girls team up against their deadly rivals the M&Ms in a race across a massive assault course – is the reputation of the Sleepover Club on the line? And when Lyndz's cat Truffle disappears, it's up to the gang to find her in Sleepover Girls Go Detective!

Three fantastic Sleepover Club
stories in one!

www.harpercollinschildrensbooks.co.uk

Order Form

To order direct from the publishers, just make a list of the titles you want and fill in the form below:

Name ....

Address ....

....

....

Send to: Dept 6, HarperCollins Publishers Ltd, Westerhill Road, Bishopbriggs, Glasgow G64 2QT.

Please enclose a cheque or postal order to the value of the cover price, plus:

UK & BFPO: Add £1.00 for the first book, and 25p per copy for each additional book ordered.

Overseas and Eire: Add £2.95 service charge. Books will be sent by surface mail but quotes for airmail despatch will be given on request.

A 24-hour telephone ordering service is available to holders of Visa, MasterCard, Amex or Switch cards on 0141- 772 2281.

HarperCollins *Children's Books*

Lightning Source UK Ltd.
Milton Keynes UK
19 November 2009
146469UK00001B/77/P